Behind the Oleander

A story from Iran

by

Sue Crampton

Published in 2019 by Sue Crampton

Book design by Lumphanan Press
www.lumphananpress.co.uk

ISBN: 978-1-9996481-1-4

This book is dedicated to Dr Elisabeth Macbean Ross from Tain in N.E. Scotland, where I lived for a short time. Dr. Ross was one of the first female doctors to qualify in Scotland and travelled to Japan as a ship's surgeon. She visited Iran and worked there becoming known as the 'Lady Doctor of Bakhtiari Land'.

She went to Serbia in 1915 to work with the Scottish Womens' Hospitals and to care for the wounded casualties in the Balkans. Three weeks after her arrival she died of typhus, as many others did too. In 2018 I visited her grave in Serbia, where each year she is honoured and remembered.

Her bravery and courage was an inspiration to me, and particularly her love and dedication to caring for the Bakhtiari tribeswomen. She is a connection to southern Iran, where I lived for a time and where this novel is set.

– *Sue Crampton, Scotland, 2019*

Thanks to the Grapevine Group in Girona, Catalonia, the Limousin Writers' Group in SW France and the extremely helpful Huntly Writers' Group in Scotland. The group members patiently listened and offered suggestions as I tried to get my story and plotting to come together. My particular thanks to Charlie Aylett (www.thestorysmith.com) who edited the raw draft.

Oleander *n.* Evergreen poisonous Mediterranean shrub (Nerium oleander) with leathery lanceolate leaves and fine red, white or pink flowers. med.L. *Concise Oxford Dictionary*

'We are no more than a moving row
Of magic shadow shapes that come and go
round with the sun-illumined lantern held
In midnight by the master of the show
But helpless pieces of the game he plays
Upon this chequer board of nights and days.'

– *Omar Khayyam*
(Persian mathematician, astronomer and poet 1048 – 1131)

Iran – The British connection

Some background to the novel

The AIOC was the UK's single largest overseas asset and a source of national pride in the British post-war era of the Labour politicians Clement Attlee, and Ernest Bevin. Even as late as the 1940s and early 1950s some high British officials still believed that Persian petroleum was actually and rightly British petroleum because it had been discovered by the British, and developed by British capital, and exploited through British skill and British ingenuity. In stark contrast, Iranian Premier Mossadegh believed the 1933 concession granted to the AIOC by Iran was "immoral as well as illegal". Mosaddeqh "challenged every aspect of the British commercial presence in Iran". The British feared that if Mosaddeqh's policies prevailed, "nationalists throughout the world could abrogate British concessions with impunity."

Nationalisation

The AIOC was nationalized by the Iranian Parliament in March 1951. In Iran this was enormously popular and seen as a long overdue staunching of the bleeding of its national wealth which could now be harnessed to fighting poverty in Iran. In Britain, the nationalisation was widely seen as an intolerable breach of contract or theft. British emissaries in the United States after the nationalisation argued that allowing Iran to nationalise the oil company "would be widely regarded as a victory for the Russians" and would also "cause a loss of one hundred million pounds per annum in the United Kingdom's balance of payments, thus seriously affecting our rearmament program and our cost of living."

British warships blockaded Abadan. On 22 August, the British cabinet imposed a series of economic sanctions on Iran. It prohibited exports of key British commodities, including sugar and steel, directed the withdrawal of all British personnel from Iranian oil fields and all but a hard core of about 300 administrators from Abadan and blocked Iran's access to its hard currency accounts in British banks.

After the withdrawal of the British workers in the fall of 1951, the Iranians felt confident that they could easily hire non-British technicians to run the industry and then quickly train their own nationals to replace them. Unfortunately, this did not prove to be the case; the United States, Sweden, Belgium, the Netherlands, Pakistan, and West Germany all refused to make their technicians available to the nationalized Iranian industry. Only Italy agreed, demonstrating that most industrialized countries supported Britain over Iran in the nationalization dispute."

In July 1952, the Royal Navy intercepted the Italian tanker *Rose Mary* and forced it into the British protectorate of Aden on the grounds that the ship's petroleum was stolen property. News that the Royal Navy was intercepting tankers carrying Iranian oil scared off other tankers and effectively shut down oil exports from Iran.

Supporters of the nationalization, including the National Poet of Iran Adib Bouroumand, sent out propaganda in the form of poetry in support of Mossadegh's movement. Poems were read out on radio broadcasts, passed out to people on paper pamphlets, and published in newspapers.

Coup d'etat of 1953

The democratically elected government of Iran was overthrown on 19 August 1953, following a coup d'etat orchestrated by the United Kingdom and the United States and the Prime Minister Mossadegh was ousted from power. During the coup, codename Operation Ajax, the CIA and MI6 restored Mohammad Reza Pahlavi to power. In August 1954, the AIOC was set under the control of an international consortium. Initially, ownership shares in the consortium proposed to be divided along the following lines: 40% to be divided equally (8% each) among the five major American companies; British Petroleum to have a 40% share; Royal Dutch Shell to have 14%; and CFP, a French Company, to receive 6%. Iran now received 25% of the profits compared to 20% of the original treaty with the AIOC. Saudi Arabia and other oil-exploiting countries of the region received up to 50% of the profits in cooperation with American oil companies at the same time.

It was only in 1980, after the US and British backed Shah regime was ousted through a people's uprising in 1979 that the oil company was nationalised into what is today known as the NIOC(National Iranian Oil Company) .

Chapter 1

Tehran 1975

'LOOK AT HER. Something's different about Elahe.' Nasreen nudged Laila. 'And she looks worried too, don't you think?' It was mid-afternoon in the newly opened canteen of Tehran University and male students sprawled around cluttered tables, while a sour, dense cloud of cigarette smoke hovered above their grey faces. A tiny number of female students sat at tables on the edges of the echoing room. Laila and Nasreen were at the back under a large arched window which looked out onto piles of gritty grey snow.

'Nonsense. Imagination,' replied Laila. 'She's just not the type. Our Elahe?' Even so Laila turned to follow Nasreen's gaze and studied their friend's progress towards them. Elahe wore her father's latest gift, a soft Italian leather coat, and carried a plate on which were three sticky almond pastries. Her shoulders were definitely hunched, Laila admitted to herself as she studied their friend coming towards them. She remembered that the day before Elahe's head had clipped a lopsided, low chandelier, as she was taller than both herself and Nasreen. That incident had all three of them laughing out loud and they'd continued to joke about the decor and how it was clinging to the past to have such a decorative item in a modern canteen. But today Elahe's posture made Nasreen apprehensive. '*Kheili mamnoonam,* Elahe. Many thanks. It'll be my turn to buy cakes tomorrow,' said Nasreen, whose hand darted forward and chose the cake farthest away but which had more almonds.

'Oh, take mine as well,' sighed Elahe, pushing the plate towards her two friends. 'I'm not hungry.'

Nasreen's large golden loop earrings dangled as she nudged Laila again. Elahe was always hungry, but managed to remain slim. Laila nibbled at the crisp pastry of her cake, sneaking looks at both Nasreen and Elahe. No, she was different, Laila thought and wondered whether it was a problem at home. It couldn't be anything to do with Elahe's studies as she always received top marks in her exams.

Elahe pulled up the sleeve of her coat and studied her tiny Swiss watch, a present from her father as a reward for her success in gaining a place at the university. Her results hadn't been as high as the 'golden sun', the words she used to describe her brother, but she knew she was her father's favourite. 'Oh sorry... sorry girls,' Elahe said, 'I've got to go. *Inshallah.* God willing, I'll be in time. Gholam, that busybody brother of mine came to find me at lunchtime. Mum and Dad want me back home. They're expecting Grandmother.' That remark confirmed Laila's suspicions.

'But you've only just arrived and we were planning to share a taxi to that new perfume shop. You know, the one that's just opened by that American food place.' Laila's quiet voice was louder than normal, and a student opposite stared across at the three of them and alerted his friend. The girls remained oblivious although previous days they would have smiled at their admirers. Laila persisted for a while, trying to persuade Elahe to come with them, but more to raise Elahe's spirits than anything.

Elahe shook her head. 'No, I can't go, I need to get home. See you both tomorrow. Not missing that poetry class.' Her last words didn't reassure the two friends although they nodded back and watched her rearrange her coat and Nasreen secretly pinched its soft leather. Just then, a waiter arrived with a grubby white apron, eager to collect up the plates and cups.

'Not ready yet, are we?' Elahe snapped. 'I'm going, but not my friends.'

He backed away with his head down.

Outside the canteen there was a cloakroom and Elahe dashed inside. She used a tissue to wipe away any traces of her pink lipstick, but her nail varnish was well and truly stuck. Well, she could hide her hands behind her back, she thought. As she unrolled a headscarf her oval face and green eyes stared back at her in the mirror. She pushed her long, thick hair beneath the scarf, but it was too late to do anything about what lay beneath her coat. Again, she looked at her watch and fumbled as she pushed the tissues back into her bag. The cold wind hit her face like a slap. Whispers of snow still clung to the crests of her beloved Elburz Mountains, where the family skied each year. As she made her way towards the line of waiting taxis, icy water splashed over her boots. It would take half an hour to reach home on the edge of the diplomats' quarter and that would be on a good day. With the latest cold weather, many cars and taxis had already broken down and been left stranded causing chaos.

She had to wait ten minutes until a yellow taxi arrived, with a driver who ignored her pleas to speed up. When they reached Elahe's house, she drew a sharp intake of breath as she spotted her great-uncle's car already parked inside the gates. She didn't bother with a tip for the taxi driver and slammed the door before realising that a quiet arrival would have made more sense. Their maid must have heard the noise as the front door opened. Elahe never bothered to find out the names of the three servants in her house. They kept out of her way and were always changing. Many were poorer relatives from her mother's home city of Qum who used the house as a launching-off point for better things in Tehran. Her mother organised them and took infinite care over their welfare, but Elahe and her brother Gholam didn't see the point. Elahe held out her coat for the woman to take and stepped out of her wet boots.

Murmurs of talk were coming from the lounge which the family only used when they had special guests. She propped herself against the wall, conscious of her heart jumping in her chest, as if it had a will of its own. The door of the room opened a crack and her mother's head appeared. She smiled when she saw her daughter had arrived and crept along the wall towards her, closing the door. Mahshid was a short woman but with Elahe's green eyes.

'Sweetheart. Good, you are here at last.' Her mother's lined face broke into another brief smile which lasted all of two seconds. 'My goodness! You can't wear that.' Her mother stared at the yellow crochet miniskirt hanging a good two inches above Elahe's knees. 'Go upstairs and change now, Elahe. You know what they're like. Please! Please! Oh dear...I knew this would happen. I just knew I...I just can't stand it. And your father is so worried about his job at the moment.' Mahshid rubbed her hands back and forth over her forehead, as if trying to calm her painful thoughts.

'Mum. You couldn't stand it when you were young, and you were fortunate and left home to marry Dad. He didn't like them either, did he?' said Elahe, but she stopped when she saw her mother's eyes widen. Mahshid put her hand over her daughter's mouth.

'Stop, Elahe,' she whispered, 'you don't understand. Times were different. I was lucky and...Tehran was a good place to come to.' Mahshid paused and clutched her throat. 'But my mother's old and become well...' By then Mahshid could barely speak although she had to try to explain somehow. 'My brother's head of the family now. He's a mullah, Elahe. We must respect that. We must, don't you see?' She squeezed Elahe's arm. 'I didn't know he would come too. Yes, both of them, Elahe. Both of them are in there. Please, please, please go and change.' Elahe couldn't bear to look at the pleading in her mother's wide green eyes, and turned her face away as she spoke.

'Change, Mum. What for? Just to please them! No, I can't.' Then she softened her tone but straightened her back. Those words about her father worried her too, and her stomach clenched like a vice. 'No time to change, Mum. And I'm young, don't forget.' Elahe stroked her mother's mouth, generating a smile. 'Maybe just a bit like you were?'

Her mother shook her head but not in answer to the last words. She clasped her daughter's hand. 'Come then. Nothing more to say.' Mahshid's face returned to stone. 'Your father's already in there. Perhaps, perhaps he can handle them like he did when we wanted to marry.'

Elahe took off her headscarf and shook out her long hair. Her skirt was short but there was a principle at stake and she wanted them to see that. Her mother's meekness and pleading had convinced her to do the opposite. She breathed in deeply as her hand shook. At the last moment, she squeezed her mother's hand and held it tight. Behind the door, Elahe saw, at first, only a bowl of blue hyacinths. She concentrated on that blue, not wanting to look or see anything else.

'How can you allow her to wear that?' The old woman's shrill voice echoed around the walls of the ornately decorated room. The great-uncle's eyes glittered at Elahe like wet pebbles on one of the Caspian beaches and Elahe's hand continued to grip her mother's as she forced herself to stare back at both of them.

Her grandmother, wrapped in a tight black chador, which she had never relinquished throughout her life, shook her fist in the air. She reached down to pluck at the bottom of her granddaughter's skirt, tugging it between her bony fingers. 'What's happened to this family?' She turned her wrinkled face towards her daughter and repeated the question again, this time stabbing her finger in the air as she drew attention to Elahe's knees, visible beneath the miniskirt, and refusing to be still.

Behind sat Elahe's father, who stood up at that point and put an arm on the back of his mother-in-law. He rubbed one hand on the front of his cotton jacket, as if he had a pain there and his face had a grey, clammy appearance. Great-Uncle Jamshyd sat sunk back on the cushions of the velvet sofa shaking his bearded face beneath his flat, black, pancake cap. Elahe bit back words that she wanted to throw at both of them, now distracted by her mother's sobs, and waited for her father to speak up for her, but to her dismay, he seemed unable to speak.

Silence hung like a taut rope pulled by two opposing teams, neither willing to ease their grip. Then the old woman shrugged off her son-in-law's arm and he staggered back onto his chair. 'What's the use?' She took three steps towards Mahshid, ignoring Elahe, and almost spat in her daughter's face. 'I blame you. I blame you. If you'd have stayed in Qum and married that cousin of yours, this would never have happened.'

A sudden strangled cry filled the room. Elahe's father lay crumpled on the floor with a hand clutching his chest.

'I knew something like this would happen,' screamed Mahshid, at last finding the strength she knew she should have used. 'Look, Mother! Look what you and your brother have done!' she said.

Elahe's screams were silenced by Gholam shoving his sister to one side as he stooped over his father's body on the floor.

Chapter 2

October 1975 – Southern Iran

THE SLATE GREY mountains spread out below Annie like smocking on a child's dress. They were grey and beige ridges folding away into the horizon. Six years before she'd seen similar pictures beamed back to earth by the Americans on the first moon landing. She stared out through the scratched, grimy window, straining to see as much as possible. The rattling plane began its descent and a flash appeared as she focused on this area and the moonscape below blossomed into a shimmering lushness. Slicing through the scene was a grid pattern of roads with solid looking houses. It was a kind of exotic suburbia, and in some ways not dissimilar to Annie's childhood town.

The plane groaned on its descent and her throat became dry with expectation. Dusty roads led away from the area towards a silhouette of a nearby town, their destination. This was the town of Bashed-i-Suleiman as she had heard it referred to, or simply Bashed, and the tidy streets and houses were where they would live.

Annie turned to wake her husband even though she still felt reluctant about sharing her excitement. A sudden loss of height had her gasping and tensing her arms and legs, too frightened to speak. The rapid descent woke Mike at last and she felt him shift his body to balance his weight as they lurched forward. 'You could have woken me, Annie,' he hissed. 'How's it going to look when the others see me half-asleep on our arrival?' His brown eyes were deep, dark pools and there were bags beneath them, from having spent three nights in different hotel beds.

'Well, you're awake now, Mike, and I did nudge you a while back but you didn't stir. Next time—' she paused and looked away, muttering under her breath '—I'll have to make sure I give you a really hard dig.' She gripped her hands on the armrests and concentrated on the shabby cloth of the seat in front. By *the others* Annie knew he meant the two other English teachers who, like him, had been recruited to teach Iranian apprentices.

'This isn't a holiday trip, you know!' He must have heard her mutterings. 'This is where I'm going to work and earn us a great deal of money. First impressions, my dear!'

Annie flinched. Why was he telling her off already? Why not squeeze her hand and give her at least a smile. He was nervous and tired. But then she was too. That's what it was, wasn't it? Could this job all be a mistake? Were they foolhardy to go to live in a foreign country and leave their permanent teaching jobs?

Annie had always been the more adventurous. She'd hitch-hiked in Europe only six years before as a teenager, and danced to the music of the Rolling Stones on a Greek beach. Her mother had remained tight-lipped and silent when she'd heard of the plans for that trip and only Annie's dad, a veteran of Montgomery's North African campaign, had supported her. Now she repeated similar words. 'You'll be fine, Mike. Aren't you the most experienced teacher? You've got nothing to worry about. Anyway, I'm here,' and Mike's tense face relaxed a fraction. 'We are in this together like always, aren't we?' She stroked his arm, but just for a moment.

Mike sat back and tugged hard at his seat belt, his mouth still a hard red line and he made a grunting sound. She sighed and turned again to the tiny window where a cloud of dust whirled to greet her, and then a windsock emerged flapping like a huge yellow dishcloth. Annie kept her body taut and rode the deceleration like the rollercoaster ride at the Battersea funfair. It shook away her negative thoughts and Mike's comments. This would be the best adventure they'd ever had together, and her excitement bubbled up again.

'OK over there?' a voice boomed from the back of the plane.

'I've lost my bag. It slid to the back of the plane,' another voice called out.

'I feel sick,' squealed Tommy, the only child with the party. Most of the journey, he'd run up and down the narrow aisle making noises with his model plane. Annie wanted to take him on her lap and distract him with a story but Mike sat in the corridor seat and refused to move.

Annie had met the other passengers in London, where they'd had their briefing. Major Castle, or Jack as he preferred to be called, had shepherded them here and sat on the opposite side to Mike and Annie. A pile of papers lay on a seat beside him, and he'd seemed absorbed reading them the entire trip. He'd not spoken very much except to give them the times and details of the journey involving two plane trips: the first plane from London to Abadan and the second to Bashed. His face bore a strained look most of the time, despite the brisk tone he adopted when speaking to them all. Once though, he did speak to her and asked whether she had managed to 'get much zizz'. It had taken her a full half-minute to understand what he meant, and she'd stuttered her 'Yes sir' feeling her cheeks redden as he grinned at her. She and Mike were four years into their marriage, both young teachers in their mid-twenties, while this man didn't look ancient but wore his authority as if he was someone much older.

Two Iranian military chaps were smoking beside the windsock and the tiny arrivals building as Annie clutched her skirt billowing around her bare legs. The effort immediately encased her body in a film of sweat. Major Castle saluted these men and then shook their hands before ushering the teachers to the cars. Annie felt the pressure of his hand resting on her back and when the hand continued to cup her elbow, she let it stay there as she bent her head before stepping into the first waiting car. She realised too late that Mike had been watching, and he shifted his tall body to the far side of the shared back seat, and remained fixed there with his head turned away.

The airstrip wasn't so far from the town, and they bounced along, passing groups of squatting men and children kicking a ball with bare feet. The town slumbered in a heat haze and the shops were closed; piles of rubbish blew around the rough walls of single-storey buildings. Behind open metal gates she glimpsed houses. Goats and dogs were picking over the rubbish, and children chased after the cars, as they swept past churning up dust. She turned her head to watch through the back window, pitying their dishevelled state, but they waved and their faces all bore wide grins. She returned the wave, pleased at last to have arrived. The colours, the heat, the smiling children, and even the dusty road. It wasn't at all disappointing. Far from it. 'What do you think, Mike? Great to arrive at last and feels so different to be actually here. That black and white film they showed us in London. Doesn't do the place justice.'

He nodded then and Annie reached over, took a limp hand in hers, and laced her fingers through his. He turned at last to speak. 'Early days, Annie, early days,' he said.

Leaving the town they followed a potholed road for about two miles, arriving at the suburban scene of bungalows surrounded by battlements of green hedges which Annie had first seen from above. A woman stepped forward and opened their car door when they arrived.

'Well, here you are at last. I'm Margaret. My husband's Major

Billy. Don't expect you two have met him yet.' She turned to each one as they nodded their agreement and extended her hand and faced Mike, giving him a warm smile. The smile had disappeared by the time she turned to Annie. 'Tafneq is the name of our little community. You know that, from those London briefings, I expect. We are all finding our feet. Not so used to desert conditions. What about you two? Lived abroad before?'

The questions came thick and fast. Annie clutched at Mike's arm but he moved away and closer to Margaret. He shook his head, and she heard him say 'No, Margaret, never. Only been to Europe a few times for holidays. Expect you've been all over the place.' His voice now sounded friendly, and his bad mood had evaporated.

Margaret gave a loud, snorting laugh. 'Jolly well have,' she said. 'All over the show with my Billy. We have a lot of army *dos*, by the way. You know the sort of thing.'

Annie saw Mike nod again and wondered if he understood what he was nodding to. She saw how eager he was to fit in. For some reason, maybe the tiredness, maybe her natural shyness or maybe both, she held herself back from them and refrained from rushing to his side.

'I know all about you teachers,' continued Margaret. 'Three of you chaps, at the moment, if I'm right.'

Mike nodded again. She gave Annie a direct look then, and her eyes flicked downwards staring at Annie's bedraggled blouse and short skirt. 'Pete and John are with their wives and then there's a child too. John and Linda's son Tommy. Lively lad so I hear.'

'Certainly is, Margaret,' said Mike.

'Some other technical engineers already arrived with their families last week,' continued Margaret, 'and I saw them settled and now it's you.' With that last remark, Margaret looked straight at Annie, who remained tongue-tied for far too long before mumbling words of thanks. Margaret didn't wait for a response, turned and continued addressing Mike.

'Like to do my bit. Well, time's getting on. Bags are being delivered later.'

Falling in behind Margaret they marched down a weed-free gravel path, passing a vegetable plot where an old man wearing baggy grey trousers bowed his head and touched his chest in a sort of greeting. Annie nodded and began to go towards him to offer her hand, but Margaret stared at her as if she were a child and she withdrew it. When Margaret turned away Annie waved at him again. He looked a sweet old man.

The bungalow would be their home for two whole years. It was far bigger than anything they had lived in before in their married life.

Inside, the rest of the talk continued to be directed at Mike, who seemed to compliment the woman each time she explained something. Annie became transfixed by the neat grey bun on the back of Margaret's head, which wobbled as she spoke. She had last seen the style worn by her grandmother. Margaret wore a necklace of pearls over a dark blue mid-calf-length dress and a sensible pair of sandals.

She took them on a tour of the bungalow and they ended up in the huge kitchen. 'Tea bags, bread, and cereal in the cupboard for the morning.' Her bossy voice reminded Annie of her geography teacher. 'Your Major Jack will be collecting you at nine sharp. I expect you're both tired. Catches up with you young gels and boys.' Margaret seemed the type who would never admit to being tired.

'So I'll leave you now,' Margaret said, 'and wish you a very good evening. Oh, that old man is the gardener. He'll be finished soon. He does the watering each evening. Those big hedges you saw round the place. Oleander. Need a lot. Expect they're strange to you. Not a British shrub. Tell him the vegetables you like to eat and he'll grow them. Most things do grow. It might look like a desert outside the compound here but there's water piped to all of our houses and gardens.'

Margaret opened the back door from the kitchen revealing rows of red tomatoes. Mike rushed forward with his hand outstretched. 'Many, many thanks, Margaret. It's so wonderful to be welcomed in such an efficient way.'

She turned briskly and headed down the path.

Mike waited before he twirled to face Annie. His eyes shone dark and cold. 'What's the matter with you? Try and be pleasant and polite, Annie, for God's sake! Where are your manners? You need to make a bloody effort! You really do. Everything is provided for us here. Aren't you grateful?' He paused and then burst out again, 'You smiled at that Major Jack. You managed to make an effort there, didn't you? Why did you let him help you into the car? Your...' His eyes were black.

'Stop it, darling, don't be silly,' Annie protested. 'What about some tea? I'm parched and expect you are too.'

'OK. I didn't mean to shout,' he said. He clenched his hands by the side of his body. 'We're tired after the long trip. Look! You go first in the shower. It's spacious, isn't it? I'll make the tea.' He swept his dark hair back from his long face. 'Let's enjoy things, eh? You were right on the plane. What did you say? It's our fresh start and I want you to be a lady of leisure now. No marking or endless preparation for you.'

Tafneq had been built in the fifties by British Petroleum and an American oil company. Some of the bungalows were stonebuilt and others like theirs were more modern, prefabricated, and spacious. While Mike had his shower, Annie inspected each room more closely. A large deep freeze hummed in the corner of the well-equipped kitchen. Settees and armchairs filled the air-conditioned lounge. A separate dining room opened out from the kitchen and she peeped into the glass door of a sideboard and saw stacks of neatly arranged dishes and glasses. There was a simple supper organised and laid out for them by Margaret on a large oval table. But when they ate, they did so in silence.

Annie had the sense that they were in a large doll's house and they were waiting for a giant hand to open up the roof after the meal and place them side by side on the bed. They'd been used to anonymity and escaping the school gates at the end of the day back in England, and to retreating to their own little flat, away from work colleagues, pupils and family. Here they would be 'on show', wouldn't they? She glanced across at Mike as he cut cheese for his bread. She needed to make things better. He had tried, hadn't he? She spoke about the comfort of the house and how it was much better than she had expected. She made the excuse of shyness with Margaret, but his continued taciturnity dampened her mood.

After the meal, Annie opened the window and leant out into the darkness. The dense, tall hedges and a gate loomed in front of a few street lamps, which were humming with clouds of fluttering insects. In the distance dogs barked, and a donkey or mule uttered a strangled honk. Breathing in the heavy, still, warm, foreign air of this corner of the Shah's domain she felt tears form in the corners of her eyes. She struggled to close the unfamiliar wooden shutters, catching her fingers. The window banged shut and she tugged hard to release the thick curtains from their cords and hide the scene. Triumphant at last, she turned back into the room only to discover that she was alone. Mike had vanished and the faint sound of his flute was all she could hear.

Chapter 3

DURING THE JOURNEY from London Major Jack Castle studied his teachers. Mike, the tall one, had been asleep or silent, hardly speaking with his wife. She seemed altogether different, always alert and interested. She had an interesting face too. Heart shaped with full lips. If she'd been *his* wife he would have held her hand and whispered sweet nothings in her ear. He'd helped her into the car, and the memory brought colour to his cheeks. His legs were stiff from the long journey and he hated that. He prided himself on his physical fitness and at forty-five knew he looked a lot younger than some of his other colleagues. But he was tired and welcomed the thought that he would have another day to himself before his wife Sheila arrived the following evening.

The next morning Jack stood with his back to the group of old buildings which had been turned into classrooms on the campus of the college. Each of the three rooms now contained a battered desk. His own desk in a small office nearby had the initials AIOC (Anglo Iranian Oil Company) and then BP (British Petroleum) stamped on the bleached and buckled wood – a relic of the past. He had run his hands over his desk, thinking about that history, and then fumbled for his cigarettes in the top pocket of his short-sleeved shirt. He stared out towards the surrounding craggy hills where those early engineers and geologists had endured all sorts of hardships in their search for oil.

His fingers had trouble lighting up but at last he inhaled the smoke down into his lungs. Nothing much for those men, he thought, but cigarettes and daily battles with disease – no water and this relentless sun. His own sweat dribbled down his back. He stooped and brushed the dust and sand from his heavy boots. He straightened his shirt and pulled in his stomach. Jack liked smartness and his uniform, but certainly not the socks. Long, thick socks! His feet yearned to be free and his body for the cold shower back at his house. Turning towards the gate he could see Reza Ali, his driver, sitting in the car. Jack waved to attract his attention and when the man failed to see the sign he marched towards the waiting car and then rapped on the window.

'Pay attention. I said six o'clock, over there.' He held up his watch and pointed to his office. They were called Paykans here for some reason, but Jack had been given the top of the range, so it didn't matter what name they'd been given. Jack settled himself inside, focusing on the road ahead. He could sense that his driver's eyes were flicking up to the mirror to study his face. The young man had helped him in the previous month when they'd been setting things up. He was also a careful driver and seemed to understand English but...

Jack undid his leather belt and threw his peaked army cap onto the car seat beside him. Unclenching his fists he rested them on the smooth, cool leather, breathing deeply, and tried to steady the feeling in his chest. The teachers had been given the keys of a small yellow Citroën which they would share, and which didn't have the benefits of air conditioning. They were only going to be given a captain's rank after all. But what Jack had failed to spot, and Reza had seen, was that another car was following theirs.

Jack's heartbeat quickened when he approached the compound

and his house where he knew his wife would be waiting. He turned to look out of the window hoping it would take his mind off things as they passed the last of the garage-style lock-up shops and shrouded women waited for the puffy unleavened bread. Reza braked as a few donkeys weighed down with elaborate woven bags ambled across in front of the car followed by two boys yelling and waving sticks at the animals. These were Bakhtiari who still trekked with their animals across the hills and Zagros Mountains.

'Be bloody careful, can't you!' Jack yelled from behind. The other car stopped too. Kids clustered round his window staring at him with wide, open eyes, framed by dark curly hair. He thought of his own four boys back home at boarding school. What would they be doing now? All studying hard, he hoped so they could get good jobs and follow his example. He took out a handkerchief and wiped his face. *Never push your men too far,* he'd been taught, and that's what he realised he might be doing already with this driver. He needed to stop that. And the orders from headquarters in London were to take care with this project. Treat all the Iranians well. The contract had been a diplomatic success with the Shah. An army apprentice college to be run and staffed by Brits with millions of pounds at stake.

'Sorry for shouting, driver,' Jack said. 'Difficult job with these bloody donkeys everywhere.'

Reza Ali nodded. The car drew closer to the green hedges and Jack had a bitter taste in the back of his throat as he glimpsed the flash of a white and red dress in his front garden.

'About time you arrived,' his wife Sheila yelled, as he got out of the car. 'Why weren't you at the airstrip to meet me?' Her last words were slurred and her lined face looked blotchy. 'He's spraying the water everywhere! Show him where the bloody tomatoes are, can you?' With that she turned, steadied herself against the wall of the house, and walked towards the open front door. Their gardener stood with baggy, wet, grey trousers while the hose writhed and spurted like one of the local snakes.

'*Baksheesh*, Major?' said Reza, wanting to do something for the old man. Jack shrugged and plunged his hand into his top pocket to search for a few toman coins.

'OK, Reza. Take him round the back to the shed, can you? Try and dry his clothes. Where's the young gardener?'

'At hospital – Hussein here is father. Son has sick child,' replied his driver.

'Alright. Back here at seven sharp tomorrow.' Jack stopped himself repeating the sentence, but he held up his watch. His driver had helped him again and he mustn't forget that. Jasper came bounding round the corner then wagging his tail. 'Here, boy. Here.' Somebody was pleased to see him. He ruffled Jasper's brown and white coat and stroked his head. The dog turned onto his back with his tongue lolling red between his teeth. Jack spent the next five minutes kneeling above Jasper's soft stomach before he could summon the strength to follow his wife into the house.

Jack wondered at what time she had started. He knew the signs of course by now. He should do after so many years of it. The soles of his shoes were wet and muddy and left a trail behind him, as he'd forgotten to wipe them. She'd most probably berate him for that too. On the dining room table he saw a glass and a half-empty bottle of gin, and when he opened the bedroom door his wife was weeping face down on the bed and her suitcase lay unpacked. Her red and white dress had risen up to her thighs and her body was shaking.

'Sheila. Come on now! What's the point of all this?'

Jack spoke from the safety of the doorway.

'Leave me! Just bugger off. Ye ken what I mean,' she shouted.

He forced himself to approach her and patted her shoulder

but she moved it away as soon as she felt his touch. His left cheek started to twitch, and he took a deep breath before sitting down on a corner of the bed. He pulled a cover over his wife and tucked it round her waist. Sheila turned over to face him, holding his eyes, and then bowed her head as she searched for her cigarettes. She lit one, brushing lank strands of hair away from her damp face and puffing the acrid smoke towards him. Sheila pushed the cover away and lowered her legs to the floor. At the window she turned to face him.

'Well, here we are again. Another house and *nothing* to do.' The familiar words still had the power to sting him. '*Nothing*.'

'Sheila!' he cooed, coaxing her to look at him as he moved towards her. He knew at the back of his mind it was hopeless but he made himself go through the motions. 'Why didn't you stay back with your mum a bit longer? She'd have loved to have you stay more. You could have gone to see the kids as well. Half-term holidays. Taken them out for a slap-up meal. Growing boys like their food, don't they? You rarely see them now.' He paused. 'God, I miss them.' He pushed his hands over his head and tensed his face but the twitching continued.

Sheila stared back, her face wreathed in smoke and her mouth an ugly slash of jagged red. Two lines of mascara lay like railway tracks on her white cheeks.

'Too many rules.' Her eyes closed tight as she inhaled more smoke. 'Fill in bloody forms if you want to see them for half an hour. Had to be back for supper. Half-term they want to go to Wales and climb mountains. How can I compete with that?' Her voice grew shrill. It dripped with contempt and bitterness. 'Staying at Mum's is nae better. Questions every time I want to go to the shops.' She threw the lighted cigarette butt on the tiled floor and Jack stamped on it with his boot. Sheila stumbled back to the bed and drew the bedcover back over her scrawny frame, turning her face and body away.

Sheila didn't appreciate what the school was doing for his sons, and in the early days she would have made light of a new posting. She'd been great at the beginning, a real fun girl. The change had happened so fast he'd not known how to cope. He still didn't know. He envied Billy. Margaret was already taking charge of the new arrivals and keeping herself busy.

'There's a swimming pool down the road.' He was speaking to Sheila's back, and he could feel his irritation mounting. 'The other wives go there and maybe you would like it.' Sheila's back remained silent. 'No bloody answer for me?' he said then moved towards the door. He'd had experience of her throwing things at him and didn't want to get that ashtray in his face. 'I've come out here and got things sorted first. Arranged for a gardener, who is now a quivering wreck, thanks to you. Furnished this house and unpacked our trunks. I struggled to get it ready and then had to go back to London for the first batch of teachers. I've spent the last four days on an exhausting trip bringing these teachers here and...and...all I get from you is this? Well?' Jack shook his head at her silent back. 'I'll leave you to it,' he said as loud as he dared. 'I'll go to the other bedroom by the way. No point in *me* sleeping in here, is there?' Jack opened the door and nearly fell over his dog waiting outside. 'Oh my,' Jack said as he stooped to ruffle Jasper's fur aware that his cheek and heart were twitching in unison.

Chapter 4

REZA ALI LEFT old Hussein propped up on a battered chair in his hut and clutching the major's coins in his hand. Hussein had given Reza a box of misshapen aubergines and tomatoes before he left, which he attached to the back of his ancient bicycle. The bike didn't have any tyres and was used to carry things to his home in Bashed and back. He had found it amongst some plastic rubbish outside Tafneq, where it had probably been thrown out when the British Army had taken over the camp. He'd lovingly repaired it with some of his father's old tools, but was still looking for rubber inner tubes and proper tyres.

As soon as he had pushed it well away from Tafneq he stopped dead and kicked the bike's precious metal frame. He couldn't help himself. '*Farangi!*' he shouted, '*Farangi* devils.' A lorry driver with a load of empty crates honked and then swerved to avoid the scattered vegetables in the road. The shrill sound of the horn shook Reza back to the present. Foolish to act like this. What was the point? Only hurting myself and my family, he thought. He had three younger stepsisters back home, all growing up fast, and not much extra money for food since the onset of his *padar's* night blindness.

Reza opened the high rusty gate and pushed his bike past the tethered donkey and the large blue plastic water drums. His home was a single-storey building with rough, unpainted block walls, small 'windows', just square holes without any glass, and loose, unpainted wooden shutters. His mother had left the key under a stone and he opened the metal door with it, after first taking off his shoes and leaving them with the five other pairs of rubber sandals.

He walked into a central space, where his family congregated to eat. A kitchen and bedrooms opened out from it. In the room he shared with his father would be a clean, pressed shirt and trousers set out on his bed. Despite all the work his mother did with her sewing machine, stitching shirts for the tailor in town, as well as housework, she always had his clothes and food ready when he arrived home. Bread, eggs, and dates were laid out on the rickety table in the kitchen.

After eating, he padded over the soft woollen carpets with their flowers and patterns in rich colours to the room he shared with his father. He passed his mother's sewing machine standing in one corner with a pile of thick cotton cloth to stitch. Bereft of other furniture the large room looked empty but when the sun slanted through the door in the morning the carpets sparkled like captured rainbows.

First though, he washed under the tap in the tiny bathroom, combing his wet hair back as he stood naked with the cool water on his skin before shaking himself and reaching for the towel. He rubbed his face hard and wiped some tears away. What to do? He liked the job for its security, but he hated himself for working in the place and taking orders from them. The feeling never left him. It was always there like a knot in his stomach after he had eaten too much goat meat in the Eid festival, and like today it just flared up, and he lost control.

His father was sleeping in the corner with his face to the wall. Reza adjusted the cotton sheet as it rose and fell on his father's chest, and kissed his cheek. His *padar* always went to bed at sunset now, before his stumbling upset them, and he liked to rise early for the mosque. Reza couldn't understand his father's faith or his belief that his night blindness was Allah's way. The doctor at the overcrowded hospital had told the family what the real reason was. 'Not unusual at all,' he had said. 'It's lack of vitamins, particularly vitamin A. We have many of your father's generation who start to stumble around at dusk. It's fortunate you were born when our mighty Shah took the country over. Now we have money and wealth and you country people are better off.' The doctor spoke with an accent from the north and Reza had never forgotten those cold words. They had chilled him even more than the words and anger from his *farangi* major.

His sisters were still murmuring with his mother next door and he called to them to be quiet. His *namoos* – his desire to protect the females – weighed heavily on his shoulders as he was the only son.

The next day before work, when the muezzin's call echoed across the sleeping town, he decided to accompany his father to the mosque.

Both father and son stooped to take off their shoes outside the only one in Bashed. Four blind beggars sat side by side and Reza's father bent down and dropped some coins into their upheld palms. *Kheili mamnoonam,* many thanks, one mumbled as the coin tinkled on his metal bowl. Reza placed his hand on his father's arm to lift him upright, feeling his thin, gristly bones through the thick felt jacket that all the Bakhtiari men wore. He wondered if his father could be thinking of the time when he might have to join the beggars to supplement his wife's sewing money. If his father lost his job at the garage that could happen. Reza already gave all his money to his *madar,* and there wasn't much left over for anything else.

In the cool interior they joined a line of bowing worshippers. A peace descended on Reza and the knot in his stomach weakened its intensity. Again, he helped his father to his feet and they turned to bow their heads at their neighbours, touch their hearts, and repeat blessings. As they emerged into the strong daylight sun, his father draped his arms round his son and hugged him.

'Chai?' his father said. There was a small, favourite cafe of theirs which sold sweet tea with cardamom and evaporated milk.

'No thanks. I need to get to the major's house, time's short. Can you drive me?'

'Of course,' replied his father, and they started to make their way towards the family's battered car, parked in the shade of a group of palms. Donkeys were tethered nearby, with goods stuffed into their woven saddlebags. The sun began to send out its feelers of heat as the two worshippers blinked and they disturbed some pigeons pecking pieces of dried bread. A group of soldiers stood talking at the entrance of the main alley into the souk, away from the mosque but with a clear view of its comings and goings. They shuffled in the dust, puffing at their cigarettes and sliding their eyes across to the mosque once in a while, as if checking for something. With the sound of squealing brakes, the pigeons ascended in a fluttering cloud to bestraddle the walls of the shops at the market's entrance. A silver Mercedes shot round the bend at the end of the street, showering the soldiers with grit and a split second after its arrival, an army colonel emerged. The soldiers reacted in a flash, by straightening their shoulders, grinding their cigarettes under their heavy boots, and then saluting. The colonel returned their salutes and turned to help two well-dressed women out of the car.

The women must be his family, thought Reza. The Iranian colonel took the older woman's arm before introducing her to the shrouded mullah who had previously been hidden behind his followers and congregation. The mullah's long black beard was sleek and dark and he looked and spoke like a young man. Perhaps the older plump woman was the colonel's wife. She adjusted an expensive flowery hijab, while the younger woman stood unsmiling and aloof, fiddling with her watch and silver bracelets. She dangled an expensive bag from her shoulder, altering its position in between adjusting her bracelets. Reza made a low whistling sound through his teeth. She looked like an exotic, frightened gazelle.

His father heard the whistle and saw the object of his son's gaze. 'You're already promised, remember?' he said as he yanked him towards the car door. 'Your cousin in Abadan. Come on, son. You'll be late for work.' But Reza resisted and continued to watch the scene opposite. Then, to catch his attention, his father whispered, 'The town's full of them now.'

'Who?'

'The army and SAVAK*, our almighty Shah's secret police. I think some work with the army, but others have arrived and loiter round the souk.'

Reza remembered then the car that had followed his major. 'How come you know all this, *padar*?' whispered Reza. 'How do you know who or what they are?' He led his father away from the other men and soldiers. He wanted to hear more but not in this public place.

'I might not see so good but that doesn't make me stupid.' His father drew up his head. 'Come, let's get away from here. They are like rotten aubergines.' He spat a large globule of spit onto the ground.'

The next day, while they sat chatting in their favourite cafe, before work, Reza realised that his father was against the Shah and the regime.

---

* **Organ of Intelligence and National Security**

'Last week, the baker disappeared, son, and when he returned a day later, he wouldn't speak about what had happened to him.' The old man stopped at that point to see if they were being overheard. Satisfied nobody could hear them, he slurped his tea and continued. 'His wife saw his bruises though and he broke down and told her. Seems like he has a rebel cousin in Tehran, who made anti-Shah speeches and they thought our baker's son might be in cahoots with him. The cousin's even a mullah. Can you believe that? Seems like mullahs have problems as well with this lot, and this Shah.' He drained his glass and slammed it down on the table in front of Reza.

Reza hadn't even had time to absorb his father's words when, that evening, on his way back home, a stranger hailed Reza from the dark shadows of the bakery. 'Salaam. Cigarette?' said the man.

Reza shook his head.

'You work up there, don't you?'

His face was hidden by the shadow of the bakery wall, but Reza could see his boots. He knew only army people wore those, and he tensed his body, sensing that he was going to be asked things he really didn't want to do. 'Look. No need to be afraid. I'm well. Put it like this. Your father...he's old and can't see... you're working for them and we want to know things. Eh?' The man paused and thrust his face closer to Reza's. Reza smelt a rotten odour of sour eggs on the man's breath, and he tried to draw back, but the man grabbed at his shirt. Reza's heart pulsed and his palms grew clammy. Maybe this man was spying on the baker's son since his return from Tehran? But he seemed to have been watching Reza and his father too. Reza struggled free and pulled his scarf around his face so that the man wasn't able to see the fear in his eyes. 'Can't help...nothing much,' Reza said. 'I don't do much. Drive the major, that's all....'

The man's rotten teeth grinned back at Reza.

'Just so. That's it, my friend.' He pulled out some torn paper money from the top pocket of his jacket and stuffed it into Reza's hand. 'Buy the old man some medicine. We'll be in touch.' And with that he turned and slunk away leaving Reza shaking and having to prop himself up by the wall. He waited till his heart beat at a steadier pace before pushing his bike the few short yards back to his house.

Chapter 5

Since their arrival Annie had spent nearly every afternoon at the pool. She'd persuaded Mike to join her from time to time, and they'd also been shopping in the exclusive, staff-only supermarket. It had briefly been like the old times back in England. But he never wanted to repeat the trips together and they didn't drive away the stiffness in his face, which had grown since his arrival. Today, leaves and bits of bark were floating on the blue water, driven there by a strong desert wind. Annie dived into the water, swimming back and forth and trying to drive away her thoughts. After she'd shaken the water off her hair and wrapped her towel around her chest toga fashion, she spotted the others. A few expat wives sat fanning themselves under colourful parasols, while their young children played chase. She needed to make more friends as Mike had told her and she forced herself to walk towards them.

The conversation stopped and their glinting sunglasses turned her way. John's wife Linda sat amongst the group and she waved. 'Hi there, how are you settling in? Haven't seen very much of you. Even here at the pool you're always in the water. Join us all for a drink?'

'Hello, Linda,' replied Annie. 'I'll go and get one first, thanks.'

Annie had a sudden thought that this might be a breakthrough and a chance to fit in. Linda smiled, but her face changed to an expression of fear as a scream sliced through the air, and she stood up, flapping her hands, and yelled, 'Tommy, Tommy, STOP THAT! STOP!' She scrambled to her feet and rushed over to her son, who was fighting with another boy in the water and in danger of drowning the poor little soul. Annie recognised the whining, spoilt child from the plane journey and escaped to the bar.

The Iranian barman looked very smart in his white uniform and spoke perfect English. She'd only ever seen one other Iranian, their old gardener, at close quarters, but this young man had stunning white teeth and a brilliant smile. She sat outside with her iced tea at an empty table, while the crisis took over the group of wives, and she began to relax a little, but a crash of tinkling glass had her standing on her feet and peering through the window to the bar counter inside. She spied a woman in a tight pink swimsuit banging her fist on the top of the bar. The nice waiter stood transfixed as glasses and bottles clattered over and crashed onto the floor.

'Take your hands off me! At once!' said the woman. Not that the nice waiter's hands seemed anywhere near her, Annie thought. The pink swimsuit turned towards the door with a drooping cigarette in its mouth and then the swimsuit staggered in an attempt to steer a path towards Annie, knocking into a table, and ended up spread-eagled in a heap. The woman lay sprawled half in and half out of the door with her head by the side of Annie's foot.

'Here.' Annie bent forward, stooping down to offer the woman her hand.

'Thanks. What a bloody mess!' the woman said as she slipped back again on the tiles. Her beach bag's contents spilled over Annie's foot and the sickly sweet smell of alcohol stung the back of Annie's throat. Shards of glass lay scattered on the tiles from a broken bottle.

'I'll try and find a broom,' said Annie.

The woman propped herself up and Annie stepped carefully around the glass, aware of the vulnerability of her bare toes. Tommy's shrieks continued, and a pain began at the back of Annie's neck. Her peaceful afternoon at the pool was rapidly becoming an unpleasant experience.

When she returned empty-handed, the woman was sitting at Annie's table attempting to light a damp-looking cigarette. She made no effort to pick up any of her bag's contents.

'Oh, leave them!' she said when Annie stooped to retrieve the sun cream and the glasses. 'One of the "boys" will come and sweep everything up, won't they?'

Predictably, one of those 'boys' appeared and started to pick up each piece of glass and then placed the contents of the beach bag on the table.

'Sheila,' the woman said, and thrust a sun-blotched arm and bony fingers Annie's way. 'Expect you're a wife of one of those teachers they've brought here, aren't you? Feel sorry for you poor wee buggers – us army lot are used to all this, but it's strange for you. I dinnae ken how ye stand it. Or why you want to come in the first place.'

'Well – it's certainly different. Name's Annie by the way, but I like this pool.' She wanted to stay polite but the woman's state shocked her. She'd never seen anyone quite so drunk. 'Nice in the hot afternoons, don't you think?' Annie was beginning to think it would have been better to have accepted Linda's invitation to be with the other women on the far side.

'Suppose it is, my dear, but I dinnae like the water,' said the woman. 'It's close to the house, that's all, and it's a bit handy to pop out to and have a...' The woman looked over to Annie at that point and didn't continue. A big girl with soft brown eyes and clear, wrinkle-free skin stared back at her. Annie smiled as she met Sheila's eyes. She didn't want her to think she was unfriendly as she had appeared to Margaret.

'I'm an army wife. Some of them are too.' She pointed with her cigarette in the direction of the other women. 'Army husbands. My God, what I know now. Well I wouldna touch them, if I had my time over again.' Sheila's thin face and red eyes met Annie's. 'I met my husband in Germany. I was an au pair with a German family. Frankfurt. Fresh like a Brodie cake straight from the oven in Aberdeen and he was at the British base.' Sheila sucked on her cigarette but kept her eyes fixed on Annie. 'I fell in love with the uniform, suppose it was. They look so smart then. But I was bloody foolish.' The smoke curled around Sheila's head. Her dark eyes looked haunted. Annie had drunk her tea and perched on the edge of her seat. She looked down at her towel and bag and made as if to leave. 'Sorry,' said Sheila. 'Dinnae mind me. Is this your first time away – well, living abroad? Here! Here! Take a cigarette. Sorry. I'm rude, aren't I? You sat there listening to my stuff and you're bored stiff.'

Annie took one of the bent cigarettes. She had started smoking, since everyone else seemed to. Not that that was a good enough reason, and now, seeing Sheila's yellow teeth, she resolved to cut down, if not give up altogether. She had told herself it was a social thing. Mike had complained about it but she managed to do it secretly beside one of the hedges in the garden. It hid her from his gaze. He was working long hours in the evenings and preparing for the start of the course and the college opening. He stayed all evening in his bedroom study, and although Annie had found the army library, she was lonely. Back home they'd always been together working on their schoolwork in the only main room in their tiny flat. At that point, as Annie tried to light the cigarette from Sheila's lighter, Sheila started to cry, and the flame went out.

'I'm sorry,' said Annie. Is there anything I can do?' Sheila's sobbing ceased as quickly as it had started and she dabbed at her mottled face with a tissue Annie had retrieved from the wet tiles.

'No, nothing, love. You're a good lassie. There.' She dabbed her face and offered Annie another light for the cigarette. 'I feel a lot better now. A good cry does ye good they say. Thanks, lassie, for being here; it's not many who'll sit with me now. Most shy away.' Sheila dabbed at her cheeks again. 'I think I ken ye. You must be Annie. I've heard your name mentioned as one of the new ones and so...well...how are things?' Her wrinkled lips curled round the end of the latest cigarette.

Annie massaged the back of her head. Then something inside seemed to break as if it had been held back behind a logjam, ever since the journey and their arrival. Her words tumbled out. 'I was a teacher, then Mike, well, Mike's my husband, got the job here and it seemed an opportunity for both of us. We've been teaching for four years in the UK and it's hard work when you're both full-time. Mind you, I did enjoy the kids and well...' Annie's voice tailed off and she turned away from the older woman. 'Mike's quite right of course,' she added, 'and tells me how fortunate it is to be a 'lady of leisure'. No more marking, that sort of thing. Takes a bit of getting used to though, that's all.' Then she realised that Sheila was a 'lady of leisure' too, and Annie made to stand up. 'I better go and get dressed, Sheila.' She had a tight feeling that she was 'blurting' as her mother called it. But Sheila strained forward, grasping Annie's arm.

'Hey, that's something. You had a job like that – pity you can't teach here. I ken you're good. But it's the men here that get the best jobs. We pick up wee bits and pieces as we trail around behind them. The only women working are secretaries and part-timers. Most of the others come to the pool, like them.' Sheila's bony fingers pointed to the group at the far side. 'Like me they spend their time idling it away at the golf club, here, or having coffee mornings. The ones who complain too much are shipped out. Oh, I expect some of them here will be flown back to the UK before too long. Sometimes I wish...' Sheila paused and searched for her lighter again.

That feeling of living like a doll or puppet in the place flooded back into Annie's mind. Sheila was frank if nothing else. The drink had loosened her tongue but Annie had learnt a few things. Maybe she herself was just homesick? Why had she said those things? Annie began to think it was a mistake, speaking to a stranger like that. Mike wouldn't approve.

'Oh! Well, I've got lots to read and I've started to enjoy cooking and I'm sure...' She looked again towards the group of young wives. Would they have the same cynicism as Sheila after a few more postings? They seemed happy enough now.

Sheila lit her cigarette. 'Most of the older kids are at boarding schools back in England so after the age of seven we dinnae see the kids. I've got four boys at schools in Harrogate. They fly them out for holidays but they're like strangers then, wee self-contained adults who think Mother is an embarrassment that stops their fun and games. They change so quickly.'

Sheila's voice faded away at last as she searched for another tissue as more tears began to fall. Annie really had to make her escape. She'd got things off her own chest, but wasn't sure if it was with the right person or the right time. She left money for her drink on the table as well as some to cover Sheila's.

'Need to go now. I really must,' said Annie. 'Expect I will see you again soon, Sheila, won't I? There's the reception. We all have to go, of course. I am a bit nervous. It's not the sort of thing I am used to. But you must have been to loads of them,' she said, realising that they must have been a big part of the older woman's life.

'You bet, certainly have.'

Annie shifted from one foot to the other as Sheila continued.

'It's all so stiff and bloody formal. I fear them, I really do. You wonder what it's all about. You end up saying the wrong thing or being told that you said the wrong thing – rubbish like that. You're new to all this, but —' Sheila looked straight into Annie's face '—sure you'll find your feet, lassie, and might get to like the place. Don't mind me.' Sheila's black-rimmed eyes crinkled into a grin. 'Hope though we meet again soon here.'

Annie nodded. Sheila didn't look so drunk now, and her own headache had vanished. 'Many thanks for listening,' said Sheila. 'First time I've let off steam about things to another woman. Most of the wives, being army ones, hold their peace. It's sort of taboo to betray the men. They think they live such dangerous lives and that the wives need to support them at all cost. It's baloney of course. They never see real action in battle, but like my Jack they have plenty of action elsewhere.'

Sheila's last sentence hung in the air and Annie stared at the goosebumps on her arm. She didn't want to face Sheila. Why hadn't she realised it before? Major Castle had told them his wife's name but she'd forgotten it. Sheila was now spilling the beans about him. She was even hinting he was a philanderer. What about those eyes in the plane and the hand on her back? She had a sick feeling and wondered if she and Mike would end up like this.

Later, as she walked back to the bungalow, there was a red and purple panorama of a sunset. The bold colours everywhere flooded the sensations. It distracted her from the previous encounter and she thought of the wet, grey evenings back home. It was a colourful picture-book landscape here, always vivid and dramatic, and all larger than life. She started to hurry, then realised she felt a bit odd. Maybe it was the cigarettes. The headache had returned. She passed the towering hedges with their bright red and pink blooms and she gripped her damp towel and bag.

Perhaps she could prepare a special meal? Steak or a chicken roast with all the trimmings? It was up to her to make things work between them and to try to recreate their closeness. To end up like Sheila and... no, she had to try.

Chapter 6

ELAHE SAT WITH her back against a pine tree, legs stretched out in front and her eyes sweeping over the surface of the water in front of her. A light wind dusted her cheeks and she smelt the clean scents of sea, land, and earth. It was a heady freshness of lemon and sandalwood, but lighter and more delicate than any of the bottled perfumes she bought in Tehran. She closed her eyes for a moment and smiled. Digging her fingers into the sandy shale she grasped two handfuls of small, polished stones. There were three fishing boats in the distance, tiny blots against the sky. Every so often the sun reappeared from behind a few clouds, casting rays of darting light across the water's surface and making the ripples of foam sparkle and shimmer. She stood up and rushed towards the water's edge, throwing the stones as far as she could, and when her young cousins arrived, they joined her in the game, gathering more pebbles and running squealing behind her. Back and forth they ran until exhausted, when they flopped down giggling, side by side.

Later, she paddled with her jeans tucked up around her legs and wandered away from the family group who were sitting under the shade of trees. She picked her way around the rocks. The sea now seemed brooding and stillness surrounded her. Her mother and auntie started to set out a picnic. Three generations of her family enjoying the warm breezes from the Caspian Sea and a weekend staying at the wooden summer house of her great-uncle. She turned to wave, but no one seemed to be looking in her direction. Their faces were all turned towards the gesticulating grey-bearded face.

A damp Elahe returned to sit beside her mother and grandmother. Her uncle turned away and with his stick hobbled towards a tree where he rested his hand and then carefully lowered himself to the ground. Her mother glanced at him over her shoulder, tried to slice some bread, and then opened her hand revealing a deep cut. As the blood seeped onto the tablecloth, she sat frozen as if comparing the white hand with the red one. Elahe saw tears dripping onto both and she leant and lifted up her mother, wondering why she was now crying, when before she'd been so happy to plan for this picnic after the dark times when her husband, Elahe's father, had taken a turn for the worse and died. Elahe had grieved and cried herself to sleep but then with the start of the new spring term had plunged herself back into her studies. She'd even forgotten about her great-uncle's criticisms. For a while she'd tortured herself as to why it had been her sweet father and not the old man who'd died. She convinced herself it was God's work and not hers to question.

'Come, quickly.' She guided her mother to the water's edge, making her crouch and dip her hand into the water, which turned a dark red. Her mother didn't speak but when she did Elahe had to move closer to hear her words.

'It's nothing. Go back, your uncle wants to speak with you. Go to him by the tree. There's nothing I can do, Elahe. I want you to remember that. He's the head of the family now, since your father died. When your brother Gholam is twenty-one then it will be him. I tried to tell Jamshyd you had to continue your studies and have more chance of a better husband when you graduated, now your father is dead, but he would have none of it.'

Elahe wondered later how life could change so much and in such a short space of time. In a blink of an eye, or so it seemed, their enjoyment and laughter had vanished to be replaced by rules and control. No wonder Rumi or perhaps Hafez, the Persian poets she had been studying at university, wrote about life's sadness and disappointment as well as happiness. Now she was beginning to understand them.

'You are the problem, Elahe.' The weather-beaten face under the white turban demanded respect. Her great-uncle gathered his black cloak about his shoulders and stood waiting, and watching, as she tried to dust sand away from her face and legs. She pulled her wet jeans down from her knees and shifted awkwardly from one foot to the other. Then she caught up her long hair, which had come loose from its plait in wisps and curls and was framing her head. She twisted as much of the hair as she could and pushed it back from her face. All the time he waited and watched her.

'In what way, Uncle?' she said at last and then realised what she'd said. No one questioned the old man. Why did she keep doing it, especially after what had taken place before, and how guilty she felt after her father's death? Even her dear father, who had questioned things in his job as a judge, never posed questions to this old man or to Elahe's grandmother.

'The old uncles are very serious and strict, Elahe,' had been her father's words. 'And they believe in the family and what is right and wrong for it. Most are well-meaning, you know.' Now she was not so sure that her father had been right. He had been lucky and left alone by the older ones to follow his career and live his life. But he was dead and the gap in her heart would never heal over.

'That is why,' her Uncle Jamshyd continued, 'you need to listen and do as I demand. Obey me.'

She bowed her head and studied the sand on her toes.

'Firstly you wanted permission from your poor widowed mother to study at the university and now you run around like a decadent slut of the west, wearing those tiny skirts, shameful.' Flecks of spit gathered at the corner of his beard. He shook his head as he sliced her heart with his next words. 'This so soon after your father's death.'

Elahe pulled away. She'd loved her father more than this old man would ever know. He never minded her wearing short skirts, just as he never minded her questioning things. Uncle's eyes were like those hard pebbles she'd held in her hand just a few hours before.

'You will be sent somewhere until you are submissive enough to understand what is required of you,' the old man continued. 'We don't want you here. Your mother is very upset, of course.'

Elahe didn't dare answer. She started to shake, not with fear but with anger. Gholam appeared and stood beside the old man. Just last year she had helped her brother settle in at the university and he had taken her to visit Laila and Nasreen, turning a blind eye to silly excursions and things they had done. Now she began to understand why he didn't smile any more at breakfast and why he had started to question her about letters with foreign stamps from friends of hers who'd gone to live with their families in the States. He threw his head back and nodded at their uncle's last words. Elahe pulled her body away from them and turned towards the vast grey expanse of water. She screamed inside her head as clouds gathered overhead, and a powerful wind blew towards her rippling its surface.

'Come, Uncle. The food is nearly ready. Let me help you.' Gholam held out his arm and both of them turned back to the others and the picnic under the trees, where the younger cousins sat with eyes downcast. Their faces and hands had been washed free of the sand. Mahshid sat back in her place, concentrating on the chicken and the *chelo* rice she had prepared. Grandmother, now fully awake after a snooze, sat cross-legged opposite Mahshid, stiff as a broom. She pulled her chador tightly round her wizened body. She had never relinquished the garment, despite the Shah encouraging them to abandon it. Her eyes followed Elahe's every move. Elahe remembered how her father had joked about the old woman. Now Elahe missed her father's jokes and the freedom he had given her. His laugh and voice still stayed in her head. He was the one who had enrolled her at the university. He was the one who would have urged her to continue. 'What do you want to study, Elahe?' he had said, kissing the top of her head as he had dropped entrance papers and a syllabus onto her lap. 'What about being a teacher? Education will get you a good job.' But he'd left her. He'd forsaken her and Elahe sat at the edge of the tablecloth, bent her head over her plate of food, and tried to stifle her sobs. There was silence amongst the others as they picked at their food, too frightened to comfort her, all except Auntie Aesha, who knelt down behind her niece and wrapped her arms around her.

It gave Elahe just the strength she needed. She refused the chicken and then took up a pomegranate and bent over her plate dissecting the seeds and sucking the juice, letting it run down her chin, a protest, showing her disgust with what had happened. Before she would have been ashamed about eating in such a way, eating just like a country dweller. Elahe's grandmother had a triumphant smile playing across her lips. Her face looked elated as she passed Gholam the most flavoursome parts of the chicken, dripping with its sauce of apricots and raisins. 'What about a husband? Who is suitable? That son-in-law of mine was far too liberal. He let Elahe do as she pleased,' she said.

'Could Elahe come and live with us, Mother?' said Aesha, and her husband Colonel Abdul turned towards his wife. 'As you know we are going to Bashed in the south next week and well, I really would like company. Maybe Elahe can help with my girls? Teach them things. They won't have a teacher for a while.'

Abdul took his cheroot out of his mouth and flicked it on the sand. He nodded in agreement. He always let his wife sort out these domestic things. This new promotion and job with the British meant extra money and status but he was well aware of the upheaval to his family, and Aesha could do with some help.

Chapter 7

THE SUPERMARKET WAS a long, low building that looked straight out of an American style shopping mall. There were advertising hoardings outside and lines of metal trolleys. It was outside the bungalow compound of Tafneq and well away from the scruffy town houses and streets of the Bakhtiari, which spread either side of the evil-smelling river. In the same complex the Americans had built a bowling alley, a cinema, a riding club with paddock, and a shiny black eighteen-hole golf course, whose surface was rolled with oil instead of by a grass-cutter.

Annie had filled her trolley. She'd chosen a piece of steak from the frozen cabinet as well as chicken and chops. She'd stood before in the centre of the shop for a good five minutes undecided about the exact choice for the special meal, and then finally grabbed several pieces of meat before pushing her trolley towards the cash desk. Linda stood in front of her, where her son Tommy was sucking on an ice lolly. The Iranian cashier smiled broadly at the boy. Linda hadn't paid for her groceries or the lolly, but he seemed unconcerned.

Annie knelt down and ruffled his hair. 'How are you today, Tommy? Having fun helping Mummy?' The boy gave no answer, and Annie looked at Linda, who grinned.

'You look happy, Annie,' said Linda. 'Doing a big shop, I see. Anything special? A party or something?'

'Well...a meal for Mike, that's all, Linda. They're working so hard, aren't they, and I don't see so much of him.' The meal was to be at the end of the week, after the first tests which all the teachers were preparing for the classes of new students. It would also be their third anniversary, but she doubted if Mike would remember and knew it would be up to her to celebrate this, and to make light of it if he'd forgotten. She'd sent away for a special flute music book which Mike had wanted and had been on tenterhooks in case it hadn't arrived on time. But fortunately it had come the day before in the army diplomatic bag.

'Well, hope it all goes well. Come along, monkey,' Linda said to Tommy, then scooped up the groceries into her bag. 'Too much to do with a child, isn't there?'

Annie felt her face flush red as Linda turned away.

'Why don't you just eat the meat, Mike? Is anything wrong with it?' said Annie. 'I thought this would be a surprise and that you would be pleased. I...' A tear splashed onto her plate. That morning, she had picked up his towels and washed hairs and soap from the sink. Both unnecessary she had thought if he had cleared up his own mess. His mother was to blame. Not that the woman had been all bad, Annie thought. She'd struggled to pay for a private education and then even arranged flute lessons. That damn flute. Now, he had rejected the music book. Well, not directly, but she saw the disappointment after he opened it. He had asked her where the money had come from, as well as telling her it wasn't exactly the right one. He'd forgotten that it was their anniversary too, of course.

She walked away and returned from the kitchen with ice cream and apple pie dessert and even attempted a smile when he looked across at her in his grim, shaggy-eyebrow look. Satisfied at what he saw perhaps, he attacked the pudding with gusto and surprised her when later he collected the dishes from the table, taking them to the kitchen. He set to washing up and her heart skipped a beat. But when she went into the kitchen to help dry the dishes, he turned to her with the old, grim expression. His black moods had increased if she accepted the truth and all the cheerfulness she could muster didn't seem to dissipate them as they had before.

'By the way, Annie'—his thick eyebrows knotted in a frown—'I don't like you getting driven to town by that driver of Jack's. I know the other wives do it, but I'd prefer you to, well'—he turned back to turn off the tap—'to wait for me to drive us in to shop and stuff. Not too happy about you joining any clubs either, though you said you have filled in the form for the riding club and so...well'—he cleared his throat and his eyes held hers—'let that one stand for the time being.'

Annie didn't have time to reply to this or to argue her case. She'd only ever commandeered the driver Reza a couple of times and he'd never spoken to her, just taken her to the post office or the supermarket and waited for her outside. This remark by Mike was just stupid and left her speechless. Mike hung up the tea towel, went to his study bedroom, and locked the door.

There was half a bottle of Shiraz wine still left on the table. This had been another thing he had queried during the meal, the price of the wine and her extravagance, also the household expenditure and the money she had each week. She pondered his objections now to her joining the riding club. He'd signed up to the golf club and that was quite expensive. She'd seen the bill. He'd insisted it was a necessity for him to mix with the others in a social capacity, and she thought he had wanted her to do the same. But it seemed like she was mistaken. She tried to reason things in her head and went through his possible motives. He'd wanted her to mix socially too. Maybe it was to mix socially only with other wives, or to mix socially only when it didn't cost money? Then he'd been unappreciative of the meal and the book. Again he had told her that it had cost too much. So now he acted as a Scrooge despite them having a better salary. She struggled to understand it all and carried on drinking until the bottle was empty. Sheila's face flashed before her then. She had sympathy for Sheila and had been so grateful for someone to talk with even though the woman had nearly fallen into her lap.

Chapter 8

Jack's desk looked cluttered with the week's mail. The first letter he opened was from the head office in Tehran and marked as 'Highly Confidential'. He had to read it twice before he could fully understand the cryptic message and even then he wasn't sure. It was worrying though. All of them had been reassured time and again that this wasn't a Kenya or a Northern Ireland posting. This was so safe and secure it wasn't even necessary to carry a gun. It was an army apprentice college they were establishing just like the ones the Shah had seen back in Blighty. No difference.

But now there was this letter which told him to take precautions about his safety when out in the town and to check all equipment and premises were locked and guarded at night. Some shootings had taken place in the far north at another army college, although the letter described those as a criminal matter and not a security problem. Still, everyone should be a little more vigilant and they wanted him to report to Tehran in a month's time for a further briefing and update. Jack made a note of the date in his diary and wrote a letter to his friend Alan who lived and worked there, suggesting that they meet up.

A letter was probably safer than the telephone since the clicks on his phone reminded him of the telephone tapping in Northern

Ireland. But he had learnt to ignore them there and would do the same here. Jack was well aware that the Shah's police appeared from time to time in the classrooms and in the compound, and this had been a comfort. Something had changed with this letter though and he would have to speak with Alan in Tehran.

In the following days he began to notice that other majors in the technical engineering block started to carry revolvers. They had probably had the same letter as him. So what was happening? Jack's army training had helped counter his natural nervous disposition. Given all the equipment, wealth, and western allies the Shah had, Jack decided to keep the information at the back of his mind. But it all added to his unease and increased his indecisiveness, about the place and everything. The slight twitch in his cheek returned. When in a tight corner or with a decision to make in his personal affairs he knew he dithered. In a previous liaison with a girl he'd met in Germany, he'd fobbed her off with his auntie's address and lied about his next posting. Sheila had been difficult then and he had wanted to leave her. But when the time came he hadn't been able to divorce Sheila and was too scared of the consequences and the damage it might do to his career. He never spoke to anyone about any of this. None of the men did. It was women's talk, after all, and personal feelings showed weakness however you tried to disguise it. The one male colleague in Bashed with whom he could feel comfortable was Billy. They went back a long way and knew each other better than most.

At the golf club he met up with Billy that week and knew the subject of the letters would be discussed. But it was wives that were on Billy's mind, a subject which was constantly on Jack's.

'It's not easy sometimes with the women here, is it?' Billy said. Each of them had sat propping up the golf club bar. Billy had shuffled his overweight body from one side of the bar stool to the other. Jack had been about to go to the driving range and to exhaust himself by letting off a few shots. He wanted to be alone with only the vast, flattened, and oiled earth around him. Without expat golfers striding out across the black 'greens' it was a desolate place and suited his mood today. A mewling call of an eagle was often the only sound, and in the afternoons, the intense heat usually kept most members away. The local Bakhtiari boys were the caddies, and there had been a handful of hopefuls waiting at his car when he'd arrived earlier. But he'd shaken his head and they'd retreated into the shade of the palms planted round the gleaming white clubhouse, where they squatted on the ground.

'I'm looking for a bit of help, Jack, to be honest. Margaret's much better when she has something to do. You know, someone else to organise and reprimand. Otherwise she's on at me all the time – wanting help with some outings or can I just get her six tables from stores for the bloody bridge parties she wants to hold.' Jack had known he was being 'softened up' for a possible part-time job for her, and frankly he did need someone. The paperwork had been mounting up on his desk and both he and his colonel were sticklers for neatness and order. He'd turned to Billy thinking fast and then realised that if he did a good turn now he could expect a favour in the future – a bit of help one day.

'It's OK, Nellie.' Jack used Billy's army nickname when there were just the two of them. Billy had a large pink face and flapping ears. They were now clamped to the side of his bald head by a golfing hat with a large sunshade. 'You probably heard that I need a secretary.' There was the constant pile of letters each week to deal with, now the college was fully functioning. 'If she wants to put up with me and organise the teachers. You know the sort of office work stuff. Your Margaret is a competent woman. Top-notch. And you're really a lucky chap. There are far worse things to have to put up with.'

Billy swallowed hard at that last remark and looked away. He'd picked up his empty glass and shaken it at one of the barmen, not speaking until it was filled with more gin. Jack was regarded as a competent officer and well liked. Sometimes a bit hard on the locals, but he got things done and Billy respected him for that. He didn't know what to say about Sheila. She caused a bit of a stir from time to time and hadn't taken to Tafneq at all it seemed.

'Your wife OK, Jack? She left early from the officers' do the other evening, didn't she?'

Jack didn't answer that question but called the barman over. 'Another one, Nellie?' said Jack.

'No, this is on me. You're having a double, old boy,' said Billy. 'I'm in your debt forever. I'll tell Margaret tonight. She'll be there bright and early tomorrow if I know my Margaret. If there's anything I can do, Jack, just say the word.'

'I will Nellie. I will. I'll remember that.'

'I'm sure Margaret will want to thank you and Sheila,' said Billy. 'Why don't you come over to our place next week for a bit of tiffin? Maybe a spot of bridge. What do you say?'

'No thanks. Not at the moment, Nellie...it's not easy what with one thing and another and you know what she's like...a bit... well, a bit temperamental and...let me buy the next drink, Nellie. Thanks all the same.'

At that moment, the clubhouse door burst open and a blast of hot air surrounded the two men. An Iranian caddy stumbled into the room searching for Jack.

'Major, sir, Major Castle.'

'Yes,' Jack replied. 'Your driver, your driver. He go. Father hospital. Arm like this. 'The caddy made his arm go limp.

What now? Jack thought. There's always something in this place.

'Looks like I'm needed, Nellie. Got to go. These natives can't cope, can they?'

Billy nodded his head in agreement.

Chapter 9

ANNIE STEPPED FORWARD and thrust out her hand. 'Hello. I'm Annie and you're the groom here, aren't you? Just signed up for some lessons, so expect I'll see you a lot. Aren't you Major Castle's driver too? You're kept busy.'

The groom stood in front of the stalls and touched his chest. He didn't reply but nodded vigorously to each of the questions. Annie withdrew her hand but kept smiling. She realised she had spoken far too quickly.

She'd been happy and smiling all afternoon as she'd learnt to sit and hold the reins from the instructor Jeff, who offered lessons to the expats. He was an American and well into his sixties, but somehow, despite his age, still worked in Bashed and drew a salary.

'I suppose your family are from Bashed,' Annie persisted. This was her first real encounter with an Iranian and a chance to converse. She'd been cooped up all week in the house and was beginning to harbour more resentment against Mike than she cared to admit. He hadn't apologised about his behaviour over the meal. His nitpicking complaints had worried her more and more. She pushed them to the back of her mind. Now she was like a canary which had escaped from its cage.

'*Dorood, Salaam Alaykum,*' the groom said. 'Yes, Madam. I coming from town.'

Annie nodded and smiled as she repeated her request for him to help her search out a carpet. 'Do you know what I mean? They lie on the floor in your house.' Annie pointed to a woven saddle-bag that was hanging on a peg in the corner of one of the stalls, and then as he stared at her she walked towards it, unhooked it, and laid it on the floor. 'There. For the house.'

He nodded. 'I speak with Major. I speak with Major,' he replied.

'Well, many thanks,' Annie said. 'I'm Annie by the way.' She went to offer him her hand again, but he backed away.

Reza had to change the straw in the stalls before the boss came back. He liked to keep things clean and tidy and was meticulous about such things. This new job with the horses wasn't easy for him but he forced himself to do it. The smell and the mess still made him queasy each time he went there. This western woman continued to watch him. She seemed the friendliest of the bunch, and one of the teachers with the major was her husband. But he hadn't worked out which one. Any one of them could have been married to her. But those young teachers had never come up to him or looked him in the face. Their eyes slid by him or sailed over his head, as if he was an invisible man. When they saw a uniform it was different and he knew he'd have got more attention if he changed himself into a new car.

Quick-witted, as well as handsome, with long, dark lashes hiding brown eyes, he'd easily found his first job in the bar for the Americans when they'd been repairing pipelines. He'd also been 'adopted' by a young American nurse. One evening she had leant forward across the bar showing a large amount of cleavage. *What about driving me back home tonight?* she had whispered. His English had progressed rapidly after that. She had even directed things and he had been quite happy to follow. Sex was something his older friends talked about but they had never described those things; it had been better than anything he had seen in the western films at the Abadan cinema. Perhaps, before, he would have been quicker to accept his uncle's offer and marry his cousin. Now he wanted something different than what was expected or allowed. His cousin in Abadan was only twelve and though sweet enough he didn't have any interest in her either.

Reza looked for a bucket to fill. He'd been shown the previous week how to clean the stalls, plait the manes and polish the leather saddles and reins. The job was mostly an evening one and it fitted easily into his work as a chauffeur. The extra money was useful but what was going to become of his sisters and mother once his father's illness became worse?

'Allah has helped us again,' his mother had cried when she'd learnt the news of his jobs and had cradled her hands round his face. 'Now I know it was a lucky thing to name you after our mighty ruler the Shah, and you can save money for your wedding to your cousin.' He didn't know what to say to her about it. She was a simple village woman and couldn't read or write, and neither could he. His sisters had a little education and were still attending school, but he had had to look after the small flock of goats they had when he was younger and had missed out on any real learning. They'd been fifty village boys in his class, no books, and they'd spent most of the time reciting the Koran. He could write his name and that had been about it. It had been *padar*, Reza remembered, who had taught him things. How to drive in the desert with the tumbleweed and startled goats, and it was his father whom he had to thank for his job as a chauffeur. As a dutiful son he didn't contradict his mother.

Padar had been sent home from the hospital after his fall, with his arm in a dirty cotton sling. It had been a shock to him and his mother that the old man had started to stumble even in the afternoon. The gloomy lighting inside the garage in town was probably responsible, but neither liked to speak to the boss about it as he would be sure to fire his father straight away. As it was the boss had agreed that *padar* could still help out around the place when the arm healed.

Reza's once immaculate dark trousers were getting soaked as he washed the chestnut stallion's back, but he'd become so lost in his thoughts, he didn't notice. He remembered the woman Annie and liked her eyes. They were wide and brown and seemed full of wonder like a gentle donkey's. That wife of his major had eyes that were hard and drilled into him as if challenging his manhood. He despised her and her drinking. He had never in all his life seen an Iranian woman drunk. He knew the shame of such a thing would have meant dishonour for any family. There were strict rules about how women were to behave in his culture. It was the same when it came to marriage, and customs which had to be followed. There would be animals and land as part of a dowry and widows could be helped to find a new husband to take care of them and any children they might have, so they were not left destitute. That had happened with his own family – his stepfather's first wife had died in childbirth and his mother had also lost her husband to typhoid. When they each remarried, his mother had been rewarded with security and a home for them both. His three sisters were his stepsisters but all a worry for him.

What would happen if he took the British woman into the souk to show her the carpets? He'd driven her to the supermarket in the minibus with the other wives and they'd never bothered to speak with him. His English from Colleen had become rusty and his major spoke too quickly and frightened him with his shouting, so that he was too afraid to admit that he didn't understand him.

This woman could help. He at least understood nearly every word she said, and it might help him to overcome his dislike of the man, whom he knew had a disobedient wife. It might lead to extra money and tips for his family. At the back of his mind lurked the sight and smell of the man in the shadows. That was the easier option, of course, and Reza knew that despite his doubts, his naivety, and his age, he hated looking at life through a rear-view mirror. He needed to seize chances and act for the future.

Chapter 10

'I've had a letter, Abdul. Abdul! Are you listening? Please, can you turn round? Come, darling, it's important. It's about Elahe.'

Abdul didn't turn to face his wife but shut his eyes and leant back on his chair.

'Please open your eyes and listen.' Aesha studied her husband seated on their large embroidered sofa. It had been three months since their arrival in Bashed. The upheaval had driven her to a frazzle. That particular sofa had been wrapped with sacking and plastic before being packed up in the three lorries they had been given by the army on hire. She'd supervised it all while Abdul had been at his meetings and briefings, and that niece of hers, whom she'd thought would try to help, had never lifted a finger.

Aesha had offered to help her grieving sister without really considering the consequences, and now the whole arrangement seemed to be failing, and falling apart. Not that Abdul needed to be too involved. It was her family and she'd arranged it. But she did need him to listen from time to time and be aware of Elahe's state.

The previous day she'd spotted how thin Elahe's arms had become when the girl had lifted up her youngest child, but she'd shoved her doubts about what she'd arranged to the back of her mind. Her widowed sister was a worry. Each time they'd spoken on the telephone, she'd noticed Mahshid's voice seemed weaker and weaker. But she needed to speak with Abdul.

'I've brought her here with us and it's not working,' Aesha said. 'I don't like to admit it, but it's not. She's up in her room all day. She's...she's...painting her nails and only speaks when she's chatting with those two friends of hers from Tehran on the telephone. Apparently that thin one who came to bid us goodbye, Laila I think her name was, well, she's getting married, dropped out of university, and she's invited Elahe. Elahe begged me... almost crying, to take her back for a visit and the wedding.' Aesha paused and readjusted her skirt stretched and now creased over her stomach. She would have to buy new things for when the baby began to show. Not that she'd said anything to Abdul yet. He was still finding his feet in the new place. Problem was it didn't seem to be getting any easier for him either. Each day he returned with more worries wrapped up in his wrinkled forehead than the day before. Today she was well aware that she was adding to them.

'Well, that's what young women do in my experience, don't they, Aesha?' Her husband opened his eyes and searched for his cheroot box on the tablecloth. The ceiling fans were ineffective and he had beads of sweat standing out on his forehead, which glistened as he spoke. His collar was already wet and his army uniform drenched. He'd made the acquaintance of the mullah at the mosque and worked out who to impress in the godforsaken place. He still couldn't make head or tail of the local language.

'Look, Aesha. I miss things too. Give me Tehran, its mountains, and the cool waters of the Caspian any day. Bashed is an arid place and I'm not looking forward to the coming summer and trying to sort out the functioning of this college.' He thought that the British weren't necessary and they made him and the rest of the Iranian officers feel inferior somehow. But it was his job to obey and he knew SAVAK were busy recruiting locally as the Shah's tentacles of power increased in strength. He had to keep his nose clean too. They could pick up on anything. Any little deal he might want to do on the black market or as a favour to his friends in Tehran. They could twist things if they wanted. He'd already seen some of his army mates in jail for trumped-up charges. He lit his cheroot with his stubby fingers and then pushed the cigar box away. He pushed it too roughly and it fell over onto the carpet scattering the cellophane parcels at his feet.

'Aesha, she's your niece, *your* niece and I thought you liked the girl, for goodness sake, what's gone wrong? Does she help with our three? Don't they like her? I can't understand though why your family and that uncle had to interfere. The girl was doing well at the university. Why stop that? All there are now are these suitors which your mother is suggesting. Wouldn't she be better off with one?' He sensed she'd been thinking the same as him, but her kindness always let her down.

He closed his eyes again and rang the brass bell for one of their house servants. 'Did Elahe write to that one from Tabriz you told me about? What's wrong with him? I know differences of age can be a problem, but not always, are they?' Abdul had been fifteen years his wife's senior when he'd married her.

''Course not,' his wife replied. 'And it's no to all your questions. It's been like a wall with Elahe. Impenetrable. I've gone ahead and invited the suitor here. I'm going to try and tempt her. It's a way she could return to Tehran and if he's not too bad, I think I can persuade her to think about it and accept him. I just hope he arrives soon because she's beginning to look too thin and unattractive.' Aesha paused. 'I'm going to suggest, Abdul, that she takes up riding again. I've got to bring some colour back into her cheeks. What do you think?'

Abdul rose then and stretched his shoulders, loosening the collar from his neck. A round copper tray table balanced on carved legs stood in front of him. He scooped up his cigars and placed them back in the box and onto the table and helped himself to a biscuit and some dates, set out on the shiny copper. The palms in the garden would yield some more like this, and he'd been impressed at first by the size of the house and its land. He'd arranged for more planting and the building of a fountain, in a shady courtyard, which he hoped would be ready by midsummer. He could make the place comfortable if nothing else and he would organise the building of their own swimming pool by then too. He wanted those things for his family.

'There's one thing we need to promise our three girls,' said Abdul, interrupting his wife, 'although I think it will be increasingly more difficult given this religious revival that seems to have started. And that's to ensure they earn their own living before marriage, and have an education. What's the point of all this money we have? The Shah is leading us forward and we mustn't go backwards like your family want to take us.'

Aesha nodded and went to him. He was a good man and wanted the best for his family. She worried now that she had caused him an extra headache. She shouldn't have taken on Elahe, despite feeling sorry for the girl and wanting to help Mahshid in her distress. Her mother was ruthless when it came to having her own way and these days seemed only to have allegiance to her brother Jamshyd.

'Aesha? You should have said.' Abdul's body had pressed against hers and seen in her eyes that his reaction was the correct one. 'Another baby?' He wrapped his arms around her and led her back to the sofa. '*Inshallah*, a boy, my sweet. What do you think?' His forehead became smooth and his face radiated warmth. He might be lucky this time.

Upstairs in her room Elahe lay with the curtains closed. A dry sandwich was on a plate beside her bed. None of the food in the place, ever since their arrival, had seemed worth eating. The previous night she'd dreamt that she was back at the university with Laila and Nasreen and eating almond pastries in the canteen in the afternoons. She'd been woken up by the crash of broken glass, and for a brief moment thought it was that lopsided canteen chandelier. Then she saw the shattered plate and pieces of bread on the tiled floor. Her throat had a sour taste. What was the point of eating anyway? A photo of a suitor from Tabriz lay beside the bread. It had been in the latest letter from her grandmother. He looked handsome, but all her friends knew that in the flesh they were more often than not physically ugly and with bad skin or decayed teeth. She turned as she heard a knock on her bedroom door. 'Oh, it's you, Auntie,' said Elahe.

'Really, Elahe. What is this? You don't appear for breakfast and look at the mess on the floor. That was the sandwich I brought you last night.'

'My eyes are sore, and last night I don't think I slept a wink.'

Her auntie walked over to the window and drew back the blinds. She kept her back towards her niece and took a deep breath before she turned to speak. She must keep calm, she told herself. She had the baby to think about and her girls, and then there was Abdul and...

'I understand,' said Aesha, 'I really do. But look, it's difficult for Abdul and me at the moment and it's been hard for your mother too, don't forget. We need to keep together and try and sort things out.' Elahe turned to face her auntie.

Aesha continued. 'We have invitations to the British events. Your uncle thought he would let us settle in first. There is a bowling club and some of the other Iranian majors' families have invited us there.' Aesha walked to stand above her on the bed. It had been difficult speaking with Abdul and now this from the girl she'd tried to help. Her patience was beginning to run out. But she did have a few ideas and had to put them into practice before things deteriorated. Her niece had to be managed, just like Abdul. 'There's a special night just for the staff from Tehran. I'm sure you'll have something to speak about with them.' Aesha had tried to find out if any of the other Iranian families had daughters of the same age as Elahe but with little success. 'There's also another surprise for you. A club with some horses, and we... I know you like riding and, well, wondered if you wanted to restart.'

Elahe's eyes and face lit up just a fraction at that point.

'I could book you lessons. What do you think? I would come with you of course and...' Aesha stopped. She studied Elahe's face. It was paler and round her eyes were dark rings. 'There's something else.'

'If it's about that suitor from Tabriz I already know,' said Elahe. Aesha's eyes widened. 'Gholam couldn't resist telephoning me the other evening when you were out. I've even been sent his photo. Do you think I've got to marry him?' What am I going to do?' said Elahe.

'Oh, I see, well that makes my job easier,' Aesha replied. 'You'll have to give him a chance. I can't see there's much choice now, Elahe.'

'But, that's impossible, Auntie, impossible.' Elahe's voice really sounded full of fear to Aesha's ears. 'I keep thinking I'm in a car hurtling out of control and I'm screaming at the driver to stop. The driver has this face. The hideous face in this photo.' She picked it up and ripped it into tiny pieces. ' Would you return if it meant marriage to this and a straitjacket life?'

'Stop!' Aesha shouted. 'Just listen.'

She took a deep breath. ' Your mother is dependent on her family money. Something seems to have happened to your father's money and his bank account was closed. Don't think she has betrayed you because she hasn't, but she's too ashamed to tell you.'

Elahe's hands flew to her head and she pulled at her dark hair hanging loose. The girl's body started to shake, and Aesha took her in her arms and held her tight. Her natural sympathy and kindness returned. 'But look, I've news about me and Abdul. I...

we...are having another child.' Aesha looked down and patted her stomach with her podgy arm.'

'Auntie, I'm sorry.' Elahe pushed her hair away from her wet face and looked directly at her auntie. Aesha gasped and placed a hand over her mouth. 'No, I didn't mean about the baby. I bet Uncle's expecting a boy, isn't he?' Aesha nodded. 'And it's good news. I'm really happy for you. Really happy and sorry I've been a nuisance about things. I'll try. I'll try more.' She wiped her face with the back of her hand. 'Blessings, Auntie. Blessings. That riding club. Yes, I'll go.'

Chapter 11

REZA SAT CROSS-LEGGED beside his father and helped him find the rice bowl. His father's arm was still wrapped up in a cloth. Some of the juice from the lamb stew stuck to the side of his father's mouth, and his sisters opposite stared at it but ate in silence having been shushed into respect by their mother.

'Will you go to Abadan soon, son?' asked his mother.

Reza nodded. He was looking forward to getting away out of Bashed. What with one thing and another and the future of his father now haunting their family, he knew he would have to speak more with his uncle. 'Well if you go at the end of the fast for the Eid holiday you must take our gifts. I'll stay at home with the girls, of course.' His mother's fingers looked red and coarse as she handed him the plate of stew. She made sure that they were all served before sitting down. There were dark circles around her eyes from long hours at the sewing machine working on special clothes for the girls and for gifts to take to Abadan. Her colourful skirts and scarves were always popular, and she sat up night after night to complete her work for the tailor, and the extra work for Eid had taken its toll.

Azzie, sitting opposite, started to cough and the harsh croaking sound made Reza start. Azzie was the eldest of his stepsisters and never in the best of health. Although thirteen she looked wizened and old. Her thin arms and matchstick legs were hidden by her clothes but the family knew by Azzie's face that she was growing visibly thinner each day and although no one said the word TB, it was prevalent in the town and many of the younger generation seemed to be suffering from its symptoms. The vaccine available was administered in Ahwaz and Abadan to the west but often ran out before it reached Bashed.

After the meal Reza opened their high metal gate and took the donkey over to the other side of the roadway where some grass and weeds grew. There was a large globe of a moon above him, which gave the road and the other houses and gates a ghostly, unreal look as if in a film set. The traffic of the town could be heard along the main road but not here where the houses were facing each other in a protective circle, as the nomadic Bakhtiari did when they pitched their black felt tents on the outside of the town. He led the donkey down through some rubble between the houses and towards the towering bulbous cacti which dotted the area. Here and there he stopped, pulling on the rope and waiting while the donkey searched for something to eat. Goats were tethered outside and watched by the neighbours' children. They eyed the donkey's progress and then as he passed by they resumed their play, scurrying and chasing each other amongst the rubble and rubbish. He let the donkey forage and then turned back towards the gate.

On the other side of the road a dark shadow emerged and he saw by the light from the moon that it was the same SAVAK agent as had approached him before. He'd not known what to do after the first encounter, but after seeing his sister's condition and knowing his father would be too disabled to work after another six months or so, the man's appearance again had perhaps come at the right time. The extra money he'd been given at the first meeting had already been spent on medicine and vitamins.

'Salaam, Reza. You have anything for me?' the man said. 'I've been waiting. What's happening with your major?'

'I just drive him. Why did you think I could help? What exactly do you want me to do?' That was the question nagging him inside. He wondered why he'd been singled out.

'You're sometimes at that golf club and now the riding club. You might get to hear things there. It's not only your major that we are interested in. We need to know about us. I mean...' The man hesitated. 'Iranians and the Iranian colonel that works with your major. Do they meet? How many times? We're not sure about him. He's come down from Tehran and well...we've heard things that show he might not be so reliable, you know, "safe".'

Reza said nothing. He hated the idea of being spoken to like this just outside his own house and where his neighbours might see. He yanked at dry grass and held it out to the donkey to munch, suddenly remembering that he had promised to show the woman teacher carpets and saddlebags in the souk. She had money to buy such things whereas his family needed money for medicines and then there was their impending poverty when his father's health completely collapsed.

'I'll do what I can, but can't promise so much, you know,' said Reza. 'I don't always understand things and it's not easy.'

'Look,' the man said, pulling out a notebook. 'Here, take this and write down your major's movements. Times and places. That will give us something to work on. We also have others who are helping us. Locals like you. I take it you can read and write?'

'Well, yes. I went to classes sometimes. I was helping on the hills but when the girls came to live with us and my father remarried, I went every day, and the girls minded the animals and the house and...' He stopped as the man lit a cigarette and blew in his face. Why was he telling the man this anyway? He probably knew everything already. Hadn't he found out where he lived and knew all about his job?

'Best to protect our Shah, isn't it?' the man said. Reza knew then that if he didn't do what the man said then they could well suffer. From what his father had told him, neighbours had already disappeared and returned showing marks of beatings. His father was wise enough to keep his mouth shut. His mother didn't involve herself in such things. He smelt the man's rank breath and nearly gagged as he took the notebook.

'OK. I'll do that,' he said then shoved it into his pocket.

The man slunk away into the shadows and left Reza with his thoughts. In Abadan he would try to find out more from his uncle. But whatever happened there, tonight he had accepted the man's offer and there would be consequences. He'd become embroiled in something unspeakable. He yanked hard at the rope and the donkey staggered.

Chapter 12

'CAN WE POACH your wife, Mike?' The major sat on the edge of a chair and leant towards her husband. Annie sat opposite the two of them and saw Mike's startled face.

'What do you mean, Major?' Mike replied. He was still calling him Major, Annie noticed, although she had opened the door and welcomed him as Jack. Jack sat further back on his seat sensing Mike's unfriendliness. 'Well, it's like this, Mike. We need more teachers and Sheila reminded me that your Annie was one.'

'Sheila?'

'My wife, Mike. She ran into Annie so it seems, at the pool.' The irony of that statement was lost on the two men, but Annie was well aware of it. She stood up and the two men's eyes swivelled round towards her. Jack smiled broadly and looked at ease. He was smart as always, in neatly ironed slacks and white shirt. Mike frowned and pushed his brown hair back with a nervous hand. His tee shirt and shorts looked scruffy in comparison.

'A cold drink, Jack?' Annie said.

'Lovely. While us men have a chat, Annie, eh?'

She forced herself to walk to the kitchen and steadied herself on the edge of the sink. Her heart was racing and she knew her cheeks were dark pink. She was fuming at her 'dismissal' to the kitchen and the way he was speaking about her to Mike. She wasn't her poor mother, a woman who had always taken second place to an elder brother, an attitude that had embittered her mum. It was lingering here and Annie could sense its presence. Two men were in her house now and talking about her future as if she didn't exist. She waited by the sink and let the cool water splash over her hands. Through the window were dark green peppers and the purple shapes of aubergines, and she fixed her eyes on them. Their gardener was stooping over something. She saw his white headcloth as he turned towards the window, and remembered the previous day he had plucked at his clothes when she passed him.

'*Baksheesh? Dokhtar*,' he'd said. She hadn't understood. Now she thought it might mean something to do with clothes and there was a word that sounded like daughter. She'd try to learn some more Farsi words. She wanted to find out about him and to be able to speak with the man. Perhaps Jack would mention her chats with his driver Reza and the times when he'd taken her on shopping trips. They went sometimes now without the other wives. She began to panic, because if that happened Mike wouldn't be best pleased.

'Here's your lemonade, Jack.' She stood in front of the major with the glass and blocked his view of Mike opposite. Jack paused mid flow and smiled up at her as he took the clinking glass. With his free hand he patted the seat beside him.

'Well, Annie. How would you like to join the team?'

At last he spoke to her directly. She stared at those blue-grey eyes, which she'd first noticed on the plane. She stopped herself doing her automatic polite smile and made him wait as Sheila's words about the man were still in her head. Her own reply was as cutting as she dared.

'Well, I am sure you are used to speaking with husbands about their wives working. It's a man's world, isn't it, Jack? Sir.'

She heard the sound of an intake of breath from both men. She hesitated then as he looked back at her startled. She deliberately didn't look at Mike. 'In the army, I mean.' Then she noticed Mike wriggle on his seat and clench his hands together. He broke the silence with one of his nervous coughs and then a forced type of laugh. But she knew her dad would have been proud of her stand. Jack sat back and a worried look darted across his face. How could she have thought him attractive or even nice? Clever at sweet talking when he wanted his own way. But he was smarmy.

'There we are, Mike. Didn't I tell you we must wait for her? Now, don't get the wrong end of the stick here, Annie. I really need some help with things. The numbers are far higher than we anticipated. Silly of me to speak with Mike like that. Only trying to be polite, and as for being a man's world, well, we protect you though, don't we? You don't need to worry your pretty little heads about all the dangers. You can count on us men. Isn't that right, Mike? Like to protect our womenfolk don't we? That's our job, eh?'

Mike's face looked longer and more serious than ever although she noticed he nodded his head in his usual doglike way. Did she really have any illusions about Mike any more either? He had never expressed anything other than this type of obsequiousness here. First there was Margaret and he'd always been deferential with Jack. She knew she had always been the more rebellious, although both were children of the sixties and had grown up with songs of protest and the war in Vietnam. She was sure now that he had no problem embracing conventionality.

He continued also to nitpick with her, despite her best efforts. He moaned about lack of salt in his potatoes or complained about her untidiness. When they were in public together she often found herself staying silent, in case he jumped on things she said and twisted them, and caused an argument when back home. He'd begun to do it more and more.

Mike and Jack were staring at her. Mike really looked

uncomfortable, and it wasn't his fault that Jack was here. She felt a brief surge of sympathy and went to sit beside him. They would look united despite things.

'We do need your help, Annie,' Jack repeated in his formal army voice this time. 'Will you have a think about it in the next few weeks? By the way, you've got my driver's English up to scratch. Thanks for chatting with him.'

'Least I can do. I try and repeat some English phrases, that's all. But well...I didn't mean to appear rude before, Jack. It's just that I'm used to making my own decisions about jobs and would have liked to be asked directly. Isn't that the case, Mike?'

Mike nodded with his mouth clenched tight. His hand tapped a rhythm on his knee.

'Duty calls. Must go. Lovely lemonade. Homemade, no doubt.' The major's shoulders beneath his thin white seersucker shirt relaxed as he prepared to leave. His blue-grey eyes were fixed on her face and he extended his hand. A certain formality had crept into the situation. She shook it and felt warm skin and a reassuring firm grip. He smiled unblinkingly at her, and she suddenly thought about not looking a gift horse in the mouth. A sort of escape route had been offered and perhaps was what she needed. It would be something to sink her teeth into and she must thank Sheila for reminding her husband. But why hadn't it been Mike? Why hadn't he thought about her or considered her capable?

When the major left, Mike sat on in the lounge. He didn't say anything for a while as if collecting his thoughts. 'That was a bit much, wasn't it?' She knew what he was referring to. He had picked up on her initial hostility, but she didn't reply. 'He came to offer you a job. Very good of him, don't you think? Why be rude at the start to the man?' It was the same sort of attack as that time they had first met Margaret. Then his tone changed to a more measured, hostile one. 'It won't be easy two of us working in the same place though, will it? Have you thought about that?' His voice grew loud. That last remark seemed at odds with what he had said before. What was wrong with him? Annie thought.

'What do you mean, Mike? We are both teachers, aren't we? I know you think that the money you get cancels out my need to work, but have you thought that I might like to teach and might be bored otherwise?' She bit her tongue as she didn't want to blurt out all the rest of the stuff she'd been storing up in her head for days.

'OK,' he said then paused. 'So, if you're so bored you'd better think about having a baby. That will give you something to do, that's for sure.' He stopped then, grabbed both her wrists, and repeated it. 'Yes, a BABY.' She was startled by his fierceness and struggled to release her arms. When free from his grasp she ran to the kitchen door.

'You stupid man,' she yelled back at him, for once not controlling her words. 'You stupid, stupid man. Do you think that will solve anything between us? Do you think that's going to make things alright, or hunky-dory?'

Mike's lips had a rim of whiteness and his eyes looked ablaze. 'And if the major wants you as a teacher,' Mike shouted, disregarding anything she'd said, 'you'll do it too. Teaching will give you something to do until the baby comes. You'll do what I say and what Jack wants. You'll fit in with things and with me. No more shopping trips with Iranians by the way.'

She turned and fumbled to open the door. 'Too late,' she yelled back. 'I've enrolled at the riding club and I'm going tomorrow for lessons. I've asked Reza to show me the souk too. Are you going to want to have the last word on that also?' She opened and slammed the door hard, running to a corner of the thick hedge, where she couldn't be seen. The heavy evening air was beginning to cool and there was a slight breeze rustling the leaves and wafting refreshing, cooler air over her bare, hot skin. She wiped the sweat and tears from her face and welcomed it. The sky still held a purple pomegranate of a sun, resting above the hills. Then she heard Mike open the back door.

'Annie. Anniee,' he called and then again and this time louder. 'ANNIEE. Where the hell are you?' He kicked the door open and walked back inside.

She crouched still and didn't answer. At that moment the sun disappeared completely and all became black. The sound of Mike's flute drifted out through his open study window, and that reminded her of how she'd spent time choosing the new music book and there'd been nothing back from him. What sort of a person had she married? Later, she found the kitchen door bolted.

'Bastard,' she muttered. That was when she decided to definitely accept Jack's offer. She watched the red trail of sparks from her last cigarette, alone in the darkness, before drifting off to sleep scrunched beneath one of the thick spiky hedges.

Chapter 13

'SHEILA, ARE YOU ready? I need to be there to check up on everything. You know that by now, so come on. Come on!' Jack sighed and then buttoned up his white mess jacket standing in front of the bedroom mirror. He adjusted the braid, tapping and straightening the collection of miniature medals and stars beneath the black bow tie. Lastly, he positioned his red cummerbund in place and pulled it secure. He could hear Sheila next door banging drawers around. She didn't answer so he knocked on the connecting door. He hesitated over barging in. He didn't want a fight now. Sometimes she made it through the evening, but invariably she'd tank herself up so much he'd have to make excuses and bundle her away.

Jasper watched him from one eye as he lay in his basket. Jack knew time was short, and the tic in his right cheek began its usual twitch. As master of ceremonies he had to be down at the golf club to make sure all was prepared. The guest of honour was the new Iranian colonel and he was in charge until his own colonel appeared later. It didn't do for the Iranians to think the Brits were in their debt, even though the deal and contract was so highly lucrative that no one could believe their luck.

The dressing up, military pecking order, and protocol had shocked him as a young recruit. In fact he hadn't really worked out how everything operated until his late twenties. He'd joined up at seventeen to escape to a job which would protect him from a bullying elder brother. At first it had made him feel secure and more confident but when one of his officers confiscated his weekend pass for a minor misdemeanour, he'd changed his mind. That officer had long since been transferred but class and privilege were always there and although you could get promoted (as he had done) from the ranks, you would never be completely 'one of them'. He'd learnt that lesson and tried to play the game. He supposed it was no different to what you had to do in some other jobs.

'You and me both, old chap. We don't really like all this dressing up, do we? We'd prefer a walk, eh?'

Jasper's large silky ears pricked up and his body quivered under Jack's hand.

'No, 'fraid not. No walkies tonight. Not tonight.'

Jasper's ears and body flopped back down.

The contract with Iran was different to his other postings. In many places you solely did your job as a military man and kept away from fraternising too much. Here fraternising had become his job, and coping with it and with Sheila it...it didn't bear thinking about. He put his right hand up to his face and pressed hard.

He cheered himself up by remembering that the grub would be good that night. He'd found that out over his first month in Bashed, at the small gatherings, when he'd been part of the team setting things up. The diplomatic bag supplemented everything; money was no object and that included pouches full of *rials*, which his colonel locked up in his safe. He'd ordered whisky – single malts, that sort of thing, for the evening ahead, although the Iranian wine was good too. The food might include local specialities like *fesenjan* chicken. He loved its sour, sweet, rich taste of pomegranate and walnut sauce. Under his orders, the

Iranian staff were to cook, prepare, and then set out plates of pickled vegetables, their fluffy *chelo* rice, and piles of delicately flavoured lamb meat, which he'd seen beaten into a soft pulp and moulded onto wooden skewers before it was grilled. He'd ordered Caspian caviar kept on ice and flown down from head office in Tehran. Money, like the booze, flowed in the place. His stomach started to grumble.

He paced back and forth, before he called again. 'Sheila? I'm needed at the beginning, you know that, we must set off now. Damn woman,' he muttered, under his breath.

'Ta-dah.' The door flew open almost knocking him down and Sheila posed awkwardly in a long, vivid red cocktail dress. Her eyes shone with a glassy sheen.

'Be, bloody, careful, can't you,' he said between clenched teeth. 'You almost broke my nose'. He gripped her arm and tried to dab at his face. He was relieved to see in the hall mirror that there were no drops of blood on his white jacket.

Jack led her out to the car, still gripping her arm like a vice, and shoved her onto the back seat. He was driving himself as he'd recruited Reza to be a temporary barman for the night, and the week before he'd also secured for him the job of groom at the riding club. That way, he reasoned, he could really make it up to the man.

When they arrived the drinking had already begun. Groups of men and separate groups of wives hovered near the lavish buffet spread out at the far end of the room. Funny how men and women always separated at social gatherings. They had drinks but nobody had started the queue for the food. He helped himself to a beer from the waiter's tray and handed Sheila a pomegranate juice. She scowled at him, shoved it back in his hand, and swayed her way over to the bar.

Annie was fiddling with her hair and Mike suddenly leant over and grabbed her hand. She pulled her body away trying to release it, but Mike held on. Jack walked towards the couple and stared at Mike's face, noticing for the first time the cold glint in the man's eyes, and Mike released Annie's hand.

'Good evening, sir,' said Mike as he took up his drink. 'Nice party. We're enjoying it, aren't we, Annie? Lots of really good food over there at the buffet. Smells delicious.'

Jack was aware of Annie's white face at that second. Even if she stood up for herself like she'd done before when he'd offered her the job, it couldn't last with a husband like that. He wanted to believe that he would put his differences with Sheila to one side if she made a bloody effort to do the same.

'Sheila's not at her best at these dos,' Jack said addressing his remarks to both of them. 'She's missing things and it takes her a while to settle anywhere.'

Annie smiled.

'I like her, Jack,' said Annie. 'She's a good woman underneath. Too much time on her hands I expect...like me. I want to take on that job offer by the way. It will be a bit different, but I think I can cope.'

Mike said nothing, but looked at Annie and then stared at Jack, who was equally surprised.

'Well, yes sir,' said Mike, shattering the silence. 'She likes to make her own decisions. I wanted her to teach too, of course,' he said, continuing in a rush, and looking back and forth at their stunned faces. 'I really did. I mean, well we haven't started a family yet so she's free, isn't she and...well.' Mike lifted his glass and gulped down his drink. Annie said nothing.

'Very good, my dear,' Jack said. 'Just what I wanted to hear. Common sense. Now, how about a twirl on the dance floor, Annie? What do you think? I'd like to fill you in on some details.'

He led her over to a space at the far side of the groups of

drinkers where there was a small band of musicians and couples dancing. Annie held her body like a shop's mannequin and he wondered if he had done the right thing.

'Are you OK about it all?' He wanted to be on good terms and maybe Sheila would be pleased too that he had arranged the contract for Annie. After all, it had been one of Sheila's better ideas.

'I haven't really thanked Sheila properly for suggesting me,' said Annie after a few stiff perambulations. 'I'll speak to her now, if you don't mind.' Annie extricated herself from his hands and stood back. 'But I do really want to start teaching. I'm ready really and don't know why I delayed. Mike agreed and it...well, it might help with things.' She stood biting her lips. He saw her face still looked pale despite the warmth in the room and her dancing. 'Thanks for the dance. I think I spotted your Sheila by the bar.'

Later, Jack spied his wife with her satin dress stretched like a drum to reveal her thin thighs as she perched on a bar stool. Annie was by her side and listening to Sheila's babble, but had her back to her husband Mike. Jack noticed Mike at one stage advance towards his wife and then retreat shaking his head. Later, Annie danced with her husband still holding her body stiff as she had done with him.

The Iranian colonel appeared at that moment by the club entrance. He wore evening dress and scrambled egg braid not dissimilar to the British military. Jack went to find his own colonel, who was talking with some of the other majors. They looked a sight for sore eyes, a group of well-dressed and splendid British officers, and he wished he had brought his camera with him for the army newsletter of his old regiment back home.

'You are most welcome, sir,' said Jack as he greeted the Iranian colonel.

The man replied in impeccable English, 'Let me introduce you to my family, Major.'

Jack shook hands and then froze as he bowed towards a young woman in the colonel's group. She could be no more than nineteen, Jack thought, but she was a stunner. The wonderful, even features and almost translucent skin were framed by an indigo scarf and a pearly white dress. Their eyes met, but her expression didn't change and as he lingered on the beauty of her face, she turned away. Later he couldn't seem to recall her name, although he must have been told it. He didn't know who she was and presumed it was the daughter.

'I've taken Sheila to the car and your driver will take her back home.'

Jack turned round startled at Annie's voice. His head started swimming.

'She'll be OK. Your driver Reza took us back home. Reza was outside getting some more beer and I asked him to take us. I hope that's alright.'

Jack steadied himself on the edge of the bar.

'Well, of course.' Jack reddened and didn't know what to say. He'd really had enough of making excuses and dealing with these awkward situations. At that moment he caught sight of the silver gown and stiff back of Margaret. She must have seen something and he knew the gossip would fly around camp the next day. Both Billy and Margaret knew him and considered themselves friends, but it didn't stop the tittle-tattle in such a small community. 'Eh, thanks Annie. She gets like this from time to time. It's the heat and missing the kids I think, as you said. You go and enjoy yourself.' He mumbled the last words and she must have seen him flustered. 'Where's that husband of yours?' He escorted her back to where the teachers were.

Mike looked up as they approached him and pushed himself

upright. 'At last...where the hell have you been...leaving me like this? I'm your husband, or did you forget that fact on the dance floor?'

Half an hour later Jack knew he'd had too many drinks. But the sound of his driver's voice and words startled him into sobriety. 'Your wife is back at the house, Major. She losing a shoe in the car and then well...she...it was difficult get her out of car. She...well... she was fighting me all the time. She fell and she...' Reza's voice faded away. He stood shuffling behind the bar and mopping up the water from the overflowing ice bucket.

'Well! What?' Jack said. 'What did she do? What happened? Speak!' Jack wanted to swear but stopped himself just in time.

'Had...had...some blood on her nose. I try give her cloth to wipe...she scream at me...dirty nigger...and...' Reza stopped. Jack's face was within an inch of his chauffeur's.

'Listen,' Jack snarled, just managing to keep his voice low. 'You're my bloody driver, that's all. But that woman is my wife. Don't forget it. Do...you...understand?' Jack clutched the side of the bar. There were still people about and he hoped they were too drunk to have heard him. He shook his shoulders, realising how much of a failure he was; one minute trying to repair relations with this bloody Iranian driver and the next shouting at him.

Half an hour later Jack had calmed himself. Music had begun again after most of the food had disappeared. Some groups had vanished. Technical chaps whom he didn't know were discussing the best ways of dismantling the gears on a tank, their voices growing increasingly loud. Before he called it a night he knew he had to find out more about the young woman he'd spotted earlier. He called to Reza at the other end of the bar. Her face had been dancing in front of his eyes. 'Who's the young woman with that colonel's party?'

Reza didn't move or turn his way. 'Do you know if she lives here in town?'

The man made as if he hadn't heard him and continued to wash some glasses. Well, if the man was sulking he couldn't blame him. Reza started to pour a drink for one of the majors from the tank maintenance department. Jack gave up and went to join Billy and Margaret.

Margaret's hair had come undone and wisps surrounded her flushed face, but apart from that she seemed to be enjoying herself and was tapping her toe to the band, which had begun to play popular songs and music from the fifties. Jack excused Sheila's absence as symptoms of flu. Billy and Margaret gave each other a secret marital glance, Jack thought, before they tut-tutted their words of sympathy. He knew, they knew, but life was all about appearances in the army and that's how he could keep going. But only just. Inside, his guts ached as if he'd had something scooped out and his cheek was in rapid motion again.

Towards the end of what had seemed an ordeal tougher than any of his army manoeuvres, Jack took his last beer to the outer terrace. A few of the guests were there and like him were enjoying the cool darkness. A slim shape walked towards him and he immediately recognised that it was the young woman from the colonel's party. As she passed he caught a whiff of her perfume and the rustle of her clothes. She looked startled by his presence.

'Excuse me,' she said, 'I...I didn't see you, sir...I'm hot in there and too much smoke... nicer here, don't you think?'

'Major Castle and pleased to meet you. Your English is excellent for someone so young, may I say. Pleased to meet you properly.' Jack held out his hand and she took it, even though he knew it was not the done thing with Iranian women young or old.

'Nice to get some fresh air at last. But it's hot here even at night, isn't it?'

The young woman nodded. 'I miss the mountains and the seasons in Tehran. I miss them so much,' she said.

He noticed her eyes glistened and she turned away. 'Don't mind me. Homesickness, my auntie and uncle tell me. They are nice people but...'

'I understand. It's difficult when you are far from home. I know the feeling. Even though I've made it my career, I still like to return back to Blighty, I mean back to England and...'

'My name's Elahe. Please call me that. Sometimes it's easier with strangers, isn't it? To speak, I mean. What do you think?'

Jack nodded hard. He pulled in his stomach and brushed his jacket. His heartbeat grew rapid.

'Can I get you some food or a drink? It's a very good buffet and there are lots of your special Iranian dishes and there may be a chance of something before it is too late.'

'No, but many thanks, Major Castle.'

'Please call me Jack,' he said, knowing he was pushing things along far too fast.

'I must return,' she said. 'My auntie's table, they will wonder. So nice to speak with you. I've never spoken with a foreign man before, you know, despite my family's connections. My father was a... He's dead now...that's why I'm here and... Well, goodbye. I expect we will meet again and many thanks for listening, Major... Jack.' At the mention of his name he saw her face colour, but she didn't flinch from his gaze.

Huddled in the car's back seat Jack automatically turned his face away from Reza's piercing eyes. He wished he hadn't drunk so much and then he could have driven himself back home. He supposed Reza knew the woman's name but had chosen not to say anything. Must have his reasons, he supposed. He didn't want to question him further or to pull rank. He'd done too much of that to him. But he didn't like this native judging him. Then an image of Elahe's dark eyes flashed into his consciousness and he sank back on his seat and relaxed for the first time that evening.

His relaxed state didn't last long. Sheila sprang out at him from the hallway brandishing a knife as soon as he switched on the light. 'What the...?

'Where is she? Where is your latest then?'

'You're out of your mind, Sheila?' he yelled then pinned her wrist to the ground, easing the knife out of her hand as it released it under pressure. She scrambled sobbing on all fours to her bedroom and kicked the door shut behind her. Jasper barked at Jack when he entered the kitchen but soon ceased as Jack returned the knife to the cutlery tray, hoping his wife wouldn't try a repeat performance. Tomorrow he would put the knives in another place and inform the cook where they were, just for safety. He'd make sure his handgun was under lock and key too, and maybe keep it in his office filing cabinet. 'Oh dear, Jasper old chap, what to do?' He knelt down beside his dog, clutched the dog's ears, and buried his face in Jasper's warm brown coat, glad to sniff the familiar smell.

Chapter 14

'WHERE'S MY HORSE?' Elahe asked, standing in the stable doorway. She slapped her riding crop against the side of her leg. 'Well, where is he?' she repeated, directing her words at Reza, who looked up, shielding his face from the dying rays of the sun. 'I presume you are the groom.'

Reza's hand trembled as he lowered a rake against the side of one of the stalls. When he turned to face her, his cheeks were damp. Beads of sweat hung on his heavy brows. He didn't look at home amongst the horses like her grooms in Tehran. It looked a poor, shabby place in comparison but at least she had her horse Nowrooz. It comforted her to think something from her old life was here. Still, the groom was young and good-looking for a local man, despite his poor clothes.

'Salaam. Salaam.' Reza stepped back and bowed his head. 'I'm new here, madam, and well, I don't know where your horse is but I go now and find him. What's he called?'

'Nowrooz. He's the best. A chestnut. Hurry, I've not the time for hanging around.' Elahe glanced at her watch. She stroked it and a memory of her father flooded her thoughts. It had been his present for her exam success.

She bent her head away from Reza's eyes, catching up her long plait and jamming it under a net and then beneath her hard hat.

Clenching her mouth in concentration, she tried to locate the stiff new fastening. Everything she wore was new. The riding things were gifts from her Uncle Abdul and her Auntie Aesha, as she'd left her old things in Tehran. Still, they'd arranged for Nowrooz to be brought down to Bashed. That had been marvellous especially when she'd thought he was lost to her forever.

'I've found him. He is ready for you,' said Reza. The horse's coat shone, and his mane had been brushed. He tethered the reins to the side of one of the stalls and watched Elahe's face brighten at the sight of her horse after her six months' absence. He represented her old life and she searched in her green jacket pocket for a carrot. After the reception she'd grown restless. The British major had spoken to her, stumbling over his words, and she'd been flattered. But his foreignness had jolted her back to the past and the world she'd come from. Memories of meeting her girlfriends in Tehran at the Kentucky Fried Chicken restaurant had flooded her mind. She missed their light-hearted banter and jokes. She also missed the university, the classes, and the teachers. She even missed Nasreen's love of pastries.

'Thank you. What's your name?'

'Reza Ali, madam.'

The tethered chestnut pawed and snorted between them. Elahe sensed Reza's eyes on her as she took time with her horse, familiarising him with her voice. She turned her back on Reza and didn't take the reins straight away. She flicked some escaping hair back under the net and adjusted her hat. Elahe smelt the rich odour again as she stroked her horse's neck and whispered words of affection close to his ears. Nowrooz pawed the stable floor impatient to be away. Elahe walked him outside, but before she put her foot into the stirrup, she handed Reza the crop. After settling herself in the saddle, she leant down and couldn't resist brushing her hand over his as she reached to take it. He fumbled and his face darkened as he undid the reins and led her out into the late afternoon heat. She somehow knew he was watching her ride away.

A few jumps for riders had been set up in a barren, dusty area which the expats referred to as the paddock, but which couldn't support one blade of grass. As soon as Elahe and her horse were through the gate, they galloped as if they were in one of the local furious horse tournaments, where all the riders clung like leeches trying to retrieve a sheep's carcass. The horse whipped up a cloud of dust and she shut her eyes for a moment, hearing the rush of air whistle past her cheeks. When she opened them she saw flecks of white spittle on her hands, and she pulled on the reins. 'Gently now,' she said. 'We must play safe. Not the jumps today. It's too soon. I'm not bold enough.' The pace slackened and her hands relaxed on the reins as the horse obeyed her request to return.

Reza looked as if he hadn't moved the whole time. 'Here, take him,' she said, and she passed the reins over to him. He did as he was told and led the horse away towards its stall, where he wrapped a blanket around its dusty, sweaty body. Elahe looked at Reza's back while he busied himself with the saddle. 'That was good,' she said. 'He rides well. Have him ready for me each week and make sure you do. Do you understand?' She'd drawn herself up to her full height after taking off her riding boots, but even so she was slight and a little thinner than when she'd first arrived in Bashed. Elahe searched for a few coins to give Reza. 'Here, take these.'

'Yes, yes. *Kheili mamnoonam* I... But...'

'But what?' she asked.

'I not the groom every day. So I not here sometimes when you come. I work for the British major. I his chauffeur.'

'Oh no. I didn't know that.' The realisation that this local, fellow Iranian was employed by her British major startled her. 'I've seen you behind the bar at the golf club and now you are here. But I didn't know you were a chauffeur too. What's it like working for one of them? I expect they pay well, at least. We had lots of British and Americans in Tehran, they came to parties at our house sometimes. I wish I was back there.' She turned and took off her hat, shaking her plait free. 'Still, after my father died, I lost my...' Elahe was about to tell this groom about the way her freedom had been curtailed, but knew that to say such things openly would be scary, like crossing a new bridge over a deep, fast-flowing river. She knew nothing about him and would never share intimacies with such a person anyway.

'My father's sick and not good. It makes problems,' said Reza, who didn't seem to hesitate in speaking openly.

She supposed she had given him money and he wanted to make things all right after their shaky beginning. He was poor and would want more tips. She hoped he wouldn't start to pester her. Why had she started to flirt with the man?

'I need jobs for money for my mother and sisters. These horses...well, new job for me. I know the drinks and bar work and others show me. But animals...only my family goats before. These big. But Nowrooz like me. I hope.' He patted the muzzle of the chestnut and lifted up some hay on the palm of his hand for the horse to eat.

The horse's breath steamed visibly in the sun's rays and scattered a chequered pattern over the mud and straw on the floor. Elahe stood beside the horse and near to Reza. He didn't speak Farsi that well and Bakhtiari words had peppered his speech, but his words sounded honest. She smiled and made no attempt to move. 'Looks as if he likes you,' she said. They continued to stand side by side listening to the horse crunch the straw. For some reason she wanted to hold the moment for as long as possible. Whereas before, she'd deliberately touched his hand just to see his reaction, now she was too scared to do so, and she didn't understand why.

A shape darted across the entrance and blocked the light for a moment. Reza's body stiffened. Elahe didn't notice, but when she walked towards her auntie in the waiting car, she saw a Citroën had been parked nearby. Then a woman she remembered briefly from the reception got out and went to the spot where she picked up her riding boots. Elahe walked over, pleased to see another woman whom she dimly remembered.

'Hello,' she said. 'You are joining the club too? Think we both were at that reception the other night, but we didn't speak. I'm Elahe.' She put out her hand towards the young woman, as she knew they welcomed that custom on first meeting someone new.

'Nice to meet you. I'm Annie. Yes, think I did see you amongst all those bow ties and white jackets. Think you wore something blue, didn't you?'

Elahe nodded. This Annie didn't look that much older than her and had a friendly face. Elahe smiled. Her auntie, looking through the waiting car window, smiled too, happy to see her niece's recent sulkiness had disappeared.

Chapter 15

ANNIE STOPPED TO buy a bottle of orange at the first tiny shop on the outside of the town. The grizzled face of the shopkeeper smiled at her and then he concentrated on prising off the metal top with a knife, before presenting it to her with a flourish. His shop faced the main street and two Bakhtiari men with the flowerpot hats and striped waistcoats passed her leading their loaded donkeys, their woollen saddlebags bouncing up and down.

She remembered what Margaret had said once at one of her coffee mornings. 'The antique ones with the vegetable dies. They're the most valuable bags. Billy bought some the other day.' She had continued to list for Annie all the kinds of things that they had collected over the years. She'd finished by mentioning the African masks they'd bought in Kenya. 'Can't bear to look at those African masks though. Bought before that Mau Mau business. Had to put them away in the attic. Had to put them out of sight. They remind me too much of that dreadful time we had in Kenya when Billy was in Nairobi. Never knew when they would come for us. Makes me shudder even now. Glad this posting is so secure. Billy couldn't take that again.' Margaret had clutched at her pearls then and turned away. Annie had stared at the bun of hair at the back of Margaret's head as she moved away, and wondered if she would be able to face something like that.

The wool for the Bakhtiari bags and rugs came from the fleeces drying on the hillsides. Bent-backed women were like tiny dots walking amongst huge drifts of wool. On the edges of the shanty town others twirled the wool on wooden spindles as they stood guard over their flocks. One of the donkeys in the street screeched as he received a thwack from a much longer piece of wood. Annie's orange spilled down her blouse. Squeals and shouts from the other animals and their owners added to the noise of the many passing scooters, always it seemed driven with damaged silencers. There were bananas and dates at the next 'godown shop' as they were called by the expats, and Annie purchased a bundle of each, pointing at what she wanted and nodding vigorously. She felt compelled to buy something, but was also tingling with the experience of being out on her own at last, out in the world by herself.

The meat shop nearby had carcasses of bloody meat covered in flies and swinging from metal hooks. Despite the sight of so much gore Annie didn't feel at all disgusted; in fact she began to smile at the passers-by. Two women started to argue over some onions which had spilled onto a patch of diesel oil. One of them had knocked into the other, who had been carrying a baby on her back and by her side had a younger child wearing a dirty, over-sized red dress. That child emitted a series of owl-like shrieks. The groups of men and shopkeepers rushed over to investigate, dragging and jerking their donkeys, whose ears shot up like large fur gloves in surprise.

They shoved Annie out of the way and her back came up against a metal shutter. She searched around for a way out of the crush, and then froze, as across the road she saw the elegant young woman who had been at the first reception and the riding club. This time, she was speaking to a man and as he turned Annie saw it was Major Jack's handsome chauffeur with the dark eyes and wavy hair. She'd spotted him working part-time at the riding club too. He handed something over to the young, elegant woman and then walked briskly away, turning his back, crossing to the other side of the street.

The nearby dispute ended with the arrival of men waving more sticks, although this time they were used to threaten the women and not the donkeys. A crowd of youngsters were left tugging at Annie's cotton trousers. She bought sweets, handed them around, and the kids ran off to display them to their mothers. Her car was parked at the side of a garage, beside piles of reconditioned tyres and puddles of diesel, and as she made her way towards it, her mind went back over what she had seen. Reza and this young woman knew each other as they would have met at the stables, Annie told herself. But why the meeting today? Was there a connection with Jack? Sheila had told her he was a philanderer and Annie herself had seen him staring at the young woman at the night of the reception.

Mike returned later that evening. Pete had given him a lift to the golf club and then John had brought him back. His face wore his sullen look and didn't change even after he opened the door into the kitchen to find it pungent with the smell of baking. The bananas and dates were now part of a cake just finishing off in the oven, and her cake was a kind of peace offering, although as soon as she had taken the cake out of the oven, she knew it was a waste of time. Mike had been dead against her trip. But, she'd wanted to see the town right from when they'd been hovering above in the plane. He'd piled up his reasons against her going away alone and lectured her. He disliked her having the use of the car for a start as it kept him housebound on Saturdays or dependent on their teacher colleagues. He'd also told her it was dangerous by herself. 'There's everything we need in our own supermarket. Last week I saw single malt whisky and even New Zealand lamb. Crazy, if you ask me, to buy anything down in those shops. God knows what dangers there are in the gloomy bazaar. My advice is not to go and don't come crying to me if you are attacked or robbed.' He didn't seem to remember that her granddad had been a market trader in the Old Caledonian Road market in London, and she loved bargain-hunting. He made no reference to her past life or her family she suddenly realised. It was as if he'd wiped them clean away and they didn't exist.

'By the way,' he said after they'd sniped at each other most of one evening, 'I've changed my mind about you teaching.'

Annie was too stunned to reply immediately. 'Too late Mike,' she replied at last. 'I've accepted the job offer from Major Jack and told him, haven't I? You'll look a fool in his eyes if you try and tell him any different. Plus you will draw attention to yourself. You know what gossip goes on. The place is small, I've found out. Don't be an idiot.'

He jumped up and hollered over her. 'Idiot, am I?'

She shrank back in her seat. 'I didn't mean it, Mike. Look, I'm sorry. We're talking at cross purposes and it's late. Let's talk about it another time. I know you said you wanted to start a family but well...a baby isn't just going to happen like that, is it? I can teach first.'

'It's not only the teaching, my little wife,' he said, lowering his voice only a fraction, 'but I don't trust Jack, or Mike, or even Pete for that matter. You'll be with other men and, well, it's all men, isn't it, except for Margaret. I...well.'

So he was jealous and suspicious it seemed and he'd confirmed that himself.

Reza stepped out of his sandals and rolled up his trousers. His father did the same and clung to his son's arm as he washed his feet in the metal trough outside the small mud-brick mosque. Many in Bashed had fallen into lazy ways and attended prayers once a day and not the customary five. Reza was one of those. A few of the mullahs had started preaching about obedience, and today ten minutes of the mullah's speech was about just that. Reza kept his eyes downcast during the lecture and vowed he would try to attend more often, if only to please his father.

It had been a busy day as his major had wanted him to collect some crates of wine for the golf club and after that he'd needed to take the major's gardener to the hospital with a cut foot. The hospital had been built at the same time as the housing compound but in another part of the town, and it had taken him an hour to get there. When he arrived he had to push his way through all the relatives who constantly pestered the nurses and doctors while camping out in the corridors. Some of those nurses were foreigners and Reza stared as some looked very similar to Colleen, the American nurse who'd befriended him.

The gardener was an old man but a hard worker, and had been recruited to tend the gardens of the compound ever since they were established. He was one of those who had planted the tall oleander hedges which now hid the bungalows of the foreigners. Most of the compound was invisible from the two roads that surrounded it and Reza had never seen it from the air as Annie and the others had. His wider family and the locals had constructed all the compounds and the clubs as well as the gardens and he was proud of his countrymen.

Namoos or pride had been the same word used by his father as they ate their chapatti and egg later, before work, but it had been to do with Reza's new job at the stables. 'Your grandfather would have been proud and happy about this. He was an excellent rider and used to compete in our tournaments. I took you to see him once. He rode like the wind. You were tiny, suppose you can't remember.' Reza had shaken his head. 'He loved his horse. I always remember it was a grey with a fierce-looking stare. He was brave even when he broke his arm and couldn't compete so much any more. Lost his edge then and the younger ones took over. Don't you remember? Dead now, of course. He hated cars though, and hated me working in a garage.' His father swallowed some egg scooped up with his chapatti at that point and Reza had stared at the lump of food travelling down his father's thin neck. He hoped his father would always feel proud of him.

Elahe had begun to take over from Colleen in his thoughts so now he made sure he always had Nowrooz ready for her. The same day as the gardener's accident Reza's major had told him to find Elahe and to hand her a letter. 'Take the old man to the hospital and give this to the colonel's niece. You know the young woman, Reza. I don't want it to be given to anyone else, only her. Is that understood?' The *farash* or gatekeeper at the house had told him that Elahe had gone to the post office in town that morning, and after his visit to the hospital he had tracked her down. He'd felt his cheeks redden as he'd handed over the letter, but she'd smiled and the transaction then seemed worth it. He had been ordered by his boss to do this errand but it was by no means a distasteful one.

Chapter 16

'You've got it all, Sheila,' her mum said. 'Why wreck it? Why not keep the lad sweet? I ken your Jack. He's OK. Better than most men.. My God – your father was a different kettle of fish. He was a tyrant and I had it really tough. But I knew it wouldn't be easy for me out on my own. That's why I stuck with the pig and wept tears of joy when he died early. Believe me, that's what women do. Tough it out. You make your bed... OK, he's had affairs, Sheila, your man. But then they all do, you must have come to realise that, my lass.'

'OK, Mum. Please stop,' said Sheila.

Her mother shoved a chair hard back under the table. Sheila's brief visit back home to escape had seemed a good idea the day before, when some of the wives had been offered empty places on the Fokker Friendship plane to Abadan, prior to taking a direct flight to London.

'Look, I'm only here for a wee while. And I needed to...well, to get away from all this stuff.'

'I am sure Jack is not the only one in his regiment who has had an affair or two,' her mother droned on.

Sheila headed for the kitchen door.

'Start to get a grip. I'm sick of you whinging to me and you're becoming a bloody lush. No wonder he has other women. Really, Sheila, if you weren't my own lass...I...well...wouldn't want.'

'What, Mum? What wouldn't you want?' shouted Sheila. 'Christ, can you stop? I'm out of this hoose tomorrow. I'm out all day seeing the boys and then I'm going to join a job agency.'

'You! Get a job?' said her mum, who by this time had turned back to wash the breakfast things and tugged at the hot water tap. The water splashed over the dishes and onto the floor, while outside a damp British sun attempted to break through low cloud.

The dripping water in the sink suddenly reminded Sheila of the swimming pool and the nice young teacher she had met the first week and who had helped her at the reception. Sheila reached for a towel to mop the floor and gave her mum a weak smile. 'You're right; you're right. Shush, look, put the kettle on, Mum. I'll...'

When she returned to Tafneq she'd try to speak to Annie. Maybe talk things over with her.

Jack's note had taken him four hours to compose. In the end he had only managed to come up with *'I would really like to meet you and speak to you privately – Major Jack'*.

Afterwards he realised that the 'really' sounded desperate, but by then it was too late and he had given it to Reza to deliver. He decided that if there was a response, and that was the possibility he prayed for, then it would make sense to ask Elahe to arrange the place and time. He knew she would be chaperoned in Bashed. His sense of what was allowed for females was sketchy, and he had to tread carefully. Despite the claims about how free the place was and the sights he'd seen in Tehran, he wasn't stupid, and here in the countryside it was different.

Jack's world had been dominated by men. The world at his all-boys school was much the same as in the military. Despite his parents' 'ordinariness', they'd found the money to send him as a day boy to a private school. There boys were appreciated for prowess at sports and general competitiveness. Any talk about women or family was in a jokey way, accompanied often by lewd gestures or a certain vulgarity that undermined the possible seriousness of the topic. They never said if they were sad when a friend died or a parent was ill. The only change in thirty years was that the officers' mess had replaced the school changing rooms. But Jack himself thought he had changed and that now he had a better idea as to how to handle his affairs and what pleased women, if only because of his experiences.

He tended to put on an act most of the time. It was an act when he barked out his orders to Reza Ali or to his gardener. It was an act when he joked with his mates at the golf club. All the time he felt he was living as another person, who lived in a uniform. Just sometimes, it wasn't an act, as in Tehran and with his friend Alan. There he had been able to speak about himself. It had unlocked feelings inside him and these had led him to Elahe. But his feelings for Sheila were all negative and he was afraid to voice those even to Alan. He was still keeping up the charade of a marriage, and he had his kids to think about. There were others maintaining the same double life with other girlfriends. He had hoped that he could be like them. But his desperation was real. He willed that Elahe would be attracted to him, as it was, he now knew, the one thing that was maintaining his sanity.

He heard the stamping and shouts outside his office of the second group of students as their officers marched them towards the classrooms. One or two of these officers had become quite friendly with his teachers. They chatted together at break time and offered cigarettes to each other. Once or twice they had been given lifts by the teachers into town. He hadn't spelt it out exactly that they could be both secret police as well as the

Literacy Corps. He didn't want the teachers to be frightened, and if relationships developed, well, so much the better. The tallest and skinniest of these officers was one of the Iranian colonel's constant companions. Jack wondered who was keeping an eye on him, because he hadn't yet noticed a tail. Perhaps he ought to think himself lucky, he reasoned, or perhaps he was small fry and just of no importance at all.

'You're late! Lunch has been bloody well ready for half an hour. I dinnae ken where you've been.'

Jack saw his wife stabbing her fork into the meat. She was clenching her knife in the other hand and she waved it at him. He backed away from the table.

'Come on, Sheila, give us a break. You only arrived back yesterday from your little holiday in the UK and I'm already in your bad books. Right? No answer?'

'Yes, I've got an answer for you,' said his wife, and with the steak knife still in her hand she pushed her chair back and stepped towards him. He made a promise then to keep his pistols in a special case with the key always on him.

'Don't want to speak to you in that mood, Sheila. You look dreadful by the way. Thought the trip would do you good. But I was obviously mistaken. If anything you're looking worse.' He knew she was unsteady and drunk and he shouldn't taunt her. 'I'm off to take a shower, so I'll be another five minutes. You carry on with your lunch and then take a nap, you may wake up in a better mood, but, well...I very much doubt it.' He said the last words to himself as Sheila had sunk back down onto her chair, staring at her plate.

Jack slammed the bathroom door and stripped off his khaki army shirt and shorts. He cooled off under the water as it sprayed over his body as he tried to relax. Writing love notes to Iranian girls was one thing but shouldn't he be doing something about this situation first? How the hell was he going to be able to meet the girl with this harridan at home? He needed his own place somewhere and to finish with Sheila completely.

Silence reigned in the house when he came out of the bathroom. Sheila had finished and her plate was on the table beside a half-empty bottle of wine. She wasn't anywhere to be seen and he felt relief oozing into him. He sat down and took off the cover from the meal their servant had prepared that morning. If only Sheila was like Margaret and ready to occupy herself with a part-time job. Why didn't she organise a little library or a social group for craftwork? Last week, Margaret had arranged a cake sale at the cricket club and the proceeds would help with equipment in one of the children's wards at the local hospital. She was a selfish bitch and a useless wife. But he was frightened of her and really couldn't bring himself to try to finish the marriage. He only wished he could.

Chapter 17

THE FOLLOWING WEEK Jack went to Tehran. He stayed at the Continental Hotel and could walk to the head office from there. At seven in the morning the road outside the hotel throbbed with yellow Paykan taxis, Toyota trucks, and beat-up scooters. The latter seemed to move the quickest, weaving their way through the mass of vehicles. Jack didn't have the same success as he tried dodging around and in front of the cars, whose drivers slammed on their horns as soon as he was seen. He clutched at a bent pole when he reached the opposite side without noticing it held a cluster of dangerous-looking cables. During the crossing, he had stepped into puddles of dirty water and now his shoes and the bottom of his trousers flapped damp and muddy on his legs. He blew his nose to get rid of the acrid taste in the back of his throat, and then tried to clean his shoes.

'Bloody drivers,' he muttered. 'Why can't you keep to the rules?' He shook his fist as a car nearly ploughed into the cables and him. The head office had requested a report and demanded that he bring it. It lay ready in his briefcase, typed up immaculately by his new secretary Margaret.

Jack was dealt with quite briskly at his appointment in Tehran. A few of the new arrivals from London were rushing around and stopped to shake his hand, then slapped him on the back with a *good job, old chap* sort of comment. The man he met was a civil servant who asked for his report straight away and then looked at his watch. He put it on his desk alongside other papers. 'All this pile,' he said pointing to them, 'are from the six other colleges we have set up now. It's quite an operation. isn't it?' But before Jack could answer he ushered Jack towards the door. 'Keep up the good work,' he said as he opened the door. 'I've heard tip-top reports. Must go now.' They shook hands and Jack was once more thrust into the throbbing traffic.

A cafe nearby looked inviting and Jack went in and ordered a coffee. Two miniskirted British girls arrived not long afterwards and sat down at a table behind him. They looked like secretaries from the head office. One of them seemed to recognise him and gave him a smile. He couldn't recall seeing her, so maybe he was mistaken. Their conversation drifted his way and he heard the city of Qum mentioned, which he knew to be one of the cities further east. Beautiful place so he'd been told, with many mosques and a religious centre. He overheard the words 'difficult' and 'problems'. He would have liked to ask them what the problems were but thought it wise to finish his coffee and this time find a taxi to take him back to the hotel for lunch and a rest.

After a sleep, he had a sinking feeling, like a solid lump that had settled somewhere in the pit of his stomach. It was anxiety about the future. Where was he going with his marriage? What did he have to look forward to in life? He looked at his figure in the bedroom mirror and ran a comb through his short hair, peering at a slight balding patch on the crown of his head. His light brown colouring made him stand out in the crowd here, as did his height. He was a good head taller than many Iranian men and attracted glances in the streets of Tehran. He wasn't so very old but he'd definitely lost his way in life. Taking up this post hadn't done much for him so far and he'd started off with such high hopes.

It was a bustling western-style city, but a glimpse of a blue-tiled minaret on a mosque or that of a murky side street smelling of rotten fruit reminded him it wasn't London or Paris. The long hair and the youngsters' fashionable clothes were the same everywhere though. But his youth had vanished and his life was hurtling along. Despite being married he was really on his own. He felt pleased that he had still kept in touch with his old school-mate Alan, who was living in Tehran. A link with his past made him feel young again even if only for a brief time.

Jack locked the door of his hotel room behind him and then he straightened his dark blue tie and tightened his belt. It felt odd now wearing civvies. But tonight he was going to try to enjoy himself. He was in Tehran – some called it the sexiest capital in this part of the world – and he would let his hair down and hope something good would happen.

The Shah's middle classes had plenty of opportunity to spend their wealth and he had seen classy cars pull up outside the hotel and had caught a whiff of expensive perfume while waiting for his taxi in the hotel's reception hall. A large chandelier dangled and reflected sparks of light above his head. They seemed to be everywhere. Feathery potted palms were grouped around low copper tables where smart Iranian men dressed in suits sat smoking and drinking tea from tiny decorative cups. These men didn't show any interest in Jack but he was aware from time to time in the hotel lift that he was often accompanied by an Iranian who didn't wear such suits or look like a businessman, but who seemed to want to scrutinise him when he thought Jack wasn't watching. Probably secret police, Jack thought, and he decided he would use the hotel stairs and slip out a side door the following day. Too late on this occasion, as he saw the waiting Alan.

'Hello, old fellow. God, you look fit.' Alan slapped Jack on the back and patted his own paunch, and they both laughed. He led Jack to a scruffy yellow taxi waiting outside the hotel. 'How's that damn heat? Don't know how you chaps can stand it. I'm glad that I will be back in the UK soon,' said Alan. 'My job here is finished for a while and I'm back in London next month for a furlough. But you chaps will have to live most of the year baked like bread in one of those open brick ovens. You have my sympathy old boy, you certainly do.'

Jack smiled and relaxed for the first time that day. His friend knew the place and he felt he was in good hands.

They settled back on the slippery seats smelling of hot plastic and watched as the driver lit up a cigarette, stubbing his last one in the already overfilled ashtray, and then switched on the radio, where the ululating music of an Iranian singer with full orchestra drowned out any attempt at further conversation. The driver switched channels halfway through and a Beatles' song drowned out the noise of the traffic. The man twisted his head round and gave them a grin. Jack smiled back and nudged Alan.

Later, in the restaurant, Jack was able to assure Alan that in fact his lifestyle had its compensations. He was his own boss and he described his servants and house and the ease with which his teachers had organised their timetables leaving him plenty of time to take up golf.

'Well, it's not so bad really, not so much excitement as here probably. What's the latest whispering in the corridors of power and oil wealth? I've got a whiff of something going on but no one seems to want to talk. Have you heard anything?'

'Not a word, old boy. Not a word,' replied Alan. 'You are probably imagining it. Safe as houses this place. But look, let's find a quiet table first.'

The conversation resumed as they sat facing each other behind large glasses of a Shiraz wine, in a window seat away from most of the other restaurant tables.

'Shah's got all the hardware and all the power. What can go wrong? The Yanks are here in force. They've got their secret service men everywhere. There are a couple in the same apartment block as me. Can't speak the bloody lingo here but have all the equipment for eavesdropping. A few Iranian stooges help them and they file their reports to their bosses at the American embassy.' Alan paused and his eyes flickered over to Jack and he saw that his friend looked tired behind his smart facade. 'Personally I think they are being paid for nothing. But it makes the Americans feel they are doing something. But as I said, the Shah is one of us – he's going to look after us while we're here.'

Alan's confidence coloured the rest of the evening. Alan ordered the foie gras and truffles and handed the menu over to Jack. 'I'm getting paid a lot, so are you, I expect.'

Jack nodded.

'My overseas allowance makes my eyes water. I expect yours does too, old boy.'

Jack nodded again and this time smiled. He noticed roast beef and apple pie on the menu.

'Then all these little nocturnal trips are free, of course – all expenses paid,' continued Alan. The waiter interrupted them with Alan's starter, and Jack pointed to the caviar. The restaurant had started to fill with large groups of Iranians at the nearby tables.

'It's a bonus to be able to see the women properly in Tehran,' said Jack, after he'd consumed the dark, tangy caviar. 'They're all in their houses in Bashed or covered up riding on a donkey. Well, except for—' Jack wiped the corners of his mouth with his white napkin '—Not that that hasn't a certain sexual appeal, don't you think? I'm told that there are women available, well, a sort of brothel in Bashed, but...'

'Well, you've got army wives to swop with if you can escape

from that Sheila of yours,' Alan exclaimed. 'Mind you, from what you've told me about your past, seems that you've not done too badly.'

Jack laughed. 'That was in my youth, Alan. Older now and more difficult to...'

'Yes, but Sheila's worse, so I heard.'

Jack's smile vanished. Had the gossip reached Tehran? he wondered.

'You know what I'm talking about. Alright for us to get blotto but she...well she goes a bit far. That's all I've heard. Not to worry. By Christ, she's not the only one. Some of these American wives here leave me speechless. Look, enough of all this. Action eh, tonight? Eat up and we'll visit that nightclub I told you about. A belly dancer there whose stomach wobbles has everyone mesmerised. Who knows, we both might get lucky.'

Chapter 18

Elahe sat in her old childhood bedroom in Tehran. Her English novels from her brief time at the university, her old pop records, and photos of her younger self taken at the Caspian still sat on her shelves. Nothing had changed. Her auntie and uncle had brought her back for a visit to see her mother. Beside her was an open, empty suitcase, which she shoved to one side as she ripped up photos and then crammed the rest of her things into the case. What did it matter if they were damaged or broken? Once she'd done that, she smiled and decided to paint her fingernails and have a bath. She stripped off her long skirt, which her auntie had made her wear in Bashed, and threw it on the floor. Tomorrow she would be off with her friends for the last chance to buy some new clothes.

After her bath she telephoned Nasreen. 'Can't meet. Sorry, Elahe,' replied Nasreen. 'Things are a bit difficult at the moment.'

'Why is that?' said Elahe. Her heartbeat quickened, scared as to what she might hear. 'I wanted to see you and...it's so dire in Bashed I thought you would want it too. What about Laila?'

'She's left.' Nasreen's flat voice sounded distant.

'What, like me? You mean moved away from Tehran?' said Elahe.

'No no,' said Nasreen.' I mean left the university. And I'm...

well, I'm thinking of it too. Not the same without you and things seem different. We went to the canteen for a while like before and then, well, some of the other students, you know, those that used to be behind us?'

'Oh, you mean those rather attractive men?' said Elahe.

'Well... '

'Well what?' said Elahe.

'They started to make remarks and...'

'My mother's life, Nasreen. Please tell me what sort of remarks.'

Nasreen had never been so reluctant to gossip before. Why the hesitancy? Elahe needed gossip and chat. Her friend's conversation was going nowhere and then she blurted out a remark which also had Elahe speechless for a moment.

'I'm getting married as well,' Nasreen said.

'What?' said Elahe.

'Yes, I...I, well, I should have written and, but, well, I'm going to the States.'

'Lucky you,' replied Elahe. 'Why didn't you write or say before? Why all the secrecy?'

'Well, you know now,' said Nasreen. 'I must go. I will write...I...' There was a gasp and a break in Nasreen's voice almost as if she was holding back tears and then a silence. 'He's old, Elahe. He's very old and I'm frightened and...but I can't see you, I just can't.'

There was a crunch at the end of the phone a moment before the call ended. It sounded as if Nasreen might be eating. Some things never change, thought Elahe, even though her friend's words had shaken her more than she realised.

A knock at Elahe's door after she'd called her other former friends brought her back to the present. She'd been lost in thinking about what they'd said, and how they'd sounded, distant and unfriendly. Aesha found her niece with tears on her cheeks sitting slumped on her bed in her pyjamas. She perched as close to her niece as she could.

'Your mother and I understand, Elahe. We really do.'

'*Kheili mamnoonam,* thanks, but it's not much good, is it, Auntie? I'm not going to be allowed to return here. It would have been better for me to stay back in Bashed. This is like torture. All my friends have gone away, others are getting married. Why? Why? Are things so different? I thought it was just me and that when I returned I could be the same. Now I don't think I can. Last year, we were all students, although my brother Gholam's still studying, of course. Mind you, it gets him away from spying on me. He started to come in here and read my diaries, you know.'

Aesha shook her head. She had found the changes unsettling too. Many shops had shut and shopkeepers didn't want to speak to her as they'd done before. Strangers were everywhere.

'Your mother said...well, she suggested it really,' said Aesha. 'She wants to go with us to see the dancers like we used to. Have a meal all together, before we have to return next week. What do you say? Come with us and enjoy yourself. I'm taking your cousins as a treat. They're a bit young but it might be the last time they get to see the place. Many of the places closed down recently.' She didn't mention the letter that had arrived, from her Uncle Jamshyd. He had a new list of suitors for Elahe and was arranging for them to visit and pay court in Bashed. Maybe she would tell her niece after their visit to the nightclub, when she might be in a better mood.

It was the first time Jack had seen dancing like it. The music was hypnotic, so that when the main dancer burst on the scene all spangles and jingling with bright brass pieces, it was such a visual and bewitching experience that the audience rose from their chairs clapping and cheering. As she danced she slid and shook her way across the stage. Her body's olive skin seemed to glisten and look almost wet. The place was packed with large families and rich customers who were delighted to be out enjoying themselves and who stood up to sway with the music and the dancer's hips.

Both men were caught up in the charged atmosphere. The lighting was low and there were candles on the tables in beautiful brass containers which flickered on the audience's faces. At one table Jack thought he caught a glimpse of that girl from Bashed. He looked again. It was a table two away from where he and Alan were sitting. He looked over a third time, and this time he stood up and carried on clapping as the main dancer left the stage. He quickly looked away. He was convinced it had been the same girl.

Jack smelt burning. In his haste to stand up and get a better view he had knocked over the candle. 'Hey! Watch out!' Alan grabbed the candle and its brass holder and set it upright. 'Nearly had the place on fire, old chap. Seen someone, have you? Bet you have. You're a bit of a dark horse. Don't say too much, do you? Never did. But there we go, takes all sorts.'

The young woman was with the older one Jack had met before, and there were three much younger girls, who hopped up and down laughing and clapping at the noise. This time she wasn't wearing a headscarf and her blouse was of some kind of silky substance. Jack glimpsed long golden earrings beneath a mass of raven hair tumbling down to her shoulders. He could admire her beauty even more without the headscarf. She turned his way and by the way her mouth opened as she drew breath and the quick turn of her head, he knew she had seen him. Jack spied the Iranian colonel sitting at the same table. The youngsters were about the same ages as his sons and their smiling faces tore at his heart for a moment. Now he had seen her twice, and a desperate urge came over him to be introduced to her properly.

'Can I buy you a drink?' said Jack. He had been watching the table like one of the eagles that circled at the golf club and he now pounced on the colonel, who had decided to go to the bar for a refill. The waiters were swamped with orders for food as the place was full to capacity. Jack had left a drunken Alan alone at their table. When he looked back his friend's head was resting on his splayed-out hands. 'I'm Major Jack Castle, sir. We met at the reception in Bashed last month. I'm in charge of the English teachers.' Jack shot out his hand as he said these words and waited for the colonel to recognise him. The colonel looked surprised to hear a British voice. Jack saw the man's face go stiff and his heart sank.

'Oh. Well, yes, a whisky, please. Single malt.'

'What a surprise to meet up like this, sir! Saw you and instantly recognised you.'

The colonel busied himself with a packet of cheroots, seeming not to listen.

'Great atmosphere and good food. Expect the cabaret will be worth the wait, don't you?' The man's face still looked stiff as a statue and he didn't answer but busied his hands with lighting a cheroot and taking sips from the glass of whisky, which had just arrived.

'Cheers.' He lifted the glass towards Jack. 'That's what you say, isn't it? I must return to my family, Major. No doubt we will meet up in Bashed at work.' He turned away in a cloud of smoke which made Jack's eyes water.

Jack wiped at his face and leant forwards as the colonel began to move. 'The cadets are making good progress, sir, you'll be pleased to hear. We've a good team of teachers, and... Your English is very clear. I expect you studied abroad.' Now he had the man's attention and the colonel faced him.

'Cambridge actually.' The man's eyes strayed back across to the table where his family were sitting, but his face remained a mask. He needed to ask the question which he had been rehearsing in his head as soon as he'd spotted her. Jack took the plunge.

'I was wondering, sir, if you would care to visit me back in Bashed one evening. I have some good Scotch and I would be very pleased if you would do me the honour. I could even take you round to those language classrooms and introduce you to the teachers personally.'

The colonel put his glass back on the bar. 'Call me Abdul, Major. I think I heard your name is Jack. Correct?' Then Abdul put the cheroot back in his mouth and Jack leant forwards with his lighter.

'You have a lovely family, Colonel...er, Abdul. That attractive girl, is she your daughter? You must be very proud.'

Abdul's dark eyes stared back at Jack's blue ones, holding Jack's gaze. 'Not my daughter, but my niece Elahe, and yes we are proud of her.'

Jack nodded and smiled. 'Yes. Yes, of course you must be. I'm proud of my sons too.'

'This is just a little break for her back with her old friends for a few days and to see her mother, my wife's sister,' the colonel said. Jack nodded again. 'My wife Aesha and the family are already lining up a few suitors for her.'

Jack's smile vanished. That sounded like a warning to him and his blue eyes gazed into the dark depths of the colonel's.

'But I really must return to my family, Major.' He ground his cheroot out in the bar ashtray and the acrid smoke stung Jack's eyes.

'Come and see me at my house, please. It's a new one in the Iranian compound. Telephone me when you return from Tehran. I also have single malts.'

It seemed to Jack an unexpected invitation after the last remarks and Jack mumbled his gratitude. Later he left the club in a mood of excitement and even Alan's vomit in the back of the taxi didn't spoil his happiness.

He went over the whole scene later in the hotel bedroom,

and before he lost consciousness whispered the name *Elahe.* He repeated her name in front of the same mirror the following morning. He'd had 'experiences', of course, as Alan reminded him. There had been a cute little Irish waitress who still wrote him letters although he had given her an auntie's address in Aberdeen. The auntie had dutifully kept them till he paid one of his yearly visits. 'It's a friend from the past, Auntie, someone who can be a bit of a nuisance. Hope you don't mind. I don't really want to tell them not to write.' Jack hadn't told her it was a woman. Maybe she had guessed, but she enjoyed her favourite nephew's visits and never questioned him. And there'd been other women, some only girls, but as soon as Sheila began to throw things and mention their names, he'd dropped them. They really hadn't been serious and Sheila had always been willing to patch things up, until recently that was. This job had come at the right time really and he'd begged Sheila to give him and their marriage one last try in a new place. She'd agreed, but despite that she hadn't stopped drinking and as she hadn't made an effort then neither would he. Not now, not when he'd just met the girl of his dreams.

The afternoon after the visit to the nightclub a large Iranian man, one of Elahe's potential suitors, visited the Tehran house. Elahe had been told very little but when he appeared at the family lunch under the chenar tree in the back courtyard, she immediately knew. His large pockmarked face broke into a grin as he was offered a seat beside Uncle Abdul and Gholam, who pointed to her whereabouts at the end of the table beside her mother. The maid was in the middle of serving iced melon. Bowls of pistachio nuts and dates had already been laid in front of the family.

All Elahe could think about when he smiled at her was how ugly he was compared to the British Major Jack or even the groom Reza. Apparently, this suitor was rich and worthy, and one of many on a list that Great-Uncle had drawn up. A wealthy lawyer who'd already had two wives who'd died in childbirth. There were three boys needing a mother and he was prepared to accept a smaller dowry if she would become wife number three. Elahe couldn't stay angry with her mother or Auntie Aesha for long. Auntie was pregnant after all and her mother was now at her wits' end as to what to do. She'd explained to Elahe that even a widow who had some money and was living in Tehran still had to follow traditions. Mahshid had received orders that she needed to return to Qum and the family home. Gholam would take over and live in the Tehran house until he chose to marry. There was never any question of consulting Elahe about her future now her father was dead.

Chapter 19

THE SOUND OF drumming boots halted outside the classroom. Annie hastily pushed back her hair, tied it up behind her neck, and then put on her glasses. She moved her papers and pens around making sure she had them ready and then decided to remove her watch. It left a red ring on her wrist as she placed it on the scratched surface of an old desk. She needed to see how the time was going as it wouldn't be a good start to the job to finish this first lesson too early or too late. On her desk and pinned to the wall were pictures in black and white of hammers and screwdrivers, the kind of thing that her students, young trainee army cadets, would have to use with their British military instructors.

Seven o'clock and the sun had already baked the mud outside to a fine dust. Reza had sprayed water over Jack's car that morning, but the brief, refreshing smell of wet earth had soon vanished to be replaced by the sweet, rank smell of sewage, which lingered at the far end of the classrooms. There, the only toilet discharged everything into the black, sluggish, murky river. Her cadet students had crossed the evil-smelling river by way of a flimsy-looking bridge – a shortcut from the other workshops of the college.

She had written her name on the makeshift blackboard and now turned to face the door, expectant and excited. It creaked open and a shaven head appeared. Her first cadet student stood at the entrance wearing a creased khaki uniform. His trousers were criss-crossed with laces at the ankle and his feet were encased in extremely large boots. He couldn't see much after the brightness until his eyes adjusted to the gloom, but when he spotted Annie, his mouth broke into a grin and he turned round to face the others scrabbling at his back. Seconds later, she heard a muffled cheer. An adult voice boomed out and then there was silence. The door creaked open again and an officer stepped inside sporting a smart peaked cap with a wrinkle-free uniform and a blue silk cravat. The teachers had been told they were members of the Shah's Literacy Corps. They were all graduates sent out to poor areas to help raise literacy levels.

Then, like the flickering reel of an old silent comedy, Annie's first students shuffled in wearing boots several sizes too large. They resembled Charlie Chaplin figures, and their antics as they scrambled and fell over one another in their quest to find a chair in the front row merely confirmed this. The chairs presented an obstacle to most of them as they were the type with small attached arms. Some tried to squirm themselves behind the wooden arms, like snails trying to return to their shells, while others stood back and waited. A few clever ones had worked out that the arms could be folded back to allow ease of access to the seats. The noise of fifty pairs of metal seat legs scraping over a concrete floor thundered under the high roof. The officer from the Literacy Corps waited looking angry and upset at their noisy entrance. He blew his whistle and shouted, and only when he had the cadets all silent and quiet did he walk over to Annie.

'Pleased to meet you, madam. My English is from Tehran. I think it is not good.'

He stared at her, his face unsmiling, and his eyes searched her face. Annie knew at once that he would be a problem. He turned and retreated to one of the chairs on the front row which he had reserved with his army cap. Annie sensed her celebrity status and the attention it commanded. Soon, fifty pairs of eyes focused on her and followed her up and down her raised platform. No one said a word until the silence was broken by a student, the class comedian, who began parroting and repeating everything as Annie pointed to pictures on the board. At the sound of his voice and the strange English words, the class burst into laughter. The officer jumped up and bellowed at them. They fell silent again, but retained their broad grins. They looked like they were enjoying things and Annie smiled back.

Annie had been well aware that a western woman teacher was a novelty for them, and the mad rush for the front seats had confirmed this. She pointed to herself and to the name on the board. She doubted that they would recognise the Roman alphabet but perhaps some would. Most she knew were illiterate, but were good at mimicry.

'What is your name? His name is...' She pointed to herself. 'My name is Mrs Brown.' The officer sat stiffly on the edge of his chair holding his cap and gloves. He turned from time to time and had started to translate but couldn't keep up with Annie. He then decided to take a seat at the back of the class, which intimidated the students, and so she walked to the back also and had various students go to the front and repeat the words and phrases.

The officer slunk to the far corner where he busied himself scribbling in a notebook, and soon the boys forgot the officer's presence, while their faces grew serious when they were called upon to repeat things. Their expressions conveyed a sort of wonder and towards the end of the lesson, many edged forward on their chairs, shooting their hands up in their enthusiasm to supply the correct answer. They even corrected each other in a friendly way.

When she had a chance to look closer at the cadets, she realised that there were older ones with crow's feet at the corner of their eyes and lines on their faces. Jack had told her that a place at the college had been in high demand. There was the offer of three square meals a day with accommodation and pocket money. Even those in the towns who were employed in the oil fields or in the markets had been tempted to apply. They had had applications from cities like Tabriz and Qum in the north as well as the country regions on the far-flung borders with Afghanistan and Turkey. She'd read about some of these and was desperate to visit and see for herself the beauty that she knew was there. So far she'd only seen photos of blue-tiled mosques and bazaars stuffed with carpets and metal goods.

Someone blasted out three notes on a bugle outside. Her watch told her that the lesson should have ended five minutes previously. The fun had distracted her from clock-watching, which had been a part of school life for teachers as well as pupils back in England. The cadets struggled to their feet. Some of the chairs toppled backwards and red-faced they set them to rights and faced the front. The officer sprang up from his chair and walked like a stiff rod to the front, brushing at the dust on his trousers. He glared again at them and then turned towards Annie and gave her a bow before folding his notebook away and stuffing it into his jacket pocket. She wondered what he had written there. Had it been satisfactory? She must ask one of the others if they had one of these graduates too.

She joined the two teachers Pete and John in the dusty heat and they watched as each class formed into rows and were marched away. Mike came out of his classroom. She turned with a smile on her face and he raised an eyebrow. 'You survived then?' he said. 'Think you will want to carry on?'

'Yes, why not?' Pete and John had by this time retreated to the office for some iced water and cigarettes.

'Well, I feel great,' she replied. 'I feel really great, Mike. It was worth coming all the way out here for this. They were magic. I'm so glad I'm back in the classroom.'

'Well, I'm glad you're happy about it. I think these conditions are impossible. No air conditioning. How are we supposed to teach so many in such classrooms? Absolutely terrible.'

'Oh darling. I'm sorry. Yes, you're right, of course. The heat does get to you after a while. I...I didn't mean it was easy, but well, it's better than being stuck in the house and...'

'And what?' said Mike. 'Ever since we arrived you've been plotting against me in some way. Now you're going to be here all the time telling everyone how wonderful things are. You're making me look a fool. Other men have their wives at home and doing something useful.' He walked away at that point back into his classroom and left Annie as she searched for her cigarettes.

'Coming for a drink, Annie?' said Pete as he strolled over to her beside the shade of the only palm where she was sitting smoking on the bench below. 'Seemed your class was a hit. Squeals of laughter was all I heard or silence. You must have tamed them or something. Mine are just a noisy rabble. My officer is useless at keeping them in order if that is what they are supposed to do. Anyway, interested?'

An hour later, Annie was ensconced in the cricket clubhouse with Pete and John. Mike's angry face appeared at the entrance and he beckoned to her. As he drove her back to Tafneq he made sure he took the corners at high speed and she slid against the thin metal door of the Citroën. Back at their bungalow she fled to the bedroom and for the first time locked the door. He yelled outside about leaving him out and him being her husband, but she blocked her ears. She had trouble now in remembering when he'd had a good mood. There were flashes of pleasantness but they lasted about as long as desert twilight.

Chapter 20

'YOUR CONTRACT HAS come through, Annie. Please take a seat by the air conditioner. It gets hot doesn't it, in this place?' Jack pulled a plastic chair from a stack behind the door and dusted it off with his handkerchief. He then placed it by his desk. He repositioned the photo of his four boys and noticed that Margaret had put new plants on the windowsill. He passed across two sheets of paper with a Tehran stamp on the top of each. The words 'local contract' were clearly written just below it. Annie bent her head and he watched her sweep her brown hair back from her face. Her hands had slender fingers and there was a glimpse of the smooth skin of her arm. A slight scattering of freckles which hadn't been there before was across the rim of her nose. She looked, at last, towards him. He could see the understandable disappointment in the frown on her face and she gathered up the papers as if to bolt.

'Just a minute, Annie. You need to read it and then sign it, please. Look at your salary and hours. What do you think?' Silly to ask such a question as he knew and could see by her face that she was expecting a contract like the men. Annie's face reddened and the freckles on her nose looked a deep crimson.

'I'm sure you know what I think, sir. It's obvious, isn't it? I've already taught for two weeks and done the same hours as the others. But this is a local contract. It's not the same as the others. Why is that, sir?'

Jack saw Margaret move behind his glass office door. She must have heard something, and so Jack kept his voice low as he answered. 'It's really all I could manage to get you, Annie, my dear. I tried, I really did, and phoned Tehran twice about it. But they wouldn't have it. All the expat women here are on a local contract and that's the way they want it. You're different, and doing the same job. I told them that,' Jack lied. 'It's probably my fault. Look, forgive me. I rushed in to ask you to join us and didn't think about the money side of it. My fault entirely.' He wanted to save himself in front of Annie somehow but didn't think he'd convinced her. He'd been pleased to see a fresh female face around the classrooms and appreciated her acquaintance with his wife. He remembered his gallantry on her arrival but now he had Elahe on his mind and in his sights, Annie looked like becoming a bit of a nuisance.

'I see,' Annie said. 'Thanks for explaining, but well, you can see I'm disappointed and I'll write direct to Tehran myself. Not your fault. You just follow orders, I know.' She turned and walked out of the office and left him silent and stunned.

Chapter 21

REZA WAS SILHOUETTED against the stable doors without Nowrooz, and Aesha immediately placed a restraining hand on her niece's arm. Elahe shrugged it away.

'Elahe, please, show some patience. Give the groom a chance. Is this your behaviour now? Wherever we go you are bad-tempered. This anger is unseemly if nothing else. Remember who we are and don't let my husband down.' Aesha moved away shaking her head. What had she done? Elahe had so far refused to be anything but difficult.

'*Salaam Aleikum*,' said Reza.

Elahe mumbled her reply. A horse nearby neighed while another whinnied at the far end of the stalls. The pungent reek of dung and straw drifted towards them. Aesha left then to climb into her air-conditioned car holding her handkerchief to her nose. She closed her eyes once inside and switched on the radio.

'Where have you been?' Elahe asked Reza. 'You're late yet again – I'm due back in an hour's time and my uncle is breathing down my neck at the moment. Do you understand?'

Reza shook his head when she repeated her question. His black eyes flickered over her head, and her hair.

'He expects me back on time and today Auntie's with me. She turned in the direction of her auntie and waved her hand at the car parked beyond the fence.

'I sorry,' Reza replied.

'Look,' said Elahe. She handed him her riding whip to hold as she balanced on one leg to pull up one of her boots. 'I didn't mean that. How's...how's your father? Is he better?'

'No, missus, no.' Reza hoisted the saddle onto the horse's back, fumbling with buckles and losing the bit and harness in the straw. It took him much longer than the five minutes it would normally take. He'd been awake most of the night listening to his father's breathing and worrying about the future. As he led the horse out of the stall he was drenched in sweat. Elahe's anger suddenly resumed and she ripped the reins from his hands and put her right boot in the stirrup, hoisting herself onto the horse's back. Losing her balance at the last moment, she fell over and Reza helped her up. She could feel his hard grip steadying her body. Mounting Nowrooz at last she kicked her heels hard into his flanks so that he almost bolted, reared his front legs, and then galloped to the other side of the enclosure.

The adrenaline rush of speed calmed her, and her anger began to dissipate. There was no point in taking it out on Reza or Auntie as she knew it just made matters worse. She couldn't carry on feeling like a fly caught in a web, waiting for something good to happen. Elahe felt close to tears and then without a warning she heard a crack as wood splintered around her head and she landed in the dust. Reza ran towards her. It looked like a slow-motion film reel.

'Nothing broken. Nothing at all. Leave me and just get the horse back. Damn nuisance! You're to blame – no, that's not fair.' She winced with pain from her grazed hand and knee.

'Look, it's me. Reza, take this hand and pull me up, can you?

The other one hurts.' Elahe stretched her arm out and Reza gripped it tight and pulled her upright. She stood close to his lean, tense body and sensed the wariness still clinging to him in the way he stood in front of her. He went and fetched some water to clean her injuries and she let him bathe her hand and bandage it. Later he helped her to a bench in the shade of a poplar tree. When he had delivered that first note from his British major she noticed he had kept his eyes away and left her immediately on the street. He was new at this job and unused to horses and the stables. Now he was helping her and she needed to show understanding. How could others understand her if she didn't try to do the same for them? 'Where did you learn your English?' she asked him in a rush. It seemed to startle Reza and he didn't reply for a minute or two.

'With the Americans when I worked at the compound.'

Elahe studied his black eyes and even teeth.

'I was a chauffeur then too and I did some work in the bar at the swimming pool.'

'Didn't you have to drive that major's wife home with that other young British woman?' He nodded. 'The women drink, don't they? Strange women. Do you know that's the first time I saw a drunk woman?' Reza remained silent.

'Look, I'm OK now. Thanks for helping. Don't tell anyone about this, otherwise I'll be banned from riding,' Elahe said. He nodded.

Elahe limped her way with Nowrooz back to the stalls. He whinnied at that point. She rubbed her hand along his soft muzzle before leaning her head forward and whispering in one of his velvet brown ears. The horse had been scared before and his ears had been flat and stiff against his head. Nowrooz twisted and struggled but Elahe whispered and stroked his head, before holding a sugar lump out to him on her palm. The horse sniffed and then nibbled at it, revealing his large teeth.

'I must go,' said Elahe. 'I'll bring some vitamins soon. For your dad.'

Reza's sad face broke into a smile. '*Kheili mamnoonam*, very kind and many thanks, missus. Next time I better with horse. Now he like me.'

The horse allowed him to stroke his back.

Cloistered back in her room in Bashed, Elahe thought about the way Reza's face had lit up when she'd mentioned vitamins and his eyes and face stayed in her thoughts for the rest of the day. She took longer to prepare herself for her next riding visit. But nothing Elahe had learnt from her girlfriends or the cinema had really prepared her for a foreign admirer, or not one like the major. Reza was attractive, there was no denying it, but the major was much more interesting. Yes, he was married, and a lot older, but then his foreignness made him interesting in a kind of exotic way. Without someone to speak to about things Elahe knew she would go mad. Her three boisterous cousins were much younger than her and her auntie wouldn't listen or speak to her as before.

'It happened at the Caspian,' Elahe said. Reza was polishing her new boots on the following visit. They were a deep golden colour, and he sang under his breath. '*Kheili mamoonam* – very grateful to you, Reza,' she said.

He looked up wondering why she was being so friendly, and then blushed under her gaze.

'I was a student at the university in Tehran before this place.' She said the last words as if they burnt her tongue. Reza concentrated on his hands as they made a circular motion with the brush. 'We went on a family picnic. My great-uncle has a summer house by the Caspian. I went to paddle and play with the other younger ones at the water's edge and I rolled up my trousers, and when we ran back the old spoilsport went to speak with my mother and made her cry.' Elahe spoke in a rush and stopped at last for breath.

Reza put his brush away and looked straight at her face.

She smiled, holding him with her eyes. 'Apparently, the paddling was the last straw. The older uncles had decided that studying at the university was not appropriate for the girls. It was too western. My poor widowed mother was unable to bring me up as she should, and I was becoming an embarrassment and getting a bad reputation. Well, I could go on. That's why I'm here. That's why I want to come riding. The colonel and Auntie Aesha know how unhappy I am and what I miss. They are sad that things are changing in Tehran and that the religious rules are being taken so seriously now. In Tehran we liked to talk about the Shah and the wonderful dresses of his queen. They have many horses and it's a real event to visit the racecourse. Do you know about our Shah?'

'Yes, of course,' said Reza. 'Cinema in Abadan and...' The Shah's new, third wife was educated in France. She'd been a rich Bakhtiari and the tribesmen in the area had held a full week of celebrations with horse tournaments and their famous musicians. But that marriage hadn't produced any heirs so their Shah had gone searching and in Paris had found and married the new, fertile, and educated one. Many of the rich Bakhtiari families were affronted by that and it had caused bad feeling in the town. They spoke about it often. Elahe stopped speaking and pulled a note from her jacket pocket.

'Here's a note for that major of yours, and something for you.'

Reza stood up and put his hand on his heart. Some money was with the note. He watched her face as she spoke. She looked a little thinner and her cheeks paler than before, but her full lips and eyebrows like two bird wings still fascinated him. He would like to reach out and pass his fingertips over their silky shape. Horse trading, he thought. The buzkashi or horse tournament in

Bashed had men showing off their horse flesh. Was she like one of those poor horses to be bought or sold to the highest bidder after they'd won in such a competition? He'd never thought in that way before. But as she recounted the details of the picnic by the Caspian he realised it was true. He could picture that place although he had never been nor was ever likely to visit it. He knew there were trees there which were so full with leaves they filled the sky when you peered upwards, their branches almost sweeping the ground, and that the water came from the snow and the mountains. Maybe it was sympathy she wanted. He didn't know why. But ever since he'd seen her at the stables he had known there was a knot of worry and anger in her which exploded at different times and he could sense it just as her horse Nowrooz could.

He needed to tell her he had the same problems. Well, they were not the same in many ways but didn't his uncle want to map out his future too and wasn't he always reminding him, like his mother, of his cousin? He wanted to have a holiday at the time of Eid and not hear that talk about his future constantly hammering in his head like a wild hornets' nest.

'I know, missus,' he said, at last gathering up his courage.

'What do you know?' Suddenly Elahe stiffened and looked surprised.

'Yes, my cousin in Abadan. We must marry. The family, like yours, insist.'

'That's not the same at all.' Elahe turned away from him pushing her hair back into her coloured scarf.

'I expect she's young,' Elahe said as her curiosity gripped her. Reza nodded. 'And pretty?' Reza nodded again. 'Well, that's not the same for a start then, is it? You know my suitors will always be older.'

'No, you right,' he replied quickly. He shouldn't have spoken.

'Still, you have a point,' she said and made a half-smile with those lips. They both were silent and Reza could hear horses munching straw and the sound of a car's tyres crunching over the gravel outside, which startled them both. Elahe stood up and brushed down her clothes. Reza gave her the boots and dusted off his trousers and straightened his shirt. His hand touched the money in his pocket. He glowed inside knowing that a rich beautiful Tehrani woman now trusted him. Never had he felt this good. The Eid holiday was approaching and he would be able to buy his mother some new material to make dresses for his sisters. She was busy cleaning the house, getting his sisters to paint eggs and gathering together all the seven items to celebrate.

When Elahe and her auntie left the riding club, a large black Toyota pulled away and followed them. Both women turned to stare out from the back of the window and tried to see if it was the SAVAK policeman that they'd spotted outside their house, who now seemed to be a permanent fixture. But the car kept its distance, and they were both pleased to return to the safety of the house and its compound. 'This surveillance is for our own protection,' the colonel had told his family not long before. 'A military compound and this contract can attract all sorts of undesirables. Don't worry,' he'd said, 'we are all on the same side.'

Chapter 22

The Iranian officers' compound was on the other side of the town, and well away from Tafneq. Jack hadn't really thought or wondered about the position of the two but he knew it made the drive today seem tedious as the only way to get there was through the centre of the town. The stench from the river infiltrated the car. Rubbish floated on the river's surface and hopeful goats populated the bank with ribbons of detritus hanging from their mouths. Jack passed shuttered shops where packs of snarling dogs fought each other over bits of raw meat and bone.

He'd telephoned the Iranian colonel the previous evening. He had made himself wait a few days after returning from Tehran and then on the telephone chatted purposely about his trip and Tehran before broaching a specific time and day which would be convenient after the colonel's invitation. Now he was on his way and feeling nervous as a kitten.

The compound had been built very recently for the Shah's army officers and was a curious mixture of buildings. There were half-built bungalows already inhabited with flapping washing, while in another part chunks of four-storey houses rose above high cement walls and large spiked metal gates. A moth-eaten group of grey palms grouped around an old man's head and cart as he sold ice lollies to groups of kids. Unlike Tafneq no oleander hedges had been planted.

'This one, Major. This is the house.' Reza went to open the door.

Jack peered out and looked up at the high, metal gate, which soon started to shudder and open. Just behind it, within the grounds, was a small corrugated and brick dwelling, where the old gatekeeper had his bed and samovar. This old man had opened the grid in the gate when he heard the car drive up outside. Jack tipped the old man and Reza got back into the car, drove it into the large driveway, and parked it beside the two Mercedes and a red BMW.

The colonel was already standing on the top step outside his front door. He looked just a little older and less flamboyant than when Jack had seen him in Tehran. The house itself was showy and imposing with white columns and marble steps, but Jack couldn't spot any outside windows only an entrance leading to an open inner courtyard with statues and tall palms in engraved brass pots.

'Good to see you. I am pleased to welcome you to my home. My wife has ready the mint tea and...well, I do hope you like such things. You British like your tea, I think.' The colonel stepped down to clasp Jack's hand. It was a much warmer greeting than before in Tehran.

'Thank you, sir. Yes, of course, very refreshing and maybe some cold water, please.'

Jack's face was already bathed in sweat and he didn't want Elahe to meet him in such a state. He followed the colonel into a large reception room. Settees stood along the edges of the room and a ceiling fan tried to refresh the stifling air as it hummed in its trapped circular path. The colonel flicked the air conditioner switch and immediately the air felt much cooler. But Jack was still hot and undid his jacket. He was tempted to take it off but his nervousness stopped him. This was the first time he had ventured inside an Iranian home. He fidgeted on the settee and fumbled with the glass of tea which the wife offered him. She also asked him to take a pastry from a large silver tray. Her entrance and the tea had given Jack a moment to start to breathe.

She was a plump, friendly-faced woman with a shiny satin skirt of a vivid red, and a matching blouse. She wore numerous gold chains and rings on her hands, and her house slippers had quite high heels which clicked on the tiled floor as she stooped and offered the refreshments. 'Here, Major. These are very delicious.' She handed the tray over to Jack and pointed out one of them. There was no evidence of any single malt whisky so maybe that had been forgotten.

The colonel's wife retreated back through one of the many doors. He could hear voices and laughter coming from another door and the smell of roasting lamb drifted in the air. He put his tea down on the table in front of him and spilled a drop in his haste and then licked the sugary residue from his fingers as the pastry melted on his tongue. The colonel was scrutinising him from behind his smoke. Jack's cheeks felt hot and then cold and he cleared his throat. The sound echoed and the chandelier above their heads tinkled. Both men looked at each other but nothing further was said, and Jack concentrated on slaking his thirst with the large glass of iced water which had also been on the tray.

Earlier that day Abdul had spoken with Aesha's Great-Uncle Jamshyd on the telephone. It had been a difficult conversation. Well, for him it had been difficult, but not for Jamshyd, who pointed out in no uncertain terms the unsuitability of the suitor in Tehran for his niece. Seemed like the man was too much a Shah's man, although Abdul thought everyone was. Uncle Jamshyd wouldn't spell it out over the phone, but said he would send a private message with a party of his followers from his mosque in Qum. They would be visiting Abadan, Ahwaz, Dezful, and arriving briefly in Bashed before journeying on to Isfahan. There wasn't much goodwill between the two men at the best of times and recently with his brother-in-law's death and their hospitality towards Elahe, Abdul had noticed things had become even more strained. He and Aesha had enjoyed their last Tehran visit and the nightclub, but some of his old favourite restaurants and clubs had closed down. They'd kept that visit a secret from the older family members. Both knew that it would be their last one for a long time.

'I'll come straight to the point, Major. You like my niece and I want to know what this is all about. You have a wife, don't you?'

Jack spluttered as he swallowed his tea too fast. Abdul had been hatching a plan after his phone conversation with Jamshyd and wanted to get on with it. That's why he had joined the army. He was a man of action and not used to matters defeating him.

'Well, sir,' said Jack.

'Call me Abdul, please. We're on the same team now, aren't we? Both trying to get this college off the ground. You've got your men and I've got mine. But we are all working together. Need to be friends too, don't we? Sometimes things don't go according to plan. Expect you've had your fill of difficulties and unexpected events. Things getting awkward. Better if we keep things running smoothly, keep in touch, all of that and work together.'

'Absolutely sir, I mean Abdul. Agree completely. Call me Jack. Glad you feel the same as me. I was wondering about a picnic and wanted to invite you all. I've been living here a bit longer and well...I managed to find a few places which are really pleasant this time of year. Down by the river. Not too far, and it flows clear above the town.'

'Good. That's settled,' said Abdul. 'Cigar?'

Jack didn't like them but accepted one of the colonel's cheroots eagerly. It was going better than expected.

'Like her, don't you?'

'Excuse me?'

'No point beating about one of your bushes, I think you say.'

Jack realised it was a joke but was still too flustered by Abdul's direct manner to reply with a smile at the joke.

'I think you are speaking about your niece and yes I do. Very beautiful and so elegant. We spoke at that reception a while back. It was only briefly, Abdul, but there seemed to be a magic, an understanding. I know I'm too old and of course there is...'

'Well, your wife, Jack. You're married. What are you getting at? Someone like Elahe deserves a good match, don't you think? Are you saying you think you could be a suitor?'

'I'm getting a divorce soon.' Jack flushed with the fierceness of his voice and he waited as his words sank in. He stubbed out the nasty cheroot and walked over to the window where he saw Reza drinking from a bottle and smoking with Abdul's gatekeeper. He had his back to Abdul and felt his eyes penetrating his jacket. Jack drew breath before turning to face him.

'Well, that could make a difference,' said Abdul. 'Now, I must go. I have an appointment with my tailor down in the souk here. Yes, let's meet again. Send word about that picnic.' Abdul ushered Jack out of the lounge and stood watching him as Jack called to Reza that he was ready to leave.

Reza had stayed in the car and from time to time switched the engine and air conditioning on to keep cool. The old gatekeeper had wanted him to share a bottle of lemonade which he had in a bucket of water at the back of his hut. Reza knew that Elahe lived in the house and that she was the colonel's niece. He'd been pleased she'd taken to speaking about herself to him. Her bad moods and anger at his incompetence had decreased, and he'd practised saddling up and dealing with the horses so that each time she came and he was working there and not chauffeuring his major, he was more proficient. He could see the pleasure she took in her riding and it gave him pleasure too, knowing that he was helping her.

But there was a fly, or perhaps many flies, in the ointment. He fiddled with his radio and tuned in to the warbles of Iranian love music. He switched it off. His major was one of the flies. He was most probably meeting Elahe and making himself more acquainted with her uncle and auntie. But his major already had a wife back in the British compound and Reza knew that the westerners would only have one wife at a time. His Shah did too and wanted everyone to follow suit. In the towns maybe this would work, but in the country such a rule was often flouted. If the woman or girl was a relative and poor then something was arranged.

He remembered when his American nurse had wanted him a while back. He hadn't had much affection for her. She was far too old for one thing. But even though Elahe seemed to like him when they saw each other at the stables, he couldn't think there would ever be anything more. Still Elahe spoke to him like one of his sisters or his cousins in Abadan. She was haughty and could be a bit mean, but he liked looking at her and he looked forward to her next visit.

Another fly in the ointment was him and his poverty. Nothing he could do about that. He fixed his eyes on a mangy cat sitting on the wall washing his coat. After a while he had to get out and he accepted the lemonade and conversation from the gatekeeeper so as to stop his thoughts.

'Well, that went well, Reza.'

'Excuse me, Major. I not understand.' The major had climbed into the back of the car.

'The colonel and I had a frank talk and well...he was friendly. Good...as we are working together on this contract but...well, I hope to plan a picnic. Those notes for the colonel's niece. They will continue by the way. Thanks for helping me out there, Reza. Maybe we understand each other more. What do you think?'

Reza made no reply.

Chapter 23

ELAHE HAD WANDERED off to explore the riverbank, and on her return heard raised voices. She moved out of sight and stood behind the thick, rough trunks of welcome palms. She held her breath as she strained to listen.

'She's got a chance with this man,' her uncle said. 'Aesha, my dear, listen to me. Just listen. He's interested. He turns up at our house and now this picnic. He's getting a divorce, by the way, so give him a chance, Aesha, my sweet. She's not going to succumb easy to marriage with one of your family's suitors. You know that!'

'Abdul, stop!' Aesha interrupted. Her everyday soft voice had vanished and Elahe increased her grip on the palm trunk. 'A divorced British major, Abdul,' continued her auntie. 'No! How can we or anyone in my family accept that? It's unthinkable. Abdul, are you mad? Oh I...'

'What is it? What's the matter, Aesha? Didn't want to alarm you and...'

'Nothing, nothing, Abdul. It's the baby, that's all, moving around and...'

'Sit back on the cushions, for my sake. Relax and leave all this to me. I'm not so stupid and want the best for us, you know that.'

Elahe took this as an opportunity to peer at them both from her hiding place and saw her auntie sitting on the ground tugging at her sunglasses, which dangled over her ample pink chest on embroidered threads. Elahe retreated behind the rough, fibrous body of the tree and scraped her cheek. The picnic at the Caspian Sea eight months earlier had been the last time Elahe could remember being truly happy. Since then her life had deteriorated. She wanted to be the tree and not an Iranian woman. Not someone who was jealous of the freedom of eagles sweeping circuits above in their search for dead fish on the riverbank.

The expat oil workers had named this particular beach and pleasant shady spot Tenby, after the seaside town on the Welsh Pembrokeshire coast. It wasn't for its landscape or situation, although both were by water, but like the Welsh Tenby it was 'Little England by the Sea'.

The party had arrived by way of an old metal bridge which had lasted since those times, and then through some steep blanched rocks of a high ravine travelling beside the gushing torrent of a tributary of the River Karun on its journey down to the *Shatt el Kebir* or Persian Gulf. No other cars had passed them and so they'd been expecting the British major to be waiting.

Aesha had chosen this shady place, a little away from the narrow track, but visible to the major. She studied Abdul's face and knew there was intelligence behind his jovial exterior. She worried about her sister Mahshid's health. Her letters had become infrequent and were peppered with '...and Gholam says...' as if her voice had disappeared with the death of her husband.

'Well, he does come to the stables to see her and is always the English gentleman,' said Aesha, 'and she's useless in the house too. No good as a teacher with the girls. They take no notice of her. I've tried to instil some discipline into them. But, well, since we left Tehran and they left their school, they're running wild, and with this baby, well I'm tired and...'

'So you agree, Aesha? The arrangement's not working, and if you don't have a better idea we must adopt mine. His last words sounded loud. 'But, well—' he searched the track and raised his head towards the road in the distance '—if the man doesn't arrive soon, I'll have to think of someone else. There's a new Iranian family moved in two doors away. They have sons and...'

Aesha made no reply and Elahe started forward ready to confront and remonstrate, thought better of it, and sank down to the ground.

At that point, Elahe's three young cousins, their mouths stuffed with sweet *senjed* fruits, ran back to show their parents a dead fish on a stick, but Aesha shooed them away when she spotted Elahe and patted a cushion beside her.

'Well, where is he? The damn British, always wanting to be boss and controlling us.' Abdul stabbed the air with his cheroot, but as if in answer, a dust cloud appeared. A car rocked to a halt and the brakes squealed in protest, the sound reverberating along the valley cliffs. The major walked towards them waving his hand.

'Sorry, so sorry not to be here for you,' he said. 'Please forgive me, Colonel – I'd forgotten that Reza, my driver, had asked for the day off to go and visit his family in Abadan and so I had to find the way myself.'

He wore slacks and a sensible, wide-brimmed hat, and even without his uniform, he had a lean, firm shape. In the stables Elahe had not noticed his body, as it seemed invisible, always parcelled up in a military uniform, but here she could compare the two men close up. Her uncle's waistline had spread and his neck was thick, whereas this major looked much the younger of the two.

'I have visited here before with a group, but I didn't take the right road this time.' He continued to speak as his eyes wandered her way. Elahe busied herself helping her auntie to her feet.

'I'm Jack by the way,' he said, 'and hope you'll call me that from now on.' Jack extended his hand in greeting to her auntie and then her uncle. She cast her eyes downwards as his hand gripped hers.

'Well, yes, late, aren't you?'

'Abdul!' Aesha said then moved closer to the major. 'Don't mind my husband, Jack. He is tired these days but we are happy to see you and it's so delightful here. You are kind to make a picnic. My children are already discovering the river.' She waved her hand in the direction of her daughters who'd returned to the sandy gravel on the bank. 'A lovely idea. Most charming of you to invite us, and it looks like you've brought a magnificent feast.'

Jack had lifted a large wicker basket from the boot of his car.

'Abdul, you haven't set up the samovar yet, and we must have tea first. Go and get it ready. Tush, my husband, Major. Needs a wife to organise him sometimes. But Iranian women make good ones if chosen well.'

'Auntie,' said Elahe, 'please...I'll help Uncle with the samovar and...'

'Yes, Elahe. I'm pleased, Major, that now she is smiling but difficult for a city girl in such a place, don't you think?'

Jack unpacked his picnic hamper and Elahe found herself watching him. She smelt the tang of her favourite chicken dish in its dark pomegranate sauce. He unpacked fresh flatbread, tomatoes, fruit, and sweet pastries. As he lifted out each item and handed it to her, she sensed his eyes searching her face, her neck, and then her body like a spotlight from a plane above and his eyes crinkled in a smile when he saw her sneak a glance at him too.

That morning, she'd taken extra care dressing. Her body was the only thing she seemed to control. She'd chosen a white blouse with a gold thread for the outing. It had long sleeves and a low neckline. As she'd opened her wardrobe, she'd inhaled the scent of leather from her Tehran coat. Pictures flashed before her eyes of the new university canteen, and she heard the sounds of her friends' laughter, and the clatter of cups and plates. She'd stroked and then screwed the supple leather between her fingers and wondered about her phone conversations with Laila and Nasreen. They often ended in silence, as if she had already receded from their world, and perhaps she had, a chapter of her life over and a crossroads reached. This major's letters had provided excitement, and there was some sense in her uncle's plan, she had to admit. She began to imagine life in an English village or town...but then, unbidden, Reza's voice and his calm brown eyes and thick dark hair invaded her thoughts.

'A feast fit for a king, Major. Or a queen in your case, isn't it?' Aesha addressed the major when they were halfway through eating. 'That delightful woman, your Queen Elizabeth. Saw her in Tehran when she came for a visit. I was only a child, of course.' Aesha giggled, putting her hand over her mouth.

'Please, my dear,' interrupted Abdul, and he shrugged his shoulders at his wife's last remark. Aesha continued to speak. Abdul muttered something and reached for the wine. After two glasses of Shiraz wine and two cheroots both men started telling each other jokes, and it was then that Aesha nudged her husband with her elbow.

'A few minutes of your time, Major,' he said. 'Will you do me the honour of accompanying me to my car? We can sit and speak there with the air conditioning to keep us cool. Did you see that SAVAK car over the hill?'

The major's eyes widened.

'But they need to do their job, don't they? We all have to put up with them. Hope you're not too bothered, eh?'

Not until they were in the car did Jack answer Abdul's remark.

'I know about our ones, Colonel, but didn't realise that you were also under scrutiny,' he said. 'Must admit that's thrown me.'

'Thrown you? What is this?'

Jack tried to explain without showing his nervousness.

When the major emerged from her uncle's car, Elahe walked with him by the river. She questioned him again about his wife, and received the same answer as her uncle. The implication was that he would be starting divorce proceedings, and all the time Elahe grinned and walked as close as she dared to his lean body. At one point he put his hand on her arm. Not a heavy touch but she felt it and, conscious of her role as seductress, withdrew a fraction from his range. She saw his face register surprise.

Before he left them, he asked about her next visit to the stables and arranged with Aesha that Elahe sit with him in his car while Aesha followed them in hers. 'I might borrow another car from the motor repair workshop,' he'd said. 'As you say, Colonel, we are all being followed, so let's play a game or two, eh?'

'Splendid.' And the colonel laughed as he patted Jack on the back before escorting him to his car.

Once he'd left, Aesha spoke. 'Well, Abdul's pleased. Are you, my dear?' Aesha searched her niece's face for an answer.

Tight-lipped, Elahe nodded. Things had happened. The conversation she'd overheard from behind the palm had sickened her, reminding her of all that had happened. So how was it she'd gone along with their plans? Why had she been so willing? She remained silent, her head spinning.

'Elahe,' said Aesha. 'Are you pleased?'

Elahe still remained silent.

'It's for the best,' continued Aesha, 'but let's hope there's enough time for him to get a divorce, what with everything else and...' She stopped speaking and played with the edge of the tablecloth.

Chapter 24

Reza flicked away some flies with his hand and went down a narrow entrance where all sorts of buckets, rope, and plastic goods were being displayed and collecting dust. Annie side-stepped the piles and her eyes adjusted to the dim light of the narrow passageway which took them into an alley full of carpets and bright woollen bags dangling from the fronts of the minuscule shops. The dealers had silky prayer mats cascading over their arms and swarmed like flies around them. The market smelt of pungent spices, leather, and damp wool. The smells flooded her senses and jostled with her increasing excitement. She stuck close to Reza with a false smile, and so the traders fell back once they realised she was with him.

Reza received countless embraces, and Annie grew impatient at their snail-like progress. 'We need to make a price for a carpet,' Reza said, at last. He looked serious and worried.

'Don't they say the price first?' Annie replied. He looked back at her fully for the first time, and he stared at her. 'We must do this slowly. First we make a price and then they make one and then we wait and shake our heads. Then we go. Do you understand, missus?'

'Go? Leave?'

'Yes! Leave and then return later and wait for new price. It may be we do same tomorrow.' Reza looked worried and serious. Annie thought she sounded like a parrot and a child. She'd have difficulty returning the next day and organising to have the car again.

'I thought we could buy it today. I was hoping we could get it now before we go to the hospital to see Tommy.'

Reza frowned. His eyes looked back at her and he shook his head three or four times. She had to follow him and trust his judgement. Why try to tell the poor man what to do here? She knew nothing about it. She changed tack and also changed her mind from a carpet purchase to buying a bag. It wouldn't be so expensive, she thought.

'What would be a fair price for that bag there?' She pointed to some saddlebags which were small, and closely woven in red, indigo, brown, and gold and spoke of places and people they had helped on their many journeys. The bags had long, plaited tassels and smelt of herbs and straw. She imagined they had carried knives and packets of salt or sugar for the wives to use for cooking, or rope and pegs for their tents. She picked out one that she favoured and looked to Reza to say a price.

The smiling shopkeeper offered each of them a tiny glass of mint tea. Reza took out cigarettes and they both smiled and started to speak. Annie hadn't a clue as to what was being said but her heart raced as the smiles and rubbing hands continued. The other shopkeepers swarmed at the entrance and then squatted on their haunches while their dark eyes darted back and forth at the scene inside the shop. A rich smell of horse flesh and burnt wood mingled with the men's smoke.

Reza stood up, startling Annie, and glared at her. He indicated with his head that they were to leave and she walked towards the entrance of the adjacent shop scattering the others, who retreated to dust off their wares. They walked about for all of twenty minutes. Reza didn't speak or turn his head towards her and she hoped it was part of Reza's strategy. But she was getting fed up with admiring plastic buckets and brooms and beginning to wonder how long it would all take. She had already been with Reza for longer than she had indicated to Jack. And then there was Mike. Fortunately, Reza turned back at that point and she stuck to him like a leech. Now she knew they were about to seal the deal and she hoped it was successful.

The old shopkeeper's brown lined face lit up and he rushed towards Reza and then nodded and went to get a ball of rope, which he proceeded to bind round the saddlebag to make a parcel. Annie held her breath. Reza's serious non-smiling expression continued. He asked for the money, which she knew was way below the amount she had mentioned back at the school. She counted out the dirty, ragged notes into his upturned palm and her fingers were left black and smelling of ink. Quick as a flash, Reza scooped up the bag in its string cocoon, shoved the money into the old man's paw, said '*Khoda Hafez*' goodbye, and was ready to leave. They emerged from the gloom some minutes later into the bright glare of the main street.

Once outside she began to breathe heavily and realised that she'd held her breath all the time she was watching the transaction. She gulped out her thanks as they hurried back to the car. As they drove away she tried to thank him again. But Reza only shook his head as if to shake it off. 'He was old that one and he had a sick wife. A bit easier to buy, missus.' Now she noticed it was 'missus' and not Mrs Brown like in the classroom. 'Some of them have a bad opinion of foreigners usually and want a big price. Sometimes don't sell. Good I tell them you help me with English.'

'What? Why the bad opinion? Why don't they like the foreign workers?'

'Too many dead. My father's father died when they were making the machines for the oil. Very big work to make the roads and drag all the things there. No water – nothing – too hot.'

She would have liked to ask him more questions about those frontier days but just then they passed the signpost for the hospital.

'The hospital now please, Reza. I want to visit the young son of the teacher – the young boy Tommy, you may have seen him, was exploring behind rocks in their garden and got himself bitten.'

'Yes, madam. Yes, but not snake as they think. Scorpion, I think you say. The one with the long fingers.' He took his right hand from the steering wheel and bent his forefinger and thumb into a pincer shape. 'Black one, I think. Not white one. The white more dangerous. Not good for a child.'

Annie should have visited the hospital before. She'd kept herself apart from the other expats more than she liked; John and Linda were neighbours after all. Mike, too, would have less to moan about if he knew she had been to the hospital as well as shopping. Although these days she could never tell what his reaction would be to anything. He was often morose or like a firework about something unimportant. But she knew he would interrogate her about the purchase and the price. More and more he controlled her spending.

It was her first visit to the hospital. The single-storey building had corridors and rooms bursting with people, and a few harassed-looking doctors and overworked nurses pushed past them. Reza found out the room number and took Annie to where Tommy lay asleep. John, her fellow teacher, was sitting by his son's bedside and had an unopened book on his lap. His eyes were fixed on his sleeping son's face. As Annie entered the room he ushered her towards the one other chair, pressing his fingers to his lips. His face had aged in the space of a week, since the incident; lines were etched on his cheeks and there were bags under his eyes. Linda wasn't visible but Annie had heard that she had been distraught and had had to be sedated back at the compound. Now Annie's guilt swamped her. Probably Margaret had made the effort and already visited the couple.

In the corridor outside John thanked her for coming and took her bananas and box of boiled sweets, purchased before they'd left the market.

'He's getting better, that's the main thing,' said Annie.

'Yes, but they don't know the long-term damage. I wish to God we had never come to the place, Annie, I really do. I feel trapped here now. When something like this happens you realise what a long way it is from everywhere. There's typhoid in the place and cholera. Do you know what Tommy said the day before he was bitten?'

Annie shook her head.

'He said that the place was spooky! In the middle of a sunny afternoon he said that and it's true isn't it – spooky and bloody dangerous.'

She was shocked into silence and then managed to blurt out more words of reassurance.

'By the way, Annie,' said John. 'I'm a bit concerned about Mike.'

Annie stood frozen in the corridor.

'Now I've got an opportunity to speak here in private. Well, I did tell Margaret.'

'Tell her what exactly, John?' said Annie, keeping her voice as calm as possible, while thoughts flashed around in her head. John was a large man and almost a head taller than her. She moved back so as to look upwards into his face and eyes.

'Difficult to explain and probably nothing. Well, you know Mike better than us, of course, and might have noticed things already. But, well, I went into his classroom and he was speaking to someone, and...but there wasn't anyone there, Annie.'

What could she say but only make some kind of explanation about...likes to practise his lesson planning like that. Then she turned away at the sound of Reza approaching down the corridor.

On her journey home Reza must have sensed something. 'The doctor say the boy OK now. It's good place'.

'Do you know about it?' Annie gulped out a question, not wanting Reza to feel she wasn't grateful for his help, even though her thoughts churned away inside, and she'd not properly thanked him.

'Yes,' said Reza. 'I had two younger brothers who were sick. The doctor tried to help but he didn't have the medicines. They both died but before the hospital come here. But now they have the medicines. They give my father vitamins and his eyes are better. *Inshallah* he will recover. So will that boy.'

'Your father's eyes are bad?'

'Yes – he is blind in the dark.'

She forced herself to speak again. The trip now seemed a bad idea and her head ached and throbbed, but it had been Reza's longest sentence as well as being the most personal.

'I am sure things will be better for Tommy and for your father. Let's hope Tommy makes a full recovery'—she realised he hadn't understood "recovery"—'better – well – soon, yes?'

Reza nodded.

Chapter 25

'Reza must know you. He works for the British so I heard.' Elahe and Annie were standing by the side of the paddock waiting for their respective horses to emerge saddled and harnessed. Reza, the groom, was leading each horse out into the bright sunshine three weeks after the Tenby picnic.

'He's a student of mine,' replied Annie, 'and my boss's driver. We thought it a good idea if he had extra English and joined some classes.'

It was odd but this was the first time the two women had met face to face. Annie had seen Elahe at the first reception and caught glimpses of her at other public festivities and here at the riding club, but they had never been close enough or had the privacy to speak. Elahe's skin looked like fragile porcelain close up but there was an air of sadness lurking in the dark eyes that made her seem older. Elahe cleared her throat a few times and her flawless skin became tinged with a pale rose colour. Annie had always thought that her boldness and dexterity in the saddle was matched in the flesh, but there was uncertainty about that judgement now.

'Umm... How do you like our country?' Elahe coughed behind her hand. 'Hot, isn't it, especially here? How I wish I was back in

Tehran and wearing a miniskirt. Might be cooler. Had to leave them all behind. Too conservative here. And now my friends have changed.'

'Changed?' said Annie, who knew that wearing cotton trousers and loose long-sleeved blouse as they had been advised to seemed the more practical and sensible option. She had a riding hat and special boots now, though loaned from the stables, but she felt shabby.

'Well, married or leaving the place, I meant. Can't seem to reach my friends now. Used to send a few letters. But I'm sure you will be glad to leave for England soon and have a holiday. Get away from all this dust and heat and...how I would love to visit your country, and I might...' She paused and hesitated.

'Well, I'm lucky now to have teaching and it keeps me busy,' said Annie.

'That's really good to hear,' said Elahe. 'And what do your students think about you? All men and boys, I think.'

'Not sure,' said Annie. 'I was told they'd never had female teachers. And I think it is only because there are so many students that I've been taken on. But they are easy, well, so far.'

Elahe smiled. 'That's the first piece of good news I've heard in the place.'

'Oh, I thought you being Iranian and...'

'Wealthy is perhaps what you think. No?

'Well, I suppose so,' said Annie, wondering if the conversation despite Elahe's good English was veering into difficulties.

'My favourite writer is Jane Austen,' Elahe said suddenly. 'She writes about marriage and trying to get married so well, doesn't she? I think I've read *Pride and Prejudice* five times, yes, at least five. What do you think about her?'

The unexpected topic left Annie at a loss as to how to reply, but at least talk about wealth had been dropped.

'I really wanted to go to the States,' continued Elahe, 'as I like American literature too. Still, can't think of that now. When you are young you have dreams, don't you?'

'It's...yes...it's sometimes the case.' Annie nodded, finding her tongue at last. She also needed to know more, her curiosity aroused by what Elahe had said. 'But what do you want to do now if you can't return to Tehran and your studies? I'm not really sure why you are here though.'

'Difficult to explain. Had to obey the older men in my family. You can probably understand.'

Annie made no reply but Mike's face flashed before her. She did understand about it and sympathised. She nodded towards Elahe, who stopped speaking and tugged hard at her riding glove.

'I don't want to be married but it seems they have a plan for me now. I did so want to study. I had one semester at the university and I managed to bring my books here.' Her voice petered out as both women heard the crunch of gravel and sounds of horses. Reza stood outside the stable and then came towards them.

Annie turned her head towards Elahe and Reza before she spoke again. 'You two are friends, aren't you?' she said.

Elahe and Reza looked at her and then Reza stumbled and retreated back towards the horses tethered outside. It seemed as if he had understood.

Elahe answered, her face serious. The friendly tone had vanished. 'With the groom?'

'Yes I saw you both in town and you seemed to know him, and...' Annie was about to add the words *quite well*, but Elahe's face told her she had already said too much and drawn the wrong conclusions.

Elahe stepped away. She turned back her cuff to look at her watch. Her reply came after she'd studied it for a moment which seemed longer than necessary.

'No, not at all. With a groom!? You are mistaken. He was...

Well, you might as well know, as you raised the subject. It's not what you think, and it's sort of arranged now.' Elahe shrugged, the haughty mood suddenly replaced by a sort of conspiratorial tone. She tugged at Annie's sleeve and pulled her further back into the stables.

'What is?' said Annie at last as all sorts of ideas buzzed around in her head.

'Jane Austen's favourite subject. Marriage, Annie, marriage. It's, it's...the major,' Elahe whispered.

'What?' Annie gasped and put a hand up over her mouth. 'You don't actually mean Major Castle, my boss, do you?'

Elahe nodded.

Two weeks later at the stables, Reza met up with Elahe. 'Is he better?' she asked him. Reza was not to know that she'd had one meeting with Jack as arranged, and he'd told her about the letters he had written to his wife and his resolve to clear the way for them to be married. He wasn't to know either that she hadn't known what to say. Things seemed to be hurtling along.

Reza spoke. 'Yes, missus, fully recovered now.'

'No! Not the horse, stupid.'

Reza's chest tightened at that last word.

'Your father. How are the eyes?'

His father's sight hadn't improved but the rapid deterioration had faltered. 'God is great and thanks be to God' had been his mother's response and there had been extra prayers at the back of the mosque in the women's quarter. Reza knew something had happened with Elahe. Her voice sounded different. Before, her words had fallen out of her unchecked like a waterfall in the hills. He calmed himself. She'd asked about his father, hadn't she? But she worried him.

Maybe she'd seen him with the spies? He so regretted the life he had to live. He'd taken money and there were two of them now. They no longer bothered about seeking him out in the shadows of an evening but had become bolder. He'd passed information to them, about Elahe's meetings with the major. He had written it all down, but each time a feeling of distaste lodged in his stomach. In his reports he left out chunks. Gave them the minimum. That made him feel a fraction better. He had to leave the notes in town at a cafe they frequented and all they did was leer and pick their teeth as he passed them lounging on the cafe terrace which faced the street. He knew that they wouldn't pay for their chelo kebab meal or their Coca-Cola drinks. The cafe before had often been busy, and a favourite place for the Bakhtiari traders. Now it always looked empty.

Once, he'd confronted the one who'd first approached him. He'd taken him behind a godown shop selling spices and pleaded that he wanted to stop things. 'Impossible,' the man had said. 'Now your major and the niece of our colonel are meeting. We are very worried. Some plotting, don't you think?' No, Reza didn't think about such things and had shaken his head as he backed away. 'More money too,' the man had said. And grabbing Reza's shoulders he had shaken him back and forth, glaring at him with his greasy pockmarked face and spewing his foul breath into Reza's face. After that encounter Reza realised he was helpless, like a sheep trapped in a ravine bleating for help.

Chapter 26

THE SADDLEBAG MADE the place a home. It hung behind the settee on the wall and already the strangeness of living with another's choice of furniture seemed to vanish. Annie had also purchased two large coloured pots and stuffed them with dried grasses from the garden. She had moved the table and chairs to one side and beneath the window placed the standard-issue machine carpet out of sight in the hall. Her next purchase would be a genuine Bakhtiari garden tribal carpet, of which this one was a copy. By asking Major Billy to share his knowledge about such things, she had hoped to make Margaret have a better opinion of her. Guilt gnawed away at her treatment of Margaret and she needed to make amends. The house decorations made her feel more cheerful and stronger for facing Mike's usual interrogation after her trip. He didn't say anything immediately and she hoped he'd forgotten.

'We should have that baby!' he said as he sat in the kitchen one morning before they left for work. Annie was cutting his hair. 'Yelp!' he said. 'Was that deliberate?' The scissors had slipped and caught Mike's ear lobe leaving a small red cut.

'Of course not,' she retorted. 'You just startled me, that's all. What's brought this idea up again, Mike? We are in the south of Iran and maybe have another year and a bit to go in this place and then we don't know where we will be or...or what jobs we will have. Won't it be a bit difficult?'—she stopped herself using the word 'silly' just in time—'and now I've started work and...'

'Yes, that bloody job. I knew it would come between us. Well, I want that baby now and I want you to have it and put paid to all this traipsing around with all and sundry and buying old things we can't afford.'

Annie concentrated on the back of Mike's head trying to control the scissors. Apart from anything, the idea seemed bizarre to her given that they had not shared the same bed for many weeks.

Annie's job had begun to protect her from what he did or said. She'd become more occupied with her students. She still had her thoughts and own ideas about what she was going to do, and how she was going to do it, after they left the place, and dreamt about finishing the marriage, but if a child arrived that would be a definite unwanted complication. What was he up to with this idea?

She blamed herself on bad days. They had been able to speak and share their thoughts when they had first met at college, surely? He had written her a few romantic letters, hadn't he? Would he ever be the kind of husband she wanted? Was that an unfair demand and was it not better to admit she had made a big mistake and cut free from him, and get rid of her doubts? She woke up to an empty bed most nights and couldn't control these questions. Annie's teaching and students helped to keep her busy but the rest of the time feelings of loneliness and panic overtook her. She wondered too how much longer she could accommodate, excuse, or protect him, before she blurted it all out. She needed to speak to someone who might understand and the only one who remotely fitted the bill was Sheila. She needed to try to meet Sheila again soon.

On a midweek afternoon when the pool had emptied of the mums and their kids Sheila appeared. But to Annie's relief she carried a can of Coke as she steered a straight path over to Annie's table. She wore a pale pink dress with a long skirt, delicate sandals, and had a new hairstyle.

'Well, this is a surprise!' said Annie. 'I thought you had returned for good to England. Haven't seen you for ages and... and...I really wanted to speak with you.' Annie bit her lip and then took hold of her glass of water.

'Yes, been with that dreadful mother of mine – but we've managed to work something out,' said Sheila.

There was something different about Sheila. She had not only had her hair restyled and swept up into an elegant French plait but her hand wasn't trembling and she didn't have a cigarette in her mouth. There were gold studs in her ears which Annie had never seen before and which suited her and matched a gold bangle round her thin, freckled wrist.

'You look different,' said Annie. 'I'm not sure what it is but...'

'Maybe it's the new bra I'm wearing.' Sheila patted her chest and gave Annie a wink.

Annie choked on her lemon squash. Sheila rushed to her side and thumped her back.

'Sheila...what? Why the sense of humour? What's happened exactly?' Annie said after a spluttering pause.

Sheila patted her nose and leant forwards on her chair. 'Well, ye ken what gossip there is in this place, lassie.'

Annie thought about how things were spread around and people's tittle-tattle had a life of its own.

'Anyway, I've been to England – and then I met someone from the past. Do I need to say anything more? It made me think and it made me start having plans. I may be able to stop the drinking... not certain but I'm going to try.' Sheila looked into the surface of the blue water a few feet away. 'By the way'—she turned to face

Annie then and the smile had vanished—'I expect ye ken who his latest bit of stuff is.'

Annie didn't answer.

'Well, I'm not going to push you if you don't want to spill the beans. It's not worth it really, is it? If things keep on the right way for me now then I'll definitely be off and his latest totty and the bloody army can have him.'

'I really do hope things work out,' said Annie.

Sheila turned away. 'But what I know is that I'll miss you if you leave the place.'

Annie panicked. 'You were the first person to treat me as a human being really rather than just a wife. I will always remember that, you know. I was feeling very lonely when I first arrived. But you helped in those first weeks. You really did.' Annie took out her packet of cigarettes offering Sheila one and lighting up before she spoke again. Her throat felt tight. 'There's something else I wanted to speak about as well about...well, about Mike.'

Sheila's forehead creased and she leant forward, her face wiped clean of any traces of anger. 'You can tell me anything, lassie, and I won't pass it on. Not like the others do. You can be sure of that. What is it, Annie?' Sheila's eyes flickered to the packet she offered and she shook her head.

Annie gulped and launched her thoughts out into the open at last. 'Mike's not himself, Sheila. He's really angry with me all the time, about the meals and how untidy I've become and...and well, there are other things too. He doesn't come out of his office at home now most evenings and he's, well, he picked up the telephone the other evening. Then he handed it to me and asked whether I could hear someone breathing at the other end. Those telephones are only for the compound, aren't they?'

Sheila nodded. 'They might be tapped though,' said Sheila. 'I've heard that the SAVAK offices listen to our calls from time to time. I don't use ours as it doesn't seem to work anyway;

otherwise I would have telephoned you from time to time. But now I'm back for a bit at least, I'll give you a wee ring when you are going to the pool. We can meet here.'

'Yes! Yes...a good idea, Sheila. I'd like that... I... I really would.'

'Nae bother, Annie. Must be a worry that Mike of yours. Could be a bit of stress and too much work. Breakdowns are common in the army. One of the other majors went on permanent sick leave last week. It's not an easy place at all, lassie.'

Annie nodded and turned away.

'It seems like forever, lassie, since we had that first meeting and I never really thanked you for rescuing me,' said Sheila, 'you know, from that reception. I've apologised to our driver as well. When I first arrived I took it out on him when it was meant for Jack. I'm ashamed of how I behaved, I'm really ashamed. But I don't forgive Jack, Annie. I've just had too much of it all.'

Those last words resonated with Annie as she passed the oleander hedges on her way back to the bungalow. Telling Sheila something about her thoughts had eased the knot of fear, but there had been no real solution offered.

Chapter 27

THE WARM COPPER-COLOURED sky of the setting sun was reflected in the surface of the greasy puddles at the bus station. Reza, conscious of his new clothes, a long striped wool Bakhtiari jacket and felt hat, avoided them and headed towards the crowds. His heart had felt like a soft lump of bread dough since his meeting with Elahe in the main street by the post office that morning. He'd left his father buying a sack of rice, dodged across the road, and thrust the major's crumpled letter into her hands. Her hasty *Kheili mamnoonam* showed him that she had at least been grateful.

As he queued for his bus ticket to Abadan he studied a small boy standing with his father. The boy had spilled his fizzy pop and was pulling on his father's coat as the orange liquid seeped away to join one of the diesel puddles. Reza squatted down, unwrapped one of his mother's pomegranates, and cut the flesh open revealing the ruby red seeds. He handed one half to the boy, and then with his knife scooped out the flesh and sucked the seeds into his own mouth. They refreshed his parched throat, which was suffering from the day's fasting. The boy's eyebrows arched in surprise.

The boy was also sporting a miniature version of the Bakhtiari striped coat. But the youngster couldn't resist pushing Reza's hat back and it fell into one of the greasy pools. Despite this, Reza smiled at the boy's cheeky face, which then disappeared behind his mother's skirts. His own mother was busy sewing new clothes for the Eid holiday and she and his sisters would all join Reza and Uncle Faraz the following day.

Outside the bus station the vehicles were grouped in a pack. A few had seen better days. Their colours were faded and bleached by the sun and their windscreens had been cracked by rocks from the dirt roads surrounding Bashed. If Reza was in one of the numerous accidents that took place on the precipitous route he would stand a better chance of survival at the back. The passengers all started waving tickets and scrambled for places. He helped a family with their sacks of belongings to board and then managed to find a place at the back, wedged beside another man about the same age as himself. Children were perched on every available lap and others clung to the broken luggage racks. There was a deafening noise and strong smell of diesel as the motors flared into life.

When the bus started to leave Bashed the hills loomed large and then dark shadows crept higher up the precipitous craggy peaks as the sun finally gave up its power. The engine screamed in protest as the bus climbed and clanked higher and higher. Burnt-out bus carcasses lay at the bottom of the deep ravines and the gorges of the River Karun. Death was a hairbreadth away. On the valley sides ragged children illuminated by the glare of their fires sat beside their black tents guarding goats and sheep. Some waved and began running as they spotted the bus, which showered them with stones and dust. Finally, the bus emerged from the gorges onto the flatter stretches of road not far from the town of Ahwaz. Here Reza ate the rest of his food his mother had packed. He shared some with the family opposite, and they gave him pistachio nuts and more fruit. Then he simply closed his eyes and went to sleep. Most of the other young men did the same, while the women were left to struggle with hungry babies or whining toddlers.

Uncle Faraz was the only one in the family who had made the Hadj to Mecca and Medina. He was a tall man with a slight limp and he dragged his left foot as he walked towards his nephew ready to greet him with outstretched arms. '*Salaam Aleikum.* Wonderful to see you, my nephew. God has granted you a safe journey. Thanks be to Allah.'

Reza embraced his uncle and smelt fresh lemon from his cologne. Both men grinned and climbed into an old Peugeot car whose engine sparked into life on the third try. Faraz wanted his eldest daughter to marry the boy and hoped this visit would secure the date for the marriage. He had six daughters to dispose of and although Parwana was not yet fifteen, the sooner she became engaged to Reza, the better. He wore a new white shirt, had thick black hair, and looked much younger than Reza's father Ali, whose face always now wore a lost look. The little work Ali still did at the Bashed garage seemed a hardship and he had begun to stoop at the shoulders and shuffle his legs.

'How is my brother Ali? How are you all managing? There is much work now in the refinery here,' said Faraz. 'Many Americans and British and many jobs. Still I heard you now have much work again, Reza.' Reza was pleased and happy to be with the older man and away from the compound, the major, and his problems. 'You are with those British?' continued his uncle. 'Do they pay well? It's good that you can speak English. I tell my daughters to study hard and my Parwana is a good student. She can speak the foreign languages too. She is learning now some French.' Faraz was displaying Parwana's good points.

Faraz looked worried when Reza didn't speak.

'My work's fine, Uncle.'

Faraz beamed and slapped Reza on the shoulder.

'We are well, although my father is low in spirits and Mother works hard with the sewing.'

Faraz nodded hard and concentrated on starting the engine of his truck. The truck roared into life and died again. After three attempts a throaty sound signified it had chugged into life. They lurched through the traffic towards Faraz's garage and house, passing the busy streets and smart-looking shops. Reza didn't see them, he saw only the stables back in Bashed.

The mosque was already full as the two men each discarded their sandals. They washed their feet and hands and then stood at the back searching for places to pray. Reza found a place beside a large man with glasses and a long jacket with large pockets. As this neighbour stooped forward to pray his glasses fell off onto the soft carpet. He hastily stuffed them into one of these pockets before the cracked soles of the man in front had a chance of damaging them. Reza turned to smile at the man but then recoiled at the ice-cold stare. He bent forward again and realised where he had seen the face before. It was a SAVAK man, a friend of his foul-breathed pest, and he'd seen him in the Bashed café where he'd left notes. Reza found himself holding his breath as he leant forward again. There was a rushing noise in his head and his stomach churned. He sat back on his heels but kept his eyes forward; the sounds of the worshippers receded as his thoughts took over.

Faraz realised there was something wrong when they were busy putting on their sandals. He was balancing and holding onto Reza's shoulder and saw his nephew's white and worried face. He had also seen the other man beside Reza and had instantly recognised the thin face and the hooded eyes. He waited until they were both in the house where a meal was waiting for them and they'd drunk glasses of refreshing mint tea. Reza didn't smoke although his uncle did, but it wasn't until the room was thick with the smoke that his uncle broached the subject of the man at the mosque.

'He's a bastard!'

'Who, Uncle?'

'That one who dropped his glasses.'

'You know him?'

'Well, it looked like you did too, Reza. Seen him around in Bashed, have you? I heard that he went to work there.' Reza didn't know what to say. His uncle continued. 'The family is well known here. But they don't usually honour us with their presence at prayer time. A bunch of heathens or Zoroastrians. He's from a well-known family here in Abadan and they're cronies of the Shah and his regime. Two of the older brothers in the family are high up in the local government administration, and another works for the national airline. A ruthless bunch, Reza. It's rare to see them at prayers though. It's money they worship and the Shah of course.'

Reza stared at the pattern of the carpet where they sat cross-legged. His uncle's words floated around in his head. The teapot steamed on a tray in front of them and he could hear the faint chatter of the women and his cousins as they prepared for bed. Fear gripped his throat and his stomach clenched into a tight lump. Was he being tailed now and followed even here? Maybe it was an innocent coincidence that he was sitting beside him in the mosque? Perhaps they were all being watched more than they realised. Should he speak with his major? Should he speak more with the other workers in the compound, his chauffeur friends and the gardeners, barmen, and house servants? But probably they already knew more than he did. Since he started his work at Tafneq and the stables, his thoughts had often been about Elahe, and he'd disregarded his own family's safety.

His uncle spoke at last, as if reading his mind. 'Don't worry about the foreigners, Reza. What is so important about them? We've all got more work these days. I'm pleased you have your job, and the city and oil is bringing a fortune into the country.

But the money isn't making us as wealthy as we should be. Where are our new cars? Why do I still have to use my donkey from time to time when this old jalopy breaks down? What's happening, Reza, is that some, a few, are getting very, very rich. Did you see that long, thick coat he wore? That bastard in the mosque?' As his uncle continued Reza remembered the soft leather of Elahe's riding boots and the Mercedes car of her uncle the colonel.

'The Shah's lot have it all, Reza, and we are being left behind. The British and Americans are his friends and doing all sorts of deals, and the worst of all is, he forgets our religion.' Uncle Faraz paused and turned away to fumble for a cigarette. He stuffed it too hard into his mouth and some of the cheap tobacco fell onto his knees. He brushed it away with an angry swipe, lit the end of the cigarette with the third match then sucked in smoke, choked, had to bang his chest, and couldn't speak until he'd swallowed more tea.

'Yes. Where was I? Thanks be to Allah that we have our saviour in Paris, he will come and rescue us. Just you see, my boy.' Reza hadn't a clue as to whom his uncle was referring. 'So worry about yourself, my boy. Worry about your own skin and your own family. Think about bringing them here and look to what you could do with your life. But keep away from that lot. That's my advice.' He reached for his mint tea. 'Well, enough of that...when are you going to be my son-in-law? That's what I want to know and that will cheer us up. What do you say? Are you ready to fix a date now?'

Reza's head was full of his uncle's words and he shook his head as if to rid his mind of them.

'Well, Reza, that's not right, is it? You're promised, you know.'

Reza reached across and grabbed his uncle's arm. 'No, it's not right and I didn't mean for you to think...I've got to get some fresh air, Uncle. I'll be back before you lock up. I need to walk and stretch my legs. The bus and the journey and...you know.'

Neither men spoke about the topic again. His mother and sisters arrived the following day and the whole extended family became immersed in celebrations for Eid. But before their return home his uncle took Reza to one side, looked directly into his nephew's face, and told him to be careful and keep in touch.

Reza returned to Bashed after the holiday with dread hovering over his head and even his mother noticed the difference in the way he looked and spoke. A week later, his father went missing. They all went out to search in the streets and amongst the market traders in the centre of Bashed. Ali had not arrived at the garage for work and hadn't been seen all day. It was several hours later as dusk was falling that he stumbled through their gate, being held upright by the same lanky SAVAK man from the mosque in Abadan.

'Keep an eye on him,' the man had said. 'I'll keep an eye out for him too. By the way, I'll be at the cafe now. Those others you used to see, well, they've gone.' He made a movement with his hand across his throat, its meaning clear.

Chapter 28

Elahe stood in silence. She nibbled at one of the small cucumber sandwiches Margaret had given them. 'What can I do, Annie? But, I hope you are my friend too?' They were at a small gathering in Margaret's new library.

Her stern face relaxed. 'Yes, yes, I am. Of course I am.' Annie pressed her hand on Elahe's arm and squeezed it. 'But I've known Sheila a while, and she's a good woman underneath that drinking. You mustn't think that she is bad just because you see her like that.'

'Come! Come and sit over here,' interrupted Elahe, 'I don't want my auntie and uncle to hear this.'

Annie followed Elahe to the opposite side of the room where some new bookshelves had been built but were empty, and where they couldn't so easily be overheard.

'I'm stuck, Annie.' Elahe picked at one of her nails, before she raised her face. 'They are not bad people either. But I can't speak with them now, or change things. They have decided Major Jack is my solution. And at least I know him and he is kind when he speaks with me.' She stopped and shrugged. 'It's always out of my hands. In Tehran and now here.'

'From what you say, Elahe, I understand how difficult it all is. They know what you think and what makes you happy but they are also considering their own family and those other older ones from Tehran. There's a lot to think about really, isn't there?'

'But Auntie and Uncle are a little more understanding and know I can't be happy at all with Great-Uncle Jamshyd's choice. They said that. And the idea about marrying Jack well... Maybe I would get a chance to study and I'm thinking it would be well... the best, *Inshallah*.'

When Annie later considered Elahe's options, she knew that Elahe didn't have much chance of changing things with Jack even if she wanted to. That much was clear. Perhaps she'd been wrong to even mention it, but somehow defending Sheila to Elahe had made her feel she'd repaid her friend and that it had been all for the best. But what to do about her own situation? She felt helpless too. What should she do about Mike? Her head was like a pressure cooker. Her mother's sole attempt at using one had left a vivid red mark on the ceiling which had never entirely disappeared.

Chapter 29

JACK AND ALAN sat drinking in Jack's lounge. Before them were empty bottles and discarded packets of cigarettes and peanuts. Sheila had left for good the weekend before and Alan had been invited down from Tehran to 'console' his friend. Sheila had told Jack that she was planning something new in her life and wanted a divorce with a good settlement. Jack was sprawled on a chair with a hand stroking Jasper's silky head, and the dog drooled and manoeuvred his body closer to Jack.

'I know it's a change for you, old boy, but you knew something like this was on the cards for a while,' said Alan.

'I agree, Alan, and at the very end it was all, well, not what I expected. Quite civilised if you can call it that. But I know her and think there'll be some kind of trouble at some point. We've had a lot of fights over the years'—although Jack wasn't going to admit to her physical attacks—'and Sheila is a drunk, but the last time she returned from Blighty, she was changed. Just more cheerful and optimistic. Don't know why and I didn't bloody well want to know why. She kept away from me and me from her. Never a good mother, you know. Never had a daughter and maybe that would have made a difference. Who knows and what's the point of that now? It's finished for good.' Jack shook his head and reached for his drink. 'And it's the fine print now, Alan. The final settlement and the sorting out. You know the sort of thing.'

Alan, as a confirmed bachelor, probably could only imagine, but he nodded and adopted a sympathetic look. He wanted to play a round of golf while in the place and looked forward to helping Jack enjoy his new-found freedom.

'I'm thinking of getting married again by the way,' Jack said, interrupting Alan's dream of a winning putt at the first hole. Alan's beer spilled down the front of his short-sleeved shirt and over his ample stomach. Alan was jealous of Jack's trim shape and wore his now damp shirt loose over his shorts in an attempt to mask his large stomach when he was with his friend. He needed to put in more hours at the pool or on the golf course, but in Tehran he was constantly under pressure from his bosses in London to complete piles of paperwork. Jasper lifted his head and growled at Alan as he cursed and staggered to his feet.

'My Christ, Jack! You don't waste any time. Who is the woman? My God!' He paused and then turned from his shirt to his friend. 'Not that young Iranian we saw in Tehran and whom you couldn't take your eyes off? You're old enough...'

'I know, I know.' Jack shrugged his shoulders and fiddled with his glass. 'I don't want to look a bloody fool. But here there's no choice. You have to marry them and here it's normal to take a younger woman as a wife. The Shah's on his third, isn't he?'

Alan nodded, sighed, and muttered again 'My God' under his breath. He reached over for some pistachio nuts, which he shovelled into his mouth, and kept his eyes fixed on Jack's face.

'Elahe's from a wealthy family, you know, Alan. Her uncle's a colonel and we get on well, I think. He respects the military. She's educated and well connected and she's, you know... you saw her. Even my bloody driver goes moon-eyed around her. She's beautiful, for Christ's sake, and she, well...she likes me.'

Alan looked into Jack's face and saw his friend was smitten and that Jack wanted his approval.

'It's your life, Jack. Your life! But do be careful. Marrying one of your own is one thing but this is...well...things are changing here. There are rumours in Tehran and our company now has three spies hanging around, even one at the head office all night. God knows what they think will happen there. You have a lot more of them. They're also a bit twitchier of late, don't you think? My phone's bugged and expect yours is too. You know the sort of thing.'

Jack didn't answer but sat twiddling with his cigarette and gazing into space.

'Come in, Annie. Margaret, a cup of tea please for us both.'

Margaret rose from her desk at Jack's words, straightened her long, pleated, flowered skirt, and turned to go through to the small kitchen area where a sink, cupboards, and cups and saucers had been recently installed. The small fridge with cold drinks had also been moved from Jack's office to the new kitchen. Mike, John, and Pete were smoking their cigarettes in the shade of the only large tree outside their classrooms and the office. Mike stood a little apart.

Jack sensed the older woman was jealous of Annie. He saw it in her face every time she spoke to Annie. But the young woman now looked troubled and Margaret was not the one to show her any sympathy immediately although he knew she had a kind heart. She had propped up Billy as they traipsed around Northern Ireland and he had heard that she had been a tower of strength when they'd been in Kenya with the Mau Mau, but she was only going to antagonise things now. He'd send her on another errand when she returned with the tea.

'I've got the new contract for next year here and I hope you will sign up.' Jack passed the papers over to Annie sitting opposite him. Jack stared at Annie's face and brown eyes. They didn't glow as they'd done before and she hadn't smiled when she entered his office as she usually did. Her hand shook a little as he passed the pen to her. She started to read through the first page and he watched her. He noticed there were definite shadows under her eyes. When she did speak her voice was so soft he had trouble understanding. She chewed the edge of her thumb.

'Sorry, I didn't catch you, Annie. Are you OK? By jove, I hope so.'

'I can't sign it now, sir, Jack, I mean. I will have to speak with Mike first,' Annie said.

'Yes, I quite understand.' Jack paused and then continued, 'Better you take the new contract home this afternoon and get him to read it through. We don't want him to...well, like last time.'

Annie nodded.

Jack stared out of the office window, where he heard noises. The teachers had disappeared and the army cadets were being drilled by their officers. Dust hung in the air and clung to the outside of his window. When he looked back at Annie, she was on the edge of her seat about to leave. He wanted her to stay and leave on a friendlier note, maybe try to find out what was troubling her, but he didn't know what words to use.

'Reza, my driver,' he said, thinking that was common ground for both of them, 'seems to be making some progress with his English, Annie. Is he still coming to some of your classes?'

'Yes sir. Jack.' Annie lifted her eyes to look back at Jack. The first time he had seen her really look at him. 'Not bad as a student. In fact I enjoy teaching all of them,' she continued, her face a little more animated, and Jack witnessed a flicker of the old Annie in her eyes. 'My students are like young, playful puppies sometimes in the class'—her face continued to lighten as she spoke '—despite that officer sat at the back. Reza sits just by the door, when he comes. But he's quieter lately.'

'Well, not surprised, Annie. Not at all. I heard from, well, doesn't matter who from, that Reza's father suffers from blindness. Difficult for the family.'

'Yes, I know, Jack. He told me a little bit on the shopping trips and on the way to the hospital.'

'Oh well, I've not always treated him so well in the past. But still, water under the bridge. Has he spoken to you about going to study in England?' said Jack.

'No. No, he hasn't. But...'

'Anyway, is there anything else, Annie?' Margaret's shape had appeared at the outer glass door.

'As a matter of fact there is,' Annie replied. Jack looked startled. Her voice sounded stronger as she began to speak about Elahe. Both she and Sheila seemed to be Annie's friends and she spoke in their defence. She hadn't wanted to speak out of turn she claimed, although he knew, and she knew, that she had. Why didn't she want to speak about her contract, but only about her friend's problems? Jack wondered.

'Is everything alright, Major?' said Margaret after Annie had left.

Jack sat staring out of his window and had made no move as Margaret knocked and entered the office.

'I'm not sure, Margaret, I'm not sure.'

Margaret picked up the tray and put the empty cups on it. She shook her head. Margaret had seen and admired Annie's competence. Her students always emerged smiling. And she'd tried to like her from the beginning, even when her offer of Billy's assistance in the purchase of a saddlebag had been politely refused. Still Margaret didn't really approve of husbands and wives working together. It often caused trouble.

Later that day at the golf club Jack was unsure about what had been negotiated or what had happened that morning. Annie's husband Mike arrived and he thought it an opportunity to make an ally of the husband just as the wife was beginning to seem difficult.

'Saw your wife today, Mike. New contract and pay rise if she wants. Said she had to speak with you first, of course, before she signs it. We both had a good chat, as well. About all sorts.' Mike flushed and Jack stopped himself from continuing. The man was touchy after all.

'Can I buy you a drink? Nice to see you here. How's your game shaping up?' Jack didn't wait for an answer but rushed ahead and complimented Mike on his progress. His handicap had indeed been steadily improving.

'Hard work though, sir,' said Mike at last. 'Your game is good, eight under par, isn't it? You must have practised many hours to reach that standard. I've a long way to go to reach your level.'

Jack was pleased to hear some praise. Different kettle of fish speaking to a man he thought. Know where you are with them. Not trying to put you at a disadvantage if you are their superior. This teacher had his sensitive places but he was still a man after all. That wife seemed to put him at a disadvantage just by looking at him.

'Well! You put me down as your partner as soon as you think your game is ready. We'll play some rounds together, eh? What do you think, old chap? Would that be OK?'

Mike stumbled out words of thanks. Billy arrived and bought both men a round of drinks. All three sat staring at their drinks until Billy broke the silence.

'It's a tough job in my machine shop. They're a bunch of idiots these Iranians sometimes. They copy you and then do something stupid.' He looked across at Jack and Mike waiting for their attention. 'Training them to be more careful with the tools and equipment is a nightmare. The other morning one of the students got his arm trapped in a lathe. It was only a fluke that he didn't lose it. Bloody difficult here, don't you think?' He turned then to face the other two directly while swallowing some beer. Some of the froth stayed on his top lip before he placed the glass down and dabbed at his mouth, his head, and then the folds in his neck with a spotted red handkerchief.

Jack nodded.

'Money's not really enough in my opinion,' continued Billy. 'It needs a fairy godmother to change goatherds and shepherds into mechanics. A fairy bloody godmother! This heat drives you mad too, eh?' He dabbed again. 'What about the English classes?' He turned to Mike. 'I expect they can't remember from one class to the next. We speak English to them, of course, in the workshops. We show them the tools and explain how the machines work. Do you think they get it?' Billy paused for Mike and Jack to answer but they both just shook their heads. Billy continued and both men strained to keep a serious look on their faces. 'No they bloody don't! Weeks it has taken my men to get them to the point of measuring and drilling holes properly in a sheet of metal. It's going to take much longer than we thought even to be able to drive a tank, let alone maintain them. They are more likely to run themselves over!' He sputtered the words out and his round face grew more red and beads of perspiration gathered on his brow. 'The poor bloody blighters. That's it really. I feel sorry for them. But they can't be helped. Almost impossible. I felt like this when we were in Kenya. Wonderful plantations and farming going on by us colonials and the next minute the murdering Mau Mau. I ask you. Any progress was shattered in a moment. They do it to themselves. I've got a feeling that things here might get nasty as well.' He uttered the last sentence in a whisper, glancing at the Iranian barman at the other end of the bar.

'It's not so bad in our language school, is it, Mike?' said Jack. 'Students are well-disciplined and now we have an extra teacher, um...Mike's wife here—' he paused and gave Mike a nod '—the classes aren't so large. Look on the bright side, I say, eh Mike?'

Mike moved his head only a fraction with a fixed smile on his face. Jack shifted the conversation then. 'Margaret's wonderful,

Billy, by the way. Great organiser. Tidied up the office and keeps all the paperwork under control.' Billy had stopped speaking and seemed to be listening. 'She's typed up the new course material which some of the teachers have prepared for the next session.'

'Awfully sorry. Awfully sorry to you both but I must go. My golf coach is waiting.'

Both Billy and Jack were startled by Mike's voice, and they turned to give curt nods.

'Didn't say much, did he? What's he like?' Billy twisted his bulk towards Jack. 'Hope I didn't frighten him with that Mau Mau stuff. I noticed his face went a bit white. No bottle these civilian chaps, have they?' Billy patted Jack on the shoulder and then heaved himself upright. The stall teetered on its long legs as he prepared to leave.

'Oh, he's OK up to a point that one, Nellie.' Jack used Billy's nickname, only he was sensitive enough to use it when alone with the man. 'Although, the other day one of the others told Margaret he'd noticed Mike seemed to be speaking to someone in the classroom. But when he ventured inside, no one else seemed to be in the room. There was only Mike sat in a corner. Seems a bit odd, don't you think, Billy? He's strange with his wife Annie too. One minute cold- shouldering her and the next minute his arms are around her shoulders.' Jack paused. 'She can speak her mind when she wants,' Jack said as he remembered that morning, 'but I've a feeling that Mike doesn't like that at all.'

Chapter 30

Annie stood in the kitchen gazing out at the oleander's pink blossoms. They didn't have any fragrance, dropped to the ground when finished blooming, and now lay in brown heaps for the gardener to sweep up over the rough, spiky grass. She clenched her hands by her sides. She'd spoken with Mike about the contract and approached it as tactfully as she could. She'd used her softer voice and peppered her words with 'darling' and 'good, the extra money'. But despite her best efforts she'd realised they had had little effect. Mike's body had remained stiff and he'd continued to glare at her. 'What game are you playing at?' he'd boomed out. Any strength then was sucked out of her like the pull of a tide.

'What do you mean? I thought you'd be pleased,' replied Annie, whose throat had become hoarse. 'I know...well...that I must have upset you before somehow.' She stopped and kept her hands at her back. 'Although I didn't mean to, really...not at all. I've changed, Mike. If...if you do want a child still then...I've been thinking...and...' Annie took a deep breath and forced herself to say it. But why she uttered those words she really didn't know. She was in a murky fog. If he was having a breakdown what could she do? Should she speak to Jack about Mike? She'd mentioned Elahe and Sheila. That seemed impertinence now. But both women were themselves confused and unhappy. Should she try to carry on as normal? Was it really only the place that was getting on everyone's nerves? Their annual leave would be in another month and she thought she'd give herself until then. But she still had to survive each day.

'Well, yes, it's OK with me now,' Annie repeated, stumbling over each word.

Mike paced up and down in front of her, his hands folded over his chest.

'I see I was wrong...so I thought. Well, the contract's a problem, isn't it? If we, well...if we both now want a child.' Why did she feel compelled to push on and say all this? Shouldn't she remain silent? His contradictions caught her out each time and she didn't know where she was with him any longer. 'What about the contract for next year? What do you think?' she said.

Mike's wide black eyes stared at her.

'Thanks for having the decency to ask *me* that question, Annie.' Mike spoke as if lecturing one of his students. But his voice had stopped booming and the volume decreased when there was a noise from the gardener outside. 'What I think is that you are flirting with Major Jack behind my back.' He'd stepped forward very close and she tried to dodge his eyes. 'And rearranging contracts and students as well as...well, as well as trips with his driver.' Despite the slightly lower volume of Mike's voice each word made her flinch. She closed her eyes and took a deep breath. He didn't stop though. 'God knows what goes on at the riding club. Don't know what you are up to any more.'

'That's unfair, Mike.' She edged away towards the lounge door, but Mike stepped forward again. 'I told him...I told him I would have to consult you and...' Annie remained silent. Her words stuck deep down at the pit of her stomach. She felt sick and when he grabbed her arm she was limp like a rag doll.

'Don't speak to me like that,' Mike started his booming again, his eyes so close to her face she saw every pore of his skin. 'I'm not one of your bloody students. And why the hell you've got that Reza in your class beats me. That's something as well that you never spoke with me about, isn't it? You've done what you bloody well liked in the place, haven't you? Maybe, just maybe, you are beginning to learn that I have bloody feelings too. Everything you've done has been selfish. Teaching jobs, contracts, buying bloody bags, even rearranging the furniture in this place. And now, oh now *you* want a baby. Now that makes it alright, I suppose. I'm trying to live *and* work here. But as for the new contract – *take the offer. Take it*,' he repeated.

Annie struggled and freed her arm at last and she flattened her back against the kitchen door. 'What else will you do with yourself? You'll probably start wanting to invite all sorts from the town as your next project if you are not employed at the school. God forbid! And the times when you actually have sex with me are so rare that there's not much chance of a baby either, *is there*?'

'But it was you that went to the...study...and...' She saw Mike's face. She stopped. Stupid to ever attempt a rational response. Stupid, stupid, she thought. Her heart thumped so hard that she didn't hear the scream she made as Mike lurched forward and dragged her by the hair into his study. He shoved her to the ground, turned, and banged the door shut, locking it from the outside. She heard his shouts and the crash of splintered wood as he seemed to be stumbling and lashing out at the furniture in the lounge.

Later, as the sounds of his anger diminished and he hadn't made any attempt to open the door where she was, she saw that streaks of light from the shuttered window lit up the walls of the room. So shocked by what had happened, she at first hadn't seen what was written on them. She put her hands up to her face, even rubbing her eyes. It didn't seem real. She'd glimpsed one wall before from the outside and noticed writing, but this just left her speechless and rooted to the spot. Interspersed with the scribble were bits of magazines and photos stuck to the wall. In the centre of one wall was a large picture of a green bush with bright red berries. When she studied it more closely she realised it was an oleander like the ones surrounding the houses. Underneath was the word *poison*. She started to shake then and sat down on the floor. Later she spelt out names and sentences everywhere but they didn't make sense at all. She tried to trace any connections with her finger but she gave up and went to sit on the single bed in the corner of the room rocking herself back and forth, before she fell into an exhausted sleep.

Annie heard Mike make a phone call to Jack and make excuses for their absence. 'Food poisoning, Jack, maybe. Both bad. Sorry but can't be helped.'

Five minutes later he had opened the study door where she'd spent a sleepless night and banged a tray with a mug of tea and bread down in front of the window on his paper-strewn desk. He opened a shutter a fraction and she saw that his face was grey and his eyes were glazed as if he'd seen something bewildering which he couldn't make sense of. A sense of pity sprang from somewhere and she thanked him, but kept her distance and eyed the doorway. She didn't have the strength to barge past him and make her escape just then, but knew that was the only option.

He kept her locked in the room all that day, allowing her to visit the bathroom but waiting outside the door each time. Her exhaustion from a sleepless night caught up with her and she must have lost consciousness for a few hours, but a noise from outside the window woke her up. The shutter was still propped open and through the window she saw Tommy's blond hair glinting in the bright sun. She knocked on the glass but Tommy didn't seem to have heard and she saw him rush to the back door where Mike stood with a bottle in his hand. What Mike said or did with the bottle Annie couldn't make out.

Later that evening Mike opened the door to the study and handed her a drink of beer. 'Peace offering,' he said. 'I just needed time to think and get myself in order. We won't talk about things for the moment, Annie, but I want you to know I am watching and keeping an eye on you. It's for both our sakes. You and I don't know this place at all or the people and we can't accept things at face value any more. Margaret, for instance.'

Startled, Annie looked up as she'd kept her eyes away for the first part of his speech.

'Well, seems like a good type,' she said, keeping her voice as calm and normal as she could.

'I thought that when we arrived,' Mike said. 'But what do we know? What does anyone really know?'

Annie nodded her head in agreement. She had to go along with everything he did or said now. All trust had vanished and if the worst came to the worst she'd have to get out of the house as fast as she could.

Linda and John usually listened to the BBC World Service during their evening meal and commented on the Callaghan government and the new social legislation to help women and parents.

'Don't you think now we'll be better off with a child back home?' said Linda. John made no reply and carried on eating. Linda sighed and started to collect the plates, but before she left for the kitchen she spoke again. 'Have you seen Annie or Mike?'

Although they lived only five minutes away, the two households had kept apart since their arrival. John with his easy-going personality found Mike a hard nut to crack. He wouldn't enter into the banter between him and Pete at work, and he didn't like his cold, arrogant behaviour with his wife Annie. She seemed a good sort when he spoke to her by herself. Not difficult at all. Quite sympathetic, he thought. He'd mentioned Mike's strangeness to Linda before Tommy's spell in hospital, but they'd both been too worried about their child to mention their neighbours again. John answered this latest question as he placed his knife and fork on his empty plate.

'Mike's phoned in sick for both him and Annie this week. Jack's had to supervise two classes, with the help of one of the Iranian officers.'

'Well, I thought it funny when the gardener came over yesterday and wanted to know what to do about the extra vegetables,' said Linda. 'He'd left them at their back door but they'd gone rotten in the sun when he arrived the following day.'

'Not to worry, Linda,' said John, 'you've got enough on your plate, keeping young Tommy occupied.' He knew his wife often couldn't cope with the lad. Tommy liked to wander off, although as the only child with blonde hair in the place, he stuck out like a sore thumb and usually someone would bring him back. The gardeners now knew where he lived after the spell with the scorpion and they often fed him some fruit while he watched them go about their work. He was a normal, curious boy, but it didn't stop both parents worrying, especially after his spell in hospital.

'I'll send Tommy round with salad stuff and a note,' said Linda.' It'll give him something to do. Annie used to be quite good with Tommy and she came to the hospital, don't forget, just to see him. He might cheer them up.'

John nodded. 'Good idea,' John said as he placed a kiss on Linda's cheek as she reached over him for his empty plate. He had his doubts that anything would improve Mike and his moodiness.

Chapter 31

ELAHE SAT IN the back of Jack's car in the shade of some of the palms outside the riding club. Jack wasn't wearing his uniform and had dodged his 'tail', or so he had thought, but a cloud of dust and sand through the back window told him otherwise. He opened the door and got into the driver's seat and started the engine.

'Where are we going?' said Elahe.'

'Sorry about this but I'm going to move us to somewhere safer,' said Jack.

'But Auntie's asleep in our car and if we disappear she'll worry, won't she?'

'A risk we'll have to take,' Jack said. How could he conduct some kind of love affair with the thought that they were being watched? It had begun to bug him more and the spies had definitely stepped up their activities. What a place! And they were here to help and train these cadets.

He knew somewhere a bit further away and it was hidden from prying eyes. He'd recced it before when Reza Ali had been busy at the golf club arranging his hours for another forthcoming reception.

They parked in the new spot, and he turned off the car engine, checking that they were on their own. Elahe remained silent pulling at her long silky, plait of hair and untwisting the end. This infuriated him just a little. Maybe she'd been listening before but she gave little indication that the last words he'd spoken had been taken in the right way. He hoped he sounded sincere, but maybe not. 'I mean we are risking upsetting some people here,' said Jack, 'but I've promised your uncle I will sort it out so we can have a life together. I'm going to do that, Elahe.'

'Yes, Jack, I hope so.'

'Of course I will,' he said, trying to convince himself and her. 'A divorce and us together, married, like your uncle and your auntie want.'

'Yes, but Great-Uncle and Grandmother want someone else for me. I'm in the middle of a rope. It's like a tug of war. I think you have it in England too? Strong men pulling a rope. We have it in Persia too and...'

'Stop,' said Jack.

Elahe looked at him at last and the plait of hair lay coiled in her lap as her fingers became idle. One or two of her fingers had bitten nails. They were no longer bright red.

'Look, I didn't mean to say that, but it's going to be different with us.'

'How, Jack? Is it because you like me a lot or something? I mean, I respect you as an older man but I just don't know you.'

'We had a good time at the picnic, didn't we?' said Jack.

Elahe nodded her head in agreement and then stared out of the window at the back of a brick wall. Jack took one of her limp hands and brought it up to his face to kiss. 'Give me a chance, Elahe. I know you think maybe I'm too old, but...'

'No, Jack, it's not age that is the problem, believe me. And really my worries are because I'm unsure about so many things. I feel lost here and I wish all this planning and plotting could finish. I wanted to be a teacher and now it's not possible.'

'Don't see why not,' said Jack, gripping her hand. 'Don't see why when we are in England, somewhere you can study and do that if you want.'

'But...you mean it could be possible? I didn't think. But you will still be in the army and you would go to other places.'

'From time to time, but we would have a home in England somewhere.' Jack squeezed her hand and she smiled back at last. He'd promised her things but he couldn't promise that he could deliver them. That was the way he'd played his courtships in the past. It was a familiar pattern. He knew he had charm and she was young. Sometimes though, he hated himself. He always seemed to be playing a game with women and never could he show them his real self. He'd wondered sometimes if other men were like that too. 'Now, it's time to return to your auntie and the car. I'll park away from the stables and you can return to her through the other entrance. Then I won't be seen.'

On their next meeting Elahe told him about her family in Tehran and how suitors were being lined up by Great-Uncle Jamshyd. Jack couldn't help himself and he whistled between his teeth when she mentioned that in less than two weeks this mullah uncle would arrive in Bashed. If a future wedding was arranged and the date fixed for the ceremony, Elahe would not be able to back out except with great difficulty. Jack understood that much. She'd asked him then about churches and religion and he had to tell her that he didn't attend church and that there wasn't one in Tafneq, although some of the men and their families went along to the American evangelical meetings. He anticipated her next question. 'Look, our wedding will have to be in Tehran at the British Embassy but can't be for a while, as there's the divorce first and...'

She'd stopped him then and put her soft fingers on his lips. They would have to have an excuse ready for the great-uncle if he did arrive when he claimed he would. But if Abdul decided Jack was the suitor then Jack could leave it to Abdul to work out. He had too much to arrange with Sheila on his side of things. His wife was blowing hot and cold, and the solicitors, as usual, were making a meal of things.

Later, that same day, Elahe stared at the dirty green water in her uncle's swimming pool. Rainwater had collected from recent heavy November showers and the pool had been left unfinished because the filter and pump were still in Tehran. The place sickened her with its backwardness and inefficiency. The gatekeeper swept leaves away from the edge but to little effect. Piles reformed elsewhere. He'd mentioned that Reza stopped by and spoke with him from time to time and her thoughts now were with Reza. She hadn't seen him at the stables, but maybe he'd been worried about her. Why else stop and tell the old man that? From Reza her thoughts drifted to Jack and their last meeting behind an Indian godown shop and piles of empty crates. It had scared her in many ways. He was a major but still had to keep a lookout for his own safety. Everything in the place seethed with danger and uncertainty despite its remoteness.

She fingered a brooch Jack had given her. 'A gift from Tehran, Elahe,' Jack had said. 'Not much, but hope it shows you what you mean to me.' She liked it. She liked presents and gifts and to feel the centre of his attention. But...he had grey flecks in his short hair. Reza's hair was deep black and his face lit up so completely when he smiled it was like the opening of a sunflower. Reza was bright and trusting and...and she had feelings for him. Once she'd upset Reza and that had troubled her and she'd tried to make it up to him by giving him more money after her ride, which had been a mistake. He seemed to have taken it the wrong way and had scuttled away as soon as she'd ridden off. Another groom had taken the reins and Nowrooz from her on her return. But now she knew Reza had been secretly visiting her and hanging around the house. It may of course be for all sorts of reasons but she hoped one of them was because he wanted to catch sight of her or be able to waylay her somehow. That thought kept a smile darting about at the edges of her mouth.

Three weeks after Alan had flown down from Tehran for that weekend visit, Jack was being driven home. Staring at the back of Reza's dark, curly hair his guilt about his treatment of the man re-emerged. He knew that misdirected anger was unfair and blamed Sheila for making him lose control. Was Reza paying him back somehow? More and more he came to represent something ominous for Jack. He didn't know when that feeling had started but it was connected with Elahe and he wondered if he had set the whole thing off by using Reza as his messenger. That initial trust and confidence he'd had in his driver had almost evaporated, but there was still his guilt.

Behind them the black car of his SAVAK officer was keeping a discreet distance and normally it wouldn't have bothered Jack but he now felt edgy about it. On the previous evening he had received two phone calls from Tehran warning him to expect the arrival of a VIP the following week and during the calls there had been clicks and a humming. Reza's eyes reflected in the mirror and Jack looked away. He concentrated on the beads of sweat trickling down the man's dark neck and blackening his collar. Jack realised that he might feel scared too about his security. Maybe he's being watched too? Or perhaps he's one of them, Jack thought. Reza had been chosen and vetted by the British and members of the man's family had been employed by the oil company since the year dot. Still, every man had his price. Jack tried to dismiss the spy idea but then confronted what was really concerning him about his driver. He'd used him as his messenger and the scene seemed to be constantly running like a piece of film in his head. Reza had been actually speaking with Elahe on his last meeting at the riding club. And they had definitely moved apart when he had walked towards them. Was it just his imagination? Was he becoming paranoid like others? He hoped that the place wasn't 'getting to him'. Even Billy had not seemed his usual loud self at the golf club and that teacher Mike was definitely shaky. Jack's shoulders tensed under his khaki shirt and he made himself sit back and roll his neck round and round pressing and massaging the top of his spine.

Even so, he still couldn't stop his mind galloping away with itself. He must look a fool to others and he looked it to himself. He'd fallen from one world into another, and even with all the coffee mornings, libraries, and cricket it was still another country. He'd started to take stock of it all, and the informers – the Shah's secret police – had started to rattle him more than he wanted to admit.

His major's voice sounded from the back of the car. Reza's hands grew wet on the steering wheel, and he braked hard as he drove the car and parked it in front of the stone bungalow, beside the rose bushes and bougainvillea, whose vivid purple and pink blossoms hung limp and dejected against the grey stone. They were suffering from the wife's frequent absences and lack of interest. His major had one of the original stone bungalows and although the weather had cooled as winter approached and there'd been a little rain, it would still be better inside. The walls were thick and substantial and so well built that he could never help but compare their neat solidity with the rough concrete blocks of his family house with mortar spewing out between the courses and no glass in some of the windows.

'What's the class like? Learning things, are you? She's quite a teacher, isn't she?'

Reza shuffled his feet on the cool, polished marble floor of the hallway of the bungalow. Jasper the dog had bounded through when he heard the front door open and sniffed at Reza's dusty sandals and feet. A clock ticked somewhere behind them, and the air conditioner made a high-pitched whistle in the lounge. Reza concentrated on the movement of hairs below the major's shorts, which were caught in the draught of cool air. 'She's asked if some of her students can get visas to study back in England and she mentioned you. Want to go, do you? Want to study there? Want to get a job?' There was silence. 'Well, answer me, Reza. Do you want a visa?'

Reza needed to reply and looked up at last at the major's face. It was red and damp, and the eyes were like those of a trapped sheep.

'I like to speak English better, that's all. I like visit your country, *Inshallah,* for sure. A good place, I know. But no money and my family need me here now. *Kheili mamnoonam, Shukran,* many thanks.'

The telephone rang at that moment in the hall and the major went to answer it. He turned towards Reza and repeated the message which had been relayed to him.

'Sorry, Reza. Your dad, father. He's in the hospital. Go now and take the car.' Jack thrust the car keys towards him and Reza stumbled over Jasper as he hurried out of the door. Reza's hand shook as he started the engine and he had to try twice before it fired into life. In the car mirror he glimpsed Jack kneeling to stroke the dog and his heart surged in his throat as he drove off.

Chapter 32

REZA'S THOUGHTS CONTINUED to churn like the car engine. Why hadn't he helped his father more when the old man wanted to go to the mosque? He could count the number of times on one hand that he had accompanied his father. Why hadn't he sorted out a marriage date with his uncle and set his mother's and everyone's mind at rest? And those people, those bastards he had been helping, those police spies, whose faces lurked at every street corner, why was he bound to them? They had trapped and cornered him like a wild wolf. He had needed the money for his family, but what good was all that money now? At the back of his throat and in the confines of the car he yelled and banged the steering wheel. Nobody knew what his pain felt like.

The neighbours on his street were gathered outside his house as he stopped the major's car. They looked surprised when he emerged but rushed towards him with their grief visible on their faces. Women were grouped squatting on the ground with their backs to the houses producing a high, ululating sound which froze his heart. His mother, sitting outside the walls of the burnt-out house, rocked her body back and forth. His sisters clung to her and then rushed towards him as soon as he arrived. The acrid smell of the fire made his eyes smart and dried the tears he had shed. His father had died some hours before and there had been a delay in finding him to deliver the message.

'Please, Reza, tell my brother. Go and telephone your uncle,' said his mother. 'Send him news. Telephone him from the post office in town. Please go now. He can be here tonight.'

All Reza could do was nod his head and gently help his mother and sisters towards the back of the house, which had remained unscathed.

The following days passed in a haze. He made arrangements for the funeral, washed down the blackened walls, and rescued as many of their meagre possessions as he could, including his mother's valuable sewing machine. It all kept him busy and prevented him from thinking about the future too much. They put up a black felt tent and slept out each night listening to their mother's weeping.

Reza's uncle stood at the bus station surrounded by families who had swarmed out of the Abadan bus. 'Salaam, welcome, Uncle. Sorry I'm late.' They embraced and Reza turned his face away for a moment not wanting the man to notice his tears. He helped Faraz into the Toyota and felt the corrugated backbone hard against his palm, which took him back to thinking about his father, thoughts which he tried to wipe away as he'd done his tears. His sisters and mother clung to them both when they arrived and led Faraz to a mat within the tent. The days had been a nightmare for Reza, and he hoped against hope that the fire was not retribution for his lack of recent information for the spies. Here was the person, his uncle, who would help solve their problems. All the family knew this and would do what he said. It was a great blessing to them that Uncle Faraz liked Reza and treated him as his own son.

The acrid smell of smoke and ashes still hung everywhere and Reza's stomach had rejected any food until today. He took up a place on a cushion and scooped a handful of rice and lamb from the large steaming plate which rested on top of a scorched carpet beneath. The fat and grease spilled over onto the cloth as he moulded some of the damp, hot mixture into a ball with his hand. He now felt very hungry. His mother had managed with the help of neighbours to prepare food. She hovered now behind the two men, passing them small enamel cups of Coca-Cola. Azzie and her younger sisters assisted their mother with more dishes of vegetables, and then sat waiting for the two men to finish. Faraz urged them to bring their plates and sit with him. In Abadan he'd bought a table and chairs and his family had their meals all at the same time, including the females. Faraz spoke then about the future and then stopped to chew a morsel of meat which Reza offered.

'What?' replied Reza. Then remembering his manners, he apologised and blushed.

'I've managed to get in contact with a foreigner in Abadan. Good customer and I repaired his car,' said Faraz. 'Now he wants to keep in touch and says he'll help if anyone in my family wants a job outside the country. He owns shops and factories in Turkey. One or two in England. He works for, well...you know, the government, the British Government.' Faraz stared at his young nephew. Reza looked leaner and tenser than their last meeting. 'What do you think?' Faraz nodded to his sister. 'Take the girls to the neighbour's, sister. I must speak with Reza about the future and it's better if the men decide it between them. We want to keep you safe.'

Azzie squealed as her mother clutched her hand and took the girls outside the tent.

'I'm not sure what you are asking of me, Uncle,' said Reza.

'No point in wandering around the mosques as they say, Reza.' He paused. 'I've come here to warn you and to help you get out.' His favourite nephew's handsome face blanched and the dark eyes opened wide with fear, but he persisted. 'Get out of Iran before it's too late. Once you're in a good, safe place we can join you. My family and yours, of course, and then we have a marriage, eh? What do you think?'

Reza sat back on his heels and reached for his drink.

'I'm not going to pretend this is easy but I am going to ask your mother to move to Abadan with the girls. If you can get a visa then get it and leave. I have enough money to give you for the fare and to make a start somewhere.'

Reza clasped Faraz's hands. 'Many thanks. Many thanks and Allah's blessings, but I don't know. I really am still not sure. I told my major the same thing when he asked me about studying and visas.'

Faraz looked serious.

'No, he is not so concerned about being followed or the spies, well, it looks like that to me,' said Reza, 'he's more concerned with the women in his life and...'

'Women?' said Faraz.

'Not to worry, Uncle. It's his affair. You know more about our country and I think it is best if I take your advice. But give me a little time. Are things that serious?'

'It's best if you don't know everything, Reza. There are too many rumours at the moment and it is difficult to work out the facts. But I want us all to be together. Now with your father's death it seems as if it is the right time. Please think hard and don't take too long. Not too long. And, well, maybe I should meet this teacher friend while I'm here?'

That last request worried Reza. It wasn't something done – any real fraternising with employers and the British, but Annie had enrolled him as her student so he supposed some sort of boundary had already been crossed. Reza promised he would try to arrange something and assured the older man that he would think about things. Reza himself had heard gossip and knew the SAVAK police had become more numerous and more inquisitive of late. He couldn't tell his uncle about his own involvement and contact. He was too ashamed and too frightened to reveal it.

Fear seemed everywhere now and haunted him at nights, and even after his uncle's visit and offer, it didn't diminish but sat in the back of his head like an evil spirit from the hills.

'Please, my son. My brother's our only hope now.' His mother gripped Reza by the shoulder before he set off for the stables. It was the day after his uncle's visit and the evening and the purple sun had disappeared behind the hills. Their gullies and folds appeared dark and treacherous. The town's few street lights flickered weakly. In contrast, the Tafneq compound lights functioned and threw up the shadows of the rectangular hedges and streets. Even from a distance they were outlined on the horizon.

'Yes, Mother. Yes.' Faraz had told her something of his plans. Reza hugged her tight before he left for work, but he knew he was still undecided. How could he leave the place when something and somebody in his heart made him yearn to stay?

Chapter 33

ANNIE CRINGED AS she saw ruts and potholes on the road in front of her and Mike. She clung to the roof strap and tried to steady her body and protect it from being flung against the thin metal of the car's door. The windscreen was covered with dust and the water in the washer bottle had evaporated hours before. Mike braked hard. 'Wipe the screen,' he said, then sank back, mopping the sweat from his face and neck. 'Be quick. It's a bloody oven. We're being baked and could be stuck for good if we break down. They wouldn't loan us a better car for the trip, do you know that, Annie? Your pal, our major, wouldn't agree. Suppose he didn't want to see us teachers riding around in cars for the bosses, eh?'

'He's not my "pal", Mike,' said Annie, keeping her voice on an even keel, 'we've been through all that. This is our chance to put things right. Your words, Mike. Please, Mike. We've both been under strain. But it's going to be alright, if we try. Let's try!' Goodness knows why she said that. But she'd been defending his behaviour to herself, covering it up, or ignoring it completely ever since their arrival. Now they were on this trip, and she knew in her heart that things would be no better afterwards. Isolated here, it increased her need to defend him more. There was no reply from Mike and the words had emptied her like a shrunken balloon. She looked back but there were no other cars in sight.

They were on their way to Isfahan, and after several more hours of bone-shaking torture, the city appeared as a shimmer on the horizon. Rocky hills and a few scrubby bushes rose up either side of them. They'd been told that there weren't any service stations or even roadside kebab places for the first few hundred kilometres of the journey, so they carried extra fuel as well as a crate of clanking bottles of orange pop on the back seat. It was their first trip away and Mike had taken it into his head that he wanted to visit the ancient city, described as 'half the world' by his class SAVAK 'officer'. Ten months earlier, living in England, Annie had been fired with the same enthusiasm while reading about the other city Shiraz and its roses and the ancient site of Persepolis. They passed a row of trucks whose drivers lay like sleeping logs beneath them. Mike didn't stop any more and spoke only when he wanted Annie to pass him another bottle of the sickly orange drink, or a biscuit.

They approached a much flatter and fertile area where there were groves of fruit trees and small mud-walled houses with docile-looking donkeys tethered to palms. Channels for water had been ploughed through the red earth and she spotted the buckets and wooden spokes of the wells where the water was raised to the surface by the harnessed donkeys. She imagined standing under one of the buckets of water and couldn't wait for the journey to end. She could see some strange shapes, large circular buildings with small niches and holes cut into the brown mud walls. 'Look there they are, pigeon houses – like large lighthouses, aren't they? I told you about them. How cute. Keeping pigeons safe from hawks, and the farmers used the droppings of the birds as fertiliser on their land. Maybe they are still in use then. What do you think?'

'Look like nothing special to me,' replied Mike, his grey face a mask of frown lines.

As they grew closer they passed more pigeon towers as well

as small herds of sheep. There were bright, fresh green-leaved orange and almond groves surrounding walls of concrete block houses. Under the vivid green umbrella of palms sat kids of all ages amongst tethered donkeys and goats. Annie privately drank in the sights and vibrant lushness of the many shades of green. No wonder it was a holy colour.

On the skyline the glinting domes and smudges of smoke grew nearer. The muezzin prayer calls drifted towards them firstly as muted sounds and then wailing sequences of *Allah Akbar*. As they came closer to the outskirts they could see more colours and sounds. The stately domes and elegant minarets of blue and white soon loomed above the other buildings. Then a blush of red and orange on the skyline appeared as the sun started to rest its chin on the earth.

The Shah Abbas Hotel was one of the world's oldest and most luxurious, and without hesitation Mike had decided to book them into it for their two nights. 'It's expensive, Mike, to stay there. Are you sure about it? You did say that we were here to save, didn't you?' She'd thrown his own words about saving money back in his face, not through malice, but because of the uncertainty of how to be with him. All the old markers and signposts on the road of their marriage had been taken down after he'd locked her in the study. She was in uncharted territory.

'Yes. I owe it to you too, Annie,' Mike suddenly said. He looked at her then, but there was almost a smirk on his face.

'What?'

'Well, you know. After what happened. Think I'd had too much to drink. You should have this hotel and trip.'

She felt bold enough to ask him the question that had been dominating her thoughts as she had lain awake many nights.

'Tommy came to the house when I was in the study, Mike. Did you give him anything?'

Mike jerked his head away and when he looked at her again his eyes were coal black holes.

'Can't for Christ's sake remember. And what has that got to do with anything now? Shut up about all that. This hotel. Just look at the size of the place, for God's sake. Have you ever seen anything so lavish? You should be pleased I've brought us, shouldn't you? Better than that poky little bazaar place in Bashed. We'll have something to tell the others – John and Pete and those majors at the club, always bragging about how tough they are and what they've done. I can't wait to see all their faces. They'll be so jealous. You wait and see. Just you wait.'

Mike flung his shirt on the bed and started to take off his trousers. 'Well, say something. Or are you going to be the difficult wife all the time? I don't know how I've put up with you here and the problems you are making. Aren't you pleased about this place? Aren't you pleased? You should be. I've plans for us and you'd be best off understanding that. This trip is going to be...' Mike stopped, and looked across at Annie. His voice had changed suddenly in pitch and volume, and she inwardly cringed at the menace in the unfinished sentence.

Instinctively, she moved away and across to the window where heavy brocade curtains framed a scene below. Sounds of laughter drifted her way from a lively group clustered around copper tables. The red tips of their cigarettes lit the darkness. She wanted to open the window and scream. Under an elaborately carved headboard, Mike lay spread-eagled and bellowed to her to close the curtains and get into bed.

The following day, Mike got her up early and marched them round the central sixteenth-century arcaded square famous for its polo. There were about two hundred one-roomed godown shops facing the square with a terrace above each. The bolts of bright fabric, shawls, and scarves were dominated by a leaf-shaped design that in England they called ‘Paisley’. Her school had had a library decorated with William Morris wallpaper and the memory of its floral loops and leaves had stayed with her. Now she recognised where the inspiration may have come from. Similar whirls and leaf shapes were on the vivid blue and coloured tiles decorating the walls and ceilings of the buildings.

At one end of the square was the main gateway into the covered market, which as Annie had read was ‘the beating heart’ of the city. A market had been there for over four hundred years, but they didn’t venture into its darkness as Mike insisted on climbing to the top of one of the terraces overlooking the main square, where he could photograph the fountains and small gardens in its centre.

They stood side by side on the ramparts of the building, and then Mike made Annie take some photos of him posing against the backdrop of the blue and white dome of the large domed mosque on the opposite side of the square. He snatched the camera away and then took just one of her. The rest of the morning he spent filming the buildings, making her pause and wait each time. As the constant hammering sound from the coppersmiths along the side streets jarred and penetrated her head, a pain began at the back of her eyes. They did not venture into the mosque but Annie followed him into the cool of the bazaar, a real rabbit warren of alleys and shops where each trade and type of shop had its own special area. She tried to keep up as they threaded their way round. But Mike never slowed down to stop or examine any of the goods. He barged ahead and even knocked into shopkeepers and family groups as they passed. Annie didn’t want to get lost and suffer his recriminations so she kept him always in sight. How she wished that it was Reza in front of her and not Mike.

He headed back to their room at last. She hadn’t unpacked properly the day before, only the clothes she had needed for the morning. Now she busied herself by sorting out her crumpled clothes and putting them in the heavy wooden wardrobe. Annie had packed some light clothing and a gauzy shawl which she could use to keep her head covered in the mosque. Sometimes, she knew, tourists were allowed in the outer parts to take photos, and she wanted to take some for herself. She managed to avoid her husband as he stripped off and took over the bathroom, and she breathed a sigh of relief as the door closed and he left her alone for the first time that day.

After his shower, Mike stomped around their large bedroom demanding that she hurry up and join him in bed. He threw back the sheets, fell on his stomach, and began snoring and Annie breathed another sigh of relief. She waited ten minutes, sitting on the bed, and then went to the bathroom to unpack her wash bag. The room was long and narrow with a full-sized bath and gold taps, but when she turned one of these taps on there was only a dribble of rusty-looking water. Maybe Mike had used up their allowance of water for their room. It was at least cold and she let it run over her feet and then managed to fill the bath with the red-coloured liquid so that she could stand in four inches of it before pouring it over her body using a glass jug. She patted her body dry, but her arms felt weak and her legs shaky.

When she reached for her packet of birth pills in her toilet bag she couldn't seem to find them. She searched around with her fingers, taking out her brush, toothpaste, and a pack of tissues. Had Mike something to do with it? Had he decided to come on the trip and to get rid of her pills? And then what? Was he planning something? She wanted to go over to the bed and pummel the body, but maybe she was jumping to conclusions. Perhaps she had just forgotten them? But despite another search they couldn't be found, and her panic and anger made her chest tighten. She brushed her hair in vigorous sweeps standing in front of the misty bathroom mirror. The headache now returned in force as she stared and continued to brush until her scalp was sore.

She managed to dress and covered herself with the thin shawl, glancing at his sleeping body. She didn't want to stay around Mike any longer and scribbled him a note before leaving the room. When she passed the reception desk she knew they would be staring at a woman venturing out on her own. They were used to tourists but that didn't mean they shared her culture. When talking with Elahe she had been surprised at how much she had in common with her, but she also realised there were huge missing chunks in her knowledge about contemporary events.

Under the domed ceiling of the mosque, rays of light shone through minuscule carved apertures so that the colourful pillars and walls looked alive. They were sparkling and speckled and she felt as if she was in the centre of a fast-flowing stream. Her head and neck started to feel better. She had the sensation she was walking over the ice of the Arctic as her bare feet slid along the marble floors. For the first time on the trip she was at peace and wanted to stay forever. She wandered around in the outer part and then outside she sat down on a long marble seat. Other tourists were fiddling with their cameras and it was there she really thought about what had happened. She asked herself the questions lurking at the back of her mind, about his strangeness and then about the pills. She walked slowly back to the hotel and was aware of a light beginning to dawn like the light inside the mosque.

'Where were you? Where the hell were you?' Mike yelled, stumbling up from the bed, his shirt undone and creased. 'At Tafneq it's you and Jack. And here I don't know who you're with.'

'I left you a note,' said Annie backing away. 'I went to the big mosque. You were sound asleep, Mike, and I didn't...'

Then he charged, shaking her until her teeth rattled and she fell back on the rumpled sheets. He pinned her wrists with one hand and with the other ripped at her skirt. She screamed when the pressure on her nose and throat had eased, but froze as she stared into his jet eyes. She twisted her head back and forth as his red lips sought her mouth. Once clamped beneath his body, unable to breathe, she became limp.

The next day was a blur. She hadn't slept with the pain from her wrists and neck where there were grazes, and a tooth was loose, and her lips were sore and red.

'I was worried about you, Annie,' Mike said, trying to justify and excuse himself, as she sat facing him trying to eat breakfast in the luxurious dining room. She couldn't speak. She tried to sip her coffee from the side of her mouth and plucked at her scarf covering her head and neck. 'It made me angry that you hadn't seen how worried I could be. You know you're a western woman. Why were you so stupid? Why were you so stupid?' he repeated in a louder voice. 'You are deliberately trying to get us in a mess here. I know it now. This trip, like everything, is being spoilt by you. In fact I hate you.'

She'd remained stunned and even embarrassed. She half blamed herself and each time she visited the bathroom she wept, stifling the sound with the back of her hand. She made sure she didn't shed tears in front of Mike. That way she kept something away and out of his reach. Something inside, which he couldn't touch.

He dragged her out after breakfast and made her walk close to him, holding her arm in a vice-like grip as they revisited both the inner courtyard of the mosque and then the main square and the fountains. It was the longest day in her life and she wanted to close her eyes on it all.

Chapter 34

ON THEIR RETURN, Annie knew it was over. Any shreds of feeling were dumped on the stony road back from Isfahan. In Bashed, she operated like a damaged machine that coughed into life when teaching and shopping needed her to act. But the swimming pool remained a haven and an escape. As soon as her bruises had healed she went there. If she timed it right she often had the place to herself and could float on her back, gazing at the blue sky and dreaming of low clouds heavy with rain scudding inland from the English coast.

Not long after the fateful trip, Sheila appeared. Annie rushed over from the side of the pool. 'Well, I'm so pleased you're here, Sheila. Didn't think you were ever returning. I was...am missing you.'

'It's that girl!' blurted out Sheila. 'That's why I'm back. As if *you* didn't know!'

'What?' said Annie, realising perhaps that the proverbial cat was out of the bag and Sheila somehow had found out about Jack and Elahe.

'Another young 'un of course. I had my suspicions but he's not getting it easy. Not this time.' Sheila's voice echoed around the pool and Annie could only stare at her friend's face, her happiness short-lived. There wasn't any sense in speaking with Sheila. She'd relapsed into inebriation. Her friend fumbled in her bag, peering into its depths to extract a crumpled packet of cigarettes, and stuck one between her lips. As she drew the smoke into her lungs, she stared back at Annie. Anger as well as vindictiveness lurked in her white face.

'Sheila, Sheila, why didn't you speak with Jack first?' said Annie. 'I'm sure he would have explained things. And I know Elahe. I've met her and...'

'What are you saying? What are you saying? That you knew what was going on? You knew, didn't you?' Sheila pushed back her chair and it crashed on the tiles. It seemed like a repeat performance of the first time they'd met.

'It's not like that, Sheila. Please I must tell you and explain.'

'Explain!' Sheila wailed. Her voice sounded like Mike's flute when he couldn't reach the right note. The instrument now lay discarded at the bottom of their bedroom wardrobe. 'I'm all ears. You explain, Annie my lass.' Sheila stood tugging at her hair, which was damp and stuck to her skull. She made an exaggerated show of setting her chair back upright facing Annie and positioned her glass on the table between them, scrutinising Annie's face. 'I thought you were a friend.' She spat out the words, 'I trusted you and I tried to help you settle in, all those months ago. You ken how I put in a good word for you about the teaching. I... You make me sick. You're as bad as the rest, aren't you?'

Annie's knees and body felt empty. How could she explain? Trying to put the pieces of herself back together after she'd hit rock bottom with Mike and the marriage had already drained her strength.

'Look, Sheila, please...please come over here and I'll...I'll explain.' Annie took Sheila's arm and managed to walk her to another poolside table, a little more private. 'It's not what you think,' said Annie as she pulled out a chair and sat facing Sheila. She breathed deeply. A smell of chlorine clung to her nose and she blew it before she spoke to clear her head. She reached over and clasped both of Sheila's wrists pinning her to the seat. 'I met this young woman at the stables, Sheila.' She clasped Sheila's wrists tighter. Sheila wriggled and turned her head away. 'I had my suspicions about Jack but I didn't want to say too much in case...in case it was a mistake. I've had my own things to work out too, Sheila.' Annie touched the loose tooth with her tongue. 'Mike and...' Annie began to shiver, and she released Sheila's wrists and clutched the sides of her own chair until she stopped. She should have told Sheila before about her suspicions about Jack. 'This might be different to what you think,' Annie managed to continue. 'I mean, this girl, Elahe, well, her uncle is the Iranian colonel in the place and it might have something... Don't you think you're well, well...?'

Sheila jumped up. 'If you were going to say interfering or something to that effect, then don't. Jack and I had agreed to a divorce before I went back but that was on the understanding he would do the decent thing and see me and the kids right first and... He promised that. Bloody friend you are. Thought you were on my side.' Sheila's voice boomed louder. 'Do you ken how I feel?'

'I do, I do, Sheila. I'm sorry, I really am but it's not so easy. I thought things were working out for you and...'

Sheila put up a scrawny arm. 'Aye, working out? Working out? When I get a letter telling me about this new one and my husband, and it arrives the day I'm about to go to a job interview back home?' Sheila stopped to find yet another cigarette in her bag. She lit it and then looked straight at Annie's face. 'I've got to stop them. Interfering, am I? Well, maybe I should have interfered and told you about the rumours about your husband.'

'What? I...' Annie stiffened.

Sheila paused and stared into space, moving her head well away from Annie's. 'They're saying he's cracking up and they want him out. Heard Jack tell Billy that he doesn't like the way you're treated by him. Had my suspicions about you and Jack at one point too, you know.'

Annie held her head in her hands, and any answering words stuck on her tongue. Sheila stopped speaking and stubbed her cigarette out in the ashtray. When Annie lifted her face, her brown freckles were now etched black on white cheeks. Sheila stood ready to walk away and then sat back down as she saw Annie's face. 'Look, look,' she said, her voice now soft. 'I'm angry, lass, forget what I said. Forget it. It'll work out. I'm older and not so stupid as I make out.'

Annie wiped at some tears forming at the edge of her eyes.

'That's better,' said Sheila.' That's better, lassie.'

After a few minutes, Sheila spoke again. 'And did you hear the real news about Tommy?'

'No...I didn't,' replied Annie, and she put her handkerchief away. She took a cigarette from Sheila and as she leant over to light it an Iranian barman appeared at the end of the bar and stared at the two women. 'What about Tommy?' whispered Annie, as she sucked in the smoke.

'Well, this time it seems he has been eating oleander berries and poisoned himself. He could have eaten them by mistake or... well, we dinnae ken.' Annie fell forward then and the last thing she heard were Sheila's screams demanding a glass of water from the barman.

It was late as Annie walked back to the bungalow, and she broke into a run knowing that Mike might make another scene. The street seemed full of shadows, and the hedges rustled, although there wasn't any breeze. She kept to the centre of the road and focused on the cypress trees and poplars in the distance just outside the compound streets. Annie knew she needed to do something, but what? Could Mike have given those berries to Tommy, maybe crushed in that bottle of pop? It wasn't just herself that was a victim of her husband's temper but it could be that others were involved too. She'd brushed away Sheila's concerns at the pool, telling her she'd not caught up with her sleep after their trip away. Both were friends again, and that at least gave Annie strength.

Chapter 35

'I DON'T KNOW, Alan. I just don't know what's for the best,' said Jack. Both men were at the Bashed Golf Club having something to eat at the snack bar. They waited for two steak sandwiches. Alan had lost weight, and his hollowed-out eyes kept darting about.

'Well, don't know what to say, Jack. Warned you there would be problems. Seems like you're in a tricky situation. Alright marrying the local German or Irish bint, but one from here. An Iranian? Different altogether, old son.' He scooped up nuts and avoided Jack's face, and then shrugged. 'Tried to warn you. Problems.'

'Yeh...know you did, but Abdul her uncle, that colonel, well he's got rank and gave his approval, so I've got the go-ahead and... It's just Sheila to sort out. And...and well...I want to be generous for the boys' sake. Still at boarding school, you know.' Alan shook his head and took up his sandwich. Jack continued. 'They need to be paid for. But I can take charge of all that.' He tried to get Alan to look at him. 'It's just that the eldest one, my Robert, look, here's a recent snap of him. Take a look. Go on.' Jack pushed the photo he always carried in his top pocket in front of Alan. 'Well, he's written a letter and sounds upset. Sheila's visited and told them a pack of lies. All lies, about never seeing them again and well...it just makes my blood boil. The bitch! No reason why

Elahe and me can't be based in England, is there, Alan, and see all the boys even more?' Alan made no reply. 'In fact, I'm going to apply for a posting back in London, and...'

'Now hold on, old chap. Hold on. Calm down,' said Alan. 'Too many plans, Jack. And no good if you are still in this place. It's complicated enough here without the problems you're landing yourself with, don't you think?' Alan hoped his friend would take the hint and stop all this nonsense. 'You might be transferred away somewhere. One of those new colleges further north. You've got another year to go here anyway. And looks like you might need to sign on for a new contract if...if, well...you are going to need more money.'

Jack nodded and his tic came to life making him grit his teeth. Nuts spilled on the floor as his hand shook when he took up the dish. His beer glass was full, but he didn't feel like drinking or eating after Alan's response. Had he been kidding himself that things would work out somehow with Elahe? Letters from Sheila's solicitors in England had been full of all sorts of unexpected recriminations and demands. At first, he didn't know what had happened between the time she'd left and her return. Then he twigged she knew about Elahe and after his son Robert's letter he knew he must consider his boys, or else, like Alan said, give up all plans to start a new life. Divorce was one thing but what about the bombshell of introducing a new woman into their lives? He had to sort things out properly.

Alan had also set him off thinking. He began to wonder about whether he could trust that Abdul at all. He was after all an Iranian and would always put his own family and their safety first. He'd not been too friendly at their first meetings either. Jack had a sneaky feeling he might be being used in the place. And then what about Elahe? She'd certainly been stand-offish at the beginning. Perhaps she was using him after she saw that he was behaving like a lovesick puppy?

'Well, you're probably right, Alan,' said Jack. 'Your flight's soon, isn't it?' Alan was leaving that night. 'Always discussing my problems, aren't we?'

Alan stood up.

'Look, I'll try and talk with Sheila tonight. This romance with Elahe may have to be put on ice for a while like you say, my boys come first, and I've definitely neglected them. Look, don't go yet, plenty of time and another drink?'

'No, Jack. Back to the guest house for me to have a snooze before the flight on that noisy Fokker Friendship tin can. Take care, old son. Hope things go the way you want.'

When Jack returned he received a call telling him Sheila had left the guest house. He hoped she'd go up to Tehran for the weekend or have second thoughts. He really just wanted time to think.

That same week, Jack sat under the front porch of the bungalow, trying to enjoy a gin and tonic before his evening meal. He'd loaned Reza his car for his father's funeral the week before and been reliant on the teachers and their car for lifts to work. He found himself glad of their friendly banter each morning and realised that their camaraderie sprang from a different place than army banter. Their jokes and chat were about home, football and sometimes BBC World Service and pop music. It helped to take his mind off things too. Alan had rattled him with his words of caution. His army reputation mattered and if the news leaked out about Elahe back at his old regiment the gossip would be damaging. Was he panicking and becoming over-sentimental? Maybe he'd try to confront Sheila if he could locate her, and suggest a 'cooling-off period', and he even toyed with the idea of a full reconciliation.

A car drew up in the distance and he heard a rasping cough. Cigar smoke wafted his way.

'How are you? Nice of you...well, please take a seat,' said Jack, and a rather dishevelled colonel stumbled towards a chair opposite a table with a whisky bottle and a glass. Jack left him to collect another glass from within the house, wondering why the man was in this state. Something must have happened. Alan's nerves and edginess was one thing but this man was a bloody Iranian. Jack poured peanuts in a dish while his brain worked overtime.

'To what do I owe the pleasure? Well, what is it you wish to speak with me about?' said Jack. Abdul's crumpled cheeks and unshaven face seemed covered in a layer of grey. He spoke at last and the cheroot slipped from his lips. He kicked it with his foot. Jack waited. Might it be an internal thing, an army thing, worrying the Iranian? There were always men trying for promotion who were often turned down or just hadn't cow tailed to enough people. He'd seen really brilliant soldiers in the British Army, who were good strategists, born leaders, who hadn't managed to pull the right strings or hadn't come up the accepted officer route. They had one lieutenant colonel serving on the project at the moment – the only one in his experience who was from the ranks. A splendid, decent chap, well liked, who'd never been the subject of gossip. He wished now he could become more like him.

'Here,' said Jack. 'Look, you better tell me why you're here. I'm going out soon and...'

The colonel picked up his glass and slurped back the last drops before holding it in front of Jack for a refill. 'Thanks, Jack... This is...a...this is private.' The man looked towards his car parked outside Jack's gate and which was without a driver.

'No driver, I see, tonight,' said Jack.

Abdul shook his head.

'But they are watching me, of course! And it's got a lot worse than one or two of them.' He chewed the end of an unlit cheroot and fumbled in his trouser pocket, but instead of his gold lighter, his hand emerged with a box of matches.

'But they are your Shah's police, after all. Surely, like you said at the picnic, nothing for us to worry about. They are protecting us...I suppose, aren't they?' Jack's chest tightened. The colonel's face studied his and a sickening thought flooded Jack's mind. God, he was stupid. Now this colonel was here at his house at night, and they knew all about him and Elahe. How must it look? He didn't have any British Army protecting him. Not in this place. Not really. They all thought they did, but danger lurked in the place for real and there was no point in hiding it. Abdul lit his cheroot and then with his free hand drained the contents of the second whisky. Jack watched the man's Adam's apple flop up and down.

'I noticed some in their smart clothes hanging...lurking... you know, round that mosque in town the other day,' said Jack. 'Conspicuous, aren't they? They don't hide or do things secretly, do they? Well dressed too compared with these Bakhtiari.'

Abdul made no reply but stared at his drink and his trembling hands. 'I need your help,' Abdul whispered. His words hung between them on the still evening air. Above their heads the eternal blanket of bright stars flickered.

'Oh! Well, what's that then, Colonel? What's it that I can do, given that this is *your* country and I know my movements are also watched? What help can I possibly give?' Jack shrugged and stood up.

'My job! My job! I think I'm about to lose it,' said Abdul.

'What the hell do you mean?' said Jack.

'Look, I know how this country works and can you listen, Major? Please listen.' Abdul's eyes stared up at Jack.

'Yes, yes, get on with it.'

'My niece!' he whispered, turning his head from side to side and leaning forwards on his chair. 'Please get her out! If you help her, then she can help us. Please! I don't know what else to do or who to turn to. But you British, you are better than those Americans. You can do something, I am sure. I am begging you... begging you.' He made to grab Jack's arm but Jack moved away and sat back on his chair, nodding his agreement as he did so, and all the time a voice in his head said, *Oh shit! Oh shit! The balloon looks like it's going up*. And despite his resolve to try to save his marriage, it now looked like that wasn't his only problem.

Chapter 36

SINCE ISFAHAN, ANNIE's daydreams had become the only place where she felt relaxed and safe. She wanted to be home. Back to her mum and dad in their suburban London home and to the refreshing drizzle. But the fantasy only helped momentarily and didn't stop her feeling isolated and betrayed. Mike's cruelty cut too deep for her to make excuses any longer to herself or to others. At the back of her mind she kept alive thoughts about applying for a job. Her survival instinct, she supposed. But first she had to focus on getting out. Maybe in a place Mike wouldn't know. Probably a big city, not London but much further away. Bristol? Manchester? But her plans would have to wait. What about Mike? She would have to betray him in order to save herself.

One evening they were on their way to a reception to celebrate the successful visit of the Shah. 'You bloody drive,' said Mike. They had the teachers' Citroën after its return from Jack. 'You only just passed the test after three attempts, didn't you?' said Mike. 'But you can drive now. You might kill us both. But what does it matter in the middle of this hole? I'm sick of it all. Even the money they pay isn't enough. I'd like to be dead.'

Annie climbed into the driver's seat, attempted to start the car, but on her fourth try Mike wrenched open his door, and pushed her out of the way. He leant forward as he turned the key, screeching in angry frustration.

'Take it easy, Mike, please.' Annie's voice was drowned out by his shouts as the car moved forward. She watched him struggle with the gear lever in front of the instrument panel, praying under her breath that the car would behave. Her light scarf draped round her neck hid the fading yellow marks. Although Mike had tended to ignore her since their trip and had eaten his meals in silence, when he did speak, it was in irritable outbursts and no amount of reasoning could calm him down.

The Citroën's headlights picked out the group of palms and poplars which lined the road outside their compound. They followed it to an older group of ex-pat buildings, where the cricket club was situated. As they started to descend, the car gathered speed until Mike began to shout that there was something wrong. His white face turned to shout, 'Bloody brakes are spongy as hell. What's that Jack done with them?'

Mike had expressed his desire to die and maybe that was to be both their fates too? Were they to die in this place? Were they to die in a car accident, which now seemed symbolic, given the state of their marriage? The car by now had begun to weave from one side to the other as Mike jerked the handbrake on and off to see if it would slow the vehicle. Annie gripped the thin metal seats with both hands and leaning backwards she shoved her feet out in front to brace her body for a possible collision. The car slowed a fraction and then Mike fiddled with the ignition and the engine died. They swerved to the roadside with Mike's curses stabbing her back to normality. The door handle fell off in her hand as she wrenched open the door.

'Bloody sardine cans,' said Mike. 'They expect us to drive these deathtraps and they swan around with chauffeurs. What did I tell you before?'

He had blood on his face from a cut on his head, and she

watched the blood darken the front of his white shirt as she tried to steady her shaking body on the car's door. By this time they were outside the buckled car and steam hissed from its engine. There were no other vehicles around although there were lights in the distance from the windows of the club, which Annie realised wasn't as far as she thought. They had travelled at least half the distance.

'But Jack was using this car last week, Mike.'

'Yes,' said Mike, and turned to face her. His eyes looked like dark pools. 'Your pal had the brakes tampered with, didn't he? So I could end up dead or at least injured and have to be sent home. I know your games. I know you have been plotting behind my back.' He walked towards her with a finger jabbing at her face. 'Why else would he keep giving you contracts? And...'

'Just stop, for God's sake, Mike. You're not making any sense.'

She could easily run to the club, if she could find her other shoe. She edged away from Mike, who was waving his arms at the fragments of windscreen glass on his shirt and shouting at her. Her neck hurt when she moved her head but nothing else seemed injured. It's not far, she thought, I'll run now for help, and she turned towards the lights.

Jack stood outside the low concrete building of the cricket club stargazing. The tiny points of shimmering light seemed to cascade down and calmed his nerves. It was the first time he had felt in control of his emotions, and he had a plan about what to do. He'd toyed with getting back with Sheila and putting his family first. He'd told Alan that and had more or less decided it was the right thing to do, but then Abdul had arrived, pleading with him, and it seemed like that man's need was a matter of life or death. He had to do something and maybe it would help him feel better about himself? Maybe restore his self-confidence, integrity, or bravery, qualities which he always thought he had. Jack turned as he heard someone approaching.

'Missus Brown, Major. Come. She's not good. It's bad,' said Reza.

What now? thought Jack, but as he turned a man's fist smashed into his head. Elahe's face flashed before his eyes then as he collapsed to his knees.

Reza had been carrying crates when he witnessed what happened, and he alerted the others inside. John rushed out and wrapped up Annie's cut and bleeding foot in his shirt and she told him about the brakes. Mike had staggered after Annie and spotted Jack in front of the club. Reza and Major Billy managed to restrain him and bundled Mike into the club. After a few seconds, badly shaken, but without any other serious injuries, Jack came round. Mike's fist hadn't done serious damage but Billy persuaded Jack to go to the hospital. Billy also decided it would be best if Mike cooled off away from everyone in a flat in the bachelors' compound, and he arranged for one of the captains from the engineering block to keep him under house arrest for the night and then get a medic to check him over. Mike's mental state looked dodgy.

Chapter 37

'IT'S KIND OF you to offer,' said Annie, 'but I think I'll be better back home.'

Major Billy nodded. Margaret raised her hand in protest. 'Well, really, my dear. You're welcome to stay another night just until you feel up to it. I'm sure that bump on Mike's head affected him.' She turned to Billy, who nodded back.

'Of course, Margaret's right. Let her take charge, eh girlie? You've been shaken up. He'll be right as rain soon, just you see, and then you can get on with things as before, can't you?' said Billy. Annie had to agree. She hadn't the energy to protest or to add anything further.

'Well, if you insist, Margaret. Thanks so much.'

The older woman smiled back at her and for once Annie liked the woman. Maybe she had been wrong to see her as a bit of a busybody?

'She means well, Annie my dear,' Billy said after his wife had left the room, almost reading her mind. 'She tries to well "pull rank" if you like and if you want to return now I'll take you.'

'Thanks, Major. But I don't want to be a nuisance.'

'You're not that, my dear. Not at all. I like showing you all my brass pots and my collections, eh what? You seem to appreciate them. Shame we never had any children, you know. But Margaret said you remind her of our niece who went on to be a career woman. That's praise indeed, isn't it?'

'Yes, I suppose so,' said Annie. She'd been brought back from the cricket club by the pair and put to bed with hot milk after her foot had been bandaged by Margaret. Margaret had also loaned Annie a nightdress and some special shampoo.

'What's up, Billy?' said Margaret, after Annie had been driven back home by Billy. 'Stop polishing those blessed trays and tell me what's really going on there. Is he cracking up, that husband of hers? Look, I've seen enough bruises and black eyes from army wives to spot when women are victims of their husband's frustration and bad temper.'

'Yes, I think you are probably right, Margaret. Poor girl.'

'And what about the contract? That's the serious thing, isn't it? Is it coming to a close? Are we carrying on here? What does Tehran say and what about London? There have been so many rumours and Jack's not happy. It maybe is his love life but there's something else too.'

Billy sighed and stopped polishing. 'Nothing for you to worry about, my dear.'

She shook her head at this and stood up shaking out the pleats of her full skirt.

Billy continued,' Internal things with these Iranians and well... you know how people can fall in and out of favour very quickly in these places.'

'That's not good enough, Billy, I want to know it all. I'm right about most things,' Margaret insisted.

'The contract is fine.' Billy's eyes flitted back from his wife's face to his trays. He coughed and said, 'Well...actually...in fact, when the Shah visited us he signed up for some more of these colleges to open.' He stopped polishing and threw his cloth down with a flourish. He rested his hands on his paunch and looked smugly back at his wife. 'Jack and I are going to Tabriz next week about it.'

Margaret put her hand to her throat and twined the string of pearls round two of her fingers, twisting and turning them till they burst from their string and spilled onto the ground. She stood still, watching them scatter on the stone slabs. She'd had them since she'd been married, a gift from Billy's mother, herself a colonel's wife. Billy eyed his wife's tight-lipped face.

'*We, don't, have, anything, to, worry, about?*' She spoke the words like a machine gun. 'You never get it, do you, Billy? You're always the last one to work it out. And I'm the one who always has to sort out the rumours from facts. This time you'd better listen to me.'

Billy pushed some of the pearls into a heap with his hand.

'Leave those blessed beads and look at me.'

Billy placed his hands back on his stomach and forced himself to stare at his wife's angry mouth. He wanted to go to the golf club at that point and swallow two or three gin and tonics, one after the other.

'I don't like what I'm hearing, Billy. Jack won't speak and avoids me. There was an important-looking letter from London yesterday. There are those ghastly SAVAK men lurking everywhere and lots of different bits of gossip.'

'Forget these things, Margaret. Be more sensible.' He stood up at that point and stepped on some of the pearls, losing his balance for a moment. I should never have got her that job in Jack's office, he thought.

'The place here is armed to the teeth and the Shah and his people are in control. What are you so worried about, Margaret? Please,' Billy said. 'And there are enough guns and equipment here to protect and save us against any kind of attack,' Billy blustered on. She needed reassurance, and although he had also heard some rumours he wasn't going to let her know that. 'Look!

Look! The Shah's a powerful and rich man and he's got us as his friends. Hasn't he? I mean, well – you know...the government and he has the backing of the Yanks. Damn powerful, all of them.'

Billy breathed a sigh of relief when she answered. 'It just better be true. It better be true, Billy. I don't like surprises. The other wives, well, the young ones, look up to me and I have to reassure them, don't I?' Margaret fanned her face.

'Yes, my dear. Yes, of course. And you do a wonderful job. A wonderful job.' He patted her arm and pushed himself up to face her. He planted a kiss on her cheek. 'Look, I'll collect those pearls and get them restrung at the bazaar tomorrow. You go outside and get a breath of air. It's cooler now.' He took her arm and led her towards the open doorway.

The garden still held the evening scent of roses and the pink of the oleander flowers glowed in the street lamps peeking over on the other side of the hedge. The recent rains had refreshed everything. At Margaret's next coffee morning with two of the other majors' wives, she'd tell them not to be silly and to ignore anything that made them worry about their safety. The British Army had certainly never let them down before.

Chapter 38

Jack stared at his plate piled high with chips and steak. A smiling houseboy had presented it on his return from a night's stay in hospital where he'd had time to think. Mike's fist had made him see stars but it had helped him see the future too. Annie's remarks, as well as his conscience and his son's letter, had persuaded him that the right thing would be to try again with Sheila. He'd already decided to be generous with her and to settle her back in a house near his boys' school. If she deigned to speak with him, other than through solicitors, he would try all he could to appease her and try again with the marriage. To hell with the colonel and his niece. As Alan had said, there were complications in pursuing that.

He forced himself to eat part of his meal and then halfway through it pushed the plate away. He grabbed his car keys on his way out, almost stepping on Jasper who'd been sitting by the table.

'Sorry. Be back soon and I'll bring someone to see you,' Jack said, whispering the words into the top of Jasper's silky head. He could rescue and hide Elahe in the house, arrange a visa, and then take her out on a flight to England, finding lodgings for her with his Scottish relatives. Sheila didn't need to know. That way he would be doing something to help her. He owed her that.

He drove fast away from the Tafneq compound towards the Iranian one. The dirt roads outside were illuminated by a white glow from a full moon. A few thin dogs scuttled away, their eyes glowing like tiny amber torches in the car's headlamps, and he was forced to slow down. When he glanced at his watch he saw that it was late. A parked lorry, full of melons, stood at one side of the road and a group of motorbikes surrounded it. Their owners squatted beside their machines. Voices and smoke drifted out to him through his open window and their laughter jarred with him and he closed the window then, wondering if he would ever laugh like that again. Pulling himself together he concentrated on finding the right house in the dark.

He recognised the large wall and metal gates of the colonel's house but they were shut and padlocked. He banged and rattled the heavy metal and the old watchman called out and then peered at him from a grid. After a painful wait he prised it open, and the man's face appeared. It folded and refolded like creases on an old map. His gaping mouth had a piece of half-chewed bread inside, and Jack glimpsed his broken and black teeth. '*Boro*,' said the man and then swallowed the bread. Jack supposed he meant that the family had left.

'Where? Where?' shouted Jack pushing his face as close as he could to the small aperture in the gate. His hands pushed the gate back and forth and the metallic clanging rang out along the road and night. The chewing mouth and face disappeared and then reappeared.

'City. City.'

'Abadan?' shouted Jack. 'Was it Abadan, you bloody idiot?'

The old man nodded and then was about to close the grill, drawing his dirty grey scarf about his head when Jack thrust some toman coins through the metal window. At this the old man perked up. He pointed to his watch and put up two fingers.

'Two hours ago?' asked Jack, and put up ten fingers while

pointing to his watch, to indicate ten o'clock. The old man nodded vigorously. Another small wad of damp bread fell from his mouth and fell at the man's feet as Jack piled up more coins in his palm. So maybe, Jack thought, his luck was in and he could sort things out. They'd only left two hours before. Jack had dithered and Abdul must be cursing himself for putting his trust in a foreigner. Could he redeem the situation and play the rescuing hero? Hope was all he had.

As he stared more closely behind the watchman, Jack saw cars parked to one side. The front door of the colonel's deserted house swung open and music drifted from inside. There were two or three shapes hidden in the shadows and the glow from the tips of their cigarettes revealed their presence. Jack knew then what had happened. The men had been ordered to arrest Abdul, but it looked like they had been too late. Under cover of darkness and with this crisis Jack might have thrown off his own tail, and the rest of SAVAK would be trying to locate the colonel's entourage on the road somewhere. There could be roadblocks and Iranian soldiers were sure to have been alerted the instant the escape had been detected.

Jack drove like a maniac back to his house, nearly knocking down one of the scooter men. He gathered up some clean shirts, food, and drink. He shoved them in the back of the car and started out again, until he hit three ruts and spun out of control. Then he slowed down and tried to picture Elahe's face in his mind and her surprise and perhaps joy when she saw him. He'd been on many military exercises when younger and once he'd got lost somehow near Bovington Camp in Dorset. Then he had been devastated and had worked hard on his compass and map-reading skills. This time his own happiness was on the line and not his job. He had to succeed. He couldn't lose his way tonight. He had to find her.

He passed the road on the right to the riding club. In the headlights he saw Reza and braked hard. 'Reza, I need you.' It wasn't an order but a plea. Jack's white face and dark eyes were framed by the open car window. 'I have to drive down to Ahwaz city and I may even need to drive further to the port and Abadan. You must drive me. You get in this car and drive towards Abadan. I'm looking for the colonel and his family.'

'Yes, Major,' said Reza, but...'

'No questions. Just get in the bloody car and drive. You know this road, and I'm tired. It's a long journey. Keep your wits about you.'

'What, Major?'

'Get in the car, man. Get in. Maybe those men, the secret agents, will be in front. Don't know. You savvy now?'

Reza nodded.

'Good. Good man. I can rely on you. Always knew that. Good.'

Reza opened the car door and Jack shifted into the passenger seat. As they left the lights of Bashed behind and began to wind their way upwards hugging the cliffs, Reza realised he had the opportunity he needed to help his major. Uncle Faraz had pointed out that the man and the teacher Missus Brown could help him with a visa and English. He'd decided to tell his mother and sisters of his plans to leave and he'd made up his mind for his second cousin to become his wife.

Reza drove for about an hour over the rough terrain and concentrated on keeping as far as possible away from the precipitous valley below. Reza dared to glance across at his major whose eyes had remained shut. The major's chin was pitted with black stubble and bounced in sequence to the ruts on the road. The car began to travel at no more than the speed of a mule, as the headlights picked out rocks or landslips at each bend. Once they passed a broken-down lorry with a mangled axle. The startled driver sprang out in front but Reza skirted round the hopeful figure and pressed on, knowing that speed was of the essence. He saw the man's fists raised in the car's rear-view mirror, and now he didn't care. His future might lie in the outcome of this journey. Maybe Elahe was in the car or maybe she'd been left back at the house. The major hadn't mentioned her name. But then what was she to him now? Now he had made up his mind about his future.

They drove for two hours. During that time his major woke and turned round to search for bottled orange, handing him the drink after he had drained half the liquid.

'God, it's black out there,' the major said. 'Hope the bloody petrol holds out.' He tapped the gauge and more or less at the same time Reza had to brake hard when the headlights hit a shape in the middle of the narrow road. He killed the engine and the major hissed, 'Lights.'

Reza switched them off and their car shuddered and stopped. A Mercedes blocked the road and three or four people huddled round its front. Reza held his breath and looked across at the quivering major. The man gripped his arm with one hand but with the other he held a gun. 'What we do, sir? Maybe police?' The car had special plates and if these men were police from Bashed they would certainly know that his major was a British one, despite the man's civilian clothes.

His major opened his door.

'Get out, Reza. Go to the back. Quick,' Jack hissed.

Jack ran a hand over his hair and mouth, which felt wet at the corners with dribbles of moisture. He shivered in his thin trousers and shirt but found comfort in the gun he clenched in his right hand. A shot echoed around the cliffs above them, and he crawled further underneath the hot metal of the car boot. Reza lay on the ground, having wedged open the door on his side for protection. Jack had caught a glimpse of another car in front of the Mercedes. It looked like one of the Iranian colonel's but he couldn't be sure. Things happened fast and there were shouts and more gunshots, like orange fireworks in the blackness. Then a woman's voice and a scream. Both Reza and Jack watched somebody coming towards them, whose gun and its rapid red blasts lit up the face of one of Reza's spies. A ribbon of blood streamed down the man's cheek as he rushed towards their car. Reza pushed Jack hard towards a ditch at the side of the road and grabbed the man's legs, wrestling with the hand which held the gun.

Jack lay frozen in the ditch, although his stomach churned beneath his thin shirt. A dark abyss loomed below. He couldn't see it but he could feel its presence. If he rolled over he would fall off the edge. The future then was like that, a leap in the dark. There was danger here on the road but if he did survive he would try to break free. The army had held him together but now he wanted to escape, make his own decisions, and not try marriage again.

Where was the gunfire coming from? He heard scuffling boots, shouts, and a gurgling like water being poured into a jug. He'd scraped his face when Reza pushed him and his whole head throbbed. His throat tightened and closed leaving him gasping like a fish as a car's engine continued to pump out fumes. Reza moaned beside Jack, clutching at his leg, and Jack realised his driver had been injured. He reached over then, clasped the man to him, and put his hand over Reza's mouth to muffle the groans. What looked like the shape of a body lay a little apart from them, but other shouts and cries indicated some sort of search was taking place. A car drove away and silence followed. Reza's moaning had ceased but the man's chest still rose and fell.

A strong smell of tobacco drifted towards the two men in the ditch. Someone tugged at Jack's arms and he was lifted up. As they carried him he glimpsed Elahe kneeling down amongst the debris beside Reza and wiping his face with her scarf.

Chapter 39

Many of the students had left for the end-of-year holiday, but Jack had not been seen for a week. The teachers filled their hours in the stuffy office with reading and practising their Farsi. John played chess with a new Iranian officer who told them openly that he belonged to SAVAK. Brian and Andy, two newly recruited teachers, smiled and tried to chat, while Pete and Annie sat trying to read under the ceiling fan. Mike's presence in the corner made her heart race. Pete had made murmurings of commiseration with both Annie and Mike when they first heard about the car accident, but now Pete chain-smoked by the window waiting and watching. Each time the entrance gates clanged as they opened or the noise of a vehicle approached, Pete's grey face turned towards the others in the room. The chess players paused mid move and the SAVAK officer placed his hand on his holster and pistol.

Jack seemed smaller and thinner when he finally reappeared. He was wearing his khaki army uniform but it was loose and there were creases and marks where there shouldn't have been. The buttons had lost their shine and his boots were dusty. He had driven himself into work and Reza was nowhere in sight. He announced he wanted to see them all after ten minutes, but at the meeting, he never lifted his head, concentrated on shuffling his papers on the desk, and all the while kept clearing his throat. The teachers waited, but the new ones, who had never met him, raised their eyebrows at each other.

'It's been difficult. This last week or so. Major Billy's told you a few things but not the full story. Well, that's impossible. You know, Official Secrets Act, which...which...you've all signed.' Jack stopped and sought his handkerchief to wipe his forehead. 'But, well, you're owed some explanation, we all realise that. I'm...I'm, well, I'm carrying on here as before but it's not so safe here as we thought.' At that Jack paused and fiddled with his papers again. 'Well, some of you youngsters might, well, want to think about leaving when this contract finishes at the end of the month. That's no problem. Know how you like to go to new places and try different things. That may be a jolly good idea for some of you.'

Annie heard Pete mutter something under his breath at that.

Jack raised his head and they could all see the shadows and marks on his face, as if he hadn't slept for months. A faint smile began at the corners of his mouth. 'But, those of you thinking of renewal—' and he paused again and this time raised his head and looked across at the teachers for the first time '—well, there are some difficulties. Problems with local dissidents, that sort of thing. But...but...well, we've put other measures in place and there are too many of these British tanks to defend us – eh? What?' His voice faltered and he looked at Annie.

'By the way—' Jack stopped as he wiped his face '—my life was saved by Reza. That I can tell you. Pushed me away from some trouble and took the shot in the leg. The one which was intended for me.'

At the word 'shot' Annie turned to Mike. It was the first time any of them knew there had been actual violence.

'But how can you say that anyone is safe here now, sir, after that. Surely not?' interrupted John. 'What arrangements are being made to get us away?' John's voice rose to a crescendo. 'Is it wise to even wait until the end of the month?'

Jack didn't answer and sat down heavily on his chair, while flapping his hand at them to indicate the meeting was over. Mike grabbed Annie's arm and thrust her through the door.

Mike retreated to his study on their return and Annie found herself wishing she could hear the sound of the flute, but instead she heard groans from within and an odd kind of sighing. Some hours later, after calling his name and rattling on the door handle, real fear took over. Why wouldn't he speak with her? Surely at this time, and after what Jack had said, he should come to his senses and be reasonable? All his bullying and anger as well as that cruel attack in the hotel had scared her, almost paralysed her into a zombielike state. Then there'd been the car accident and his night in hospital, where he'd been given tablets and then, somehow, been allowed home. But now, now, she had to act.

She fled outside, leaving the kitchen door wide open. Hurtling down the street, she passed Jack's unlit bungalow and then diverted her path towards Billy and Margaret's house, where sounds of classical music floated on the still, heavy night air. The couple's faces registered surprise as she burst through their gate, unable to speak as she tried to catch her breath, her hands pointed in the direction of her house. She collapsed onto the ground and Margaret rushed forward.

'It's Mike. He's locked himself in his room. Won't speak and I'm...I'm worried he...' Annie's body started to shake and she couldn't seem to make it stop.

'Billy, get some water. The poor girl. Quick,' said Margaret.

Later, Annie found herself led to a cool bedroom, fed some soup, and given a sleeping tablet. The panic and fear that had engulfed Annie so completely for the last months diminished and she drifted off to sleep.

The next morning, as Billy handed Annie a cup of coffee, she knew he wanted to speak but she had to thank him first.

'I don't know what I'd have done, Major. It's been a worrying time for us and more so for Mike, I suppose.' She heard herself still trying to protect him.

Margaret came towards them with a tray of breakfast things, and Annie's eyes filled with tears. They were both so kind and she couldn't prevent herself telling them the full story: about the Isfahan trip, the scribbles on the wall, even Mike's jealousy. She opened the floodgates until she had exhausted herself. They put their arms around Annie's shoulders when she finished.

'Well, you're here with us oldies and nothing bad is going to happen now,' said Margaret. Neither had interrupted her, realising that they needed to know all that had happened, if they were to be able to help.

Later, Margaret spoke to Annie alone. 'Oh well, dear thing, only pleased that we could do something. My niece is a career girl, like you. She's got her head screwed on and so have you. You cheer up now, I'm fond of you, too, don't forget,' said Margaret.

'Fond of me?' Annie repeated.

'Yes I admire you. I do, Annie, and if you want, Billy can speak to that husband of yours and suggest you would both be better apart. I think that's best, isn't it?'

Annie nodded.

The next morning, Billy told her that he had organised a car to take Mike to the hospital again. Later, Margaret accompanied Annie back home. 'Get a few things and come and stay with us. No point in you being in an empty house with all this going on. By the way, Annie, don't worry about Sheila. Jack's going to buy a house for her back home, I saw the letter, and she's quite close to the sons. She's loud and aggressive when she's drunk. I heard about that last outburst at the pool. But, she'll be OK.'

'Thanks for telling me, Margaret. Thanks for being, well, being so strong. I'm sorry I must have seemed rude to you before about the carpets and, well, everything.'

'Please don't apologise, dear girl. I'm a bit of a tartar but I know what's what and you've had a rough time and held your own in the place. When you're back home, things will work out.'

Despite Jack's speech about how safe they all were, no one believed him. The teachers had already seen furniture being loaded up and there were plans being put into place for extra planes to stand ready for the beginnings of a partial evacuation of family members. When Annie returned to collect some clothes after accepting Margaret's offer, she found Mike had scrawled a note and pinned it to the bedroom door. It must have been before Billy had taken him down to the hospital. She wanted to be sick but forced herself to read it. He wrote that the place was 'going to the dogs' and he was glad to leave if the truth were told. She could do what the hell she liked. Billy had promised he would get his bonus and money if he left now and that was what he wanted.

A month later, Annie boarded the plane on the first leg of her return trip to England. It seemed a million years since their arrival when her excitement had kept her on the edge of her seat with her eyes glued to the window. The seat beside her was empty. Mike had been flown out before and sent to an army clinic in London to recuperate. This time she focused on the back of the seat facing her and kept her eyes shut. She waited as the high-pitched engine sounds and the squeal of retracting landing gear finished. She opened them only when her stomach had flopped back to its familiar position.

Back in England, Annie applied for and was recruited into a new teaching job in England. Mike had decided to settle near his family. One evening she answered the telephone at her new flat.

'Hello. Is the fan of Jane Austen there?' a familiar voice asked.

'Elahe! How are you and my goodness, where are you?' replied Annie.

'I'm in England. In London with some cousins.' Her voice sounded like bubbles of happiness. 'That groom Reza's OK too. He got out as well, you know.'

Annie's lips curled into a smile. 'He was given a visa with your Major Jack's help and decided to come to England first. He married his cousin before he left Iran.'

Elahe paused before whispering her next sentence. 'I don't know where Major Jack is, by the way.'

'Oh,' said Annie, 'I see...' Although she didn't really see anything.

'He helped us a lot though, and saved our lives one terrible night, but now, well...we've lost touch with him.' Her voice grew stronger then. 'But in Iran, you must have heard, Annie... it's going from bad to worse. Even Grandmother has decided to leave. But...well, how are you? I managed to get your address from the army office in London. I'm a student again here, by the way. It's so much fun and...' Elahe giggled.

'Pleased for you, Elahe,' said Annie. 'Glad to hear your family is OK and good news about Reza.' She couldn't mention Mike or her divorce. Things were too raw.

After the telephone conversation Annie felt able to pin up some photos of Iran in her new flat. That thick hedge figured in a few of them and she remembered how it had shut her off from so much and shut her in. But she unpacked the saddlebag as well and placed it on the back of her small second-hand settee. Its colours brightened up the whole room. She drew her bright blue home-made curtains. Maybe Sheila and Jack were back together, but even if not, her two Iranian friends were safe and well. They had future plans and so did she.

The End